I0678200

PATCHWORK INDIGO

A novel by: J.B. Sommerset
Published in association with Origin Inc.

<u>Acknowledgements:</u>

To my friends and family who encouraged me. To my dreams and the dark and wonderful places they took me, and then forced me to see while my eyes were shut. Also, to those imaginary things which waited and never were, to all the music and all the words I never used although I wanted to. There is much more to this tale, and I killed it to write this.

Thank you for the sacrifices.

The music in the margins:

As you read through this you may notice that in certain sections, song titles and band names are scribbled in the bleed. These melodies are the songs of my life and they capture the mood and tone which accompany the key elements. Feel free to see the back of the book for a complete list of these songs in the order they appear. I feel sometimes words need companions, and like so much in life, music can enhance what is already there. These songs are not a part of the story, but I find that they add shading to the picture and highlight more depth.

ACT I: The child I want to see again.

1. Childhood.

This is the summary of my childhood and I was like any other boy of six. Being young was a carefree, and there were many pleasures and easily found comforts, in part, because of the simplicity of being youth.

I played with toys and I daydreamed. I loved ice cream, soda pop and junk food. I liked late night scary movies and camping in the back-yard during the month of August. I loved shiny new toys and sunny days when I could be outside. I liked the things other children seemed to like. My heart was full of adventure and my thoughts were still creative and pliable. There was a child-like plasticity in my ways. Looking back, I know every moment was a gift. I miss those days, when my time was tied in ribbons of imagination, wrapped in paper of optimism, and hemmed with wonder. Those were times when I found happiness in the hours of the day despite the bee stings and the scraped knees.

It would be accurate to say my youth was ripe with opportunity. From early morning, when my eyes opened to the last words of my bed time stories, I was dedicated to being the best boy I could be. I practiced such a task under the tutelage of my parents, who kept my curiosity from killing me. It was a splendid time in my life and, in part, I owe it to the parenting skills of my mother and father. As my recollection allows, they were the best parents a child could ever have.

I saw my mother and father as heroes. My dad

could be anything or do anything, and my mother was no different. They interacted with each other in harmonious ways, but also displayed a well-balanced duality for me to observe. When father was a playful pirate and scoundrel, she pretended to resist him but swooned nonetheless. When she was a queen he was her servant and kept her satisfied. When he was a knight in shining armor she was a maiden in a tower guarded by a dragon.

This all made sense to me because, as my father explained, "Most women want a man to break the rules for them, most men want a queen to serve. Without a maiden Lancelot is nothing more than a tin man... and fairy tales have more validity than we give them credit for." Needless to say, stories were a big part of my childhood.

This was the example set for me. It was their dynamic and a condition which both parents were willing victims to. They were hopeless in the magnetic pull of their attraction to each other. This magnetism stemmed from their mutual love of each other's company. In all my years I have never seen a love so strong and balanced. It was my belief they could have starved happy as long as they were within each other's reach. It was my pleasure to be a part of that wonder and emotional dependency, even though it grew from illusion and childlike substance.

I tell you about them to establish where my values are truly rooted and how what they were carried to my adulthood. My parents were happily married and I benefited greatly from their devotion.

I planted my values during those formative years and modeled them after what I observed. My values are family, friends and company with fellow humans. There was never a time when I felt distaste for my parent's public or private behavior. In fact, I have tried to emulate it my entire life. They were happily tangled in each other's lives and that made them special.

They served my growth well but also facilitated my survival. They rescued me from any troubles I had while still letting me make mistakes and learn. Later in life, this reflected in my own behavior- a benevolent neglect combined with exploratory caution. Although I never had biological children, I did have a child to practice parenting on. All good parts of my parents are also the best parts of me and I gave them to him in hopes that he would pass them down.

There are many mistakes I made along the way, many things I would change but never my childhood. I feel childhood is the only part of a person's life when patterns are not repeating. Everything is new and therefore wondrous. This is what makes it special and why I think mankind places so much importance in it. There is a blissful unawareness of danger and a refreshing breath of optimism in the interactions of most young boys and girls. This gives them an invincible and sometimes fearless approach to life.

I acknowledge from my own experience that

children are better at life than most adults and they are also better at celebrating it. I think most children have bigger and better dreams than adults do. I know I did. I have never known a child who wanted to work in a labor position but I have known a number of them who wanted to be astronauts, princesses, ninjas, race car drivers or magicians.

We created many opportunities to enjoy our happiness and parties were common in our house- with or without guests. We had birthdays, holidays, and *just for fun* days. We were never bored and we were rarely lazy. My favorite times were the holidays. When I grew old I didn't celebrate them as much because the eagerness in my bones had faded and my friends were all gone. They had left me in another time and place. However, I never forgot what it was like.

My favorite holiday was Christmas. I was in love with the lights, enthralled with the merriness and, of course, the presents.

As I grew, these things took back seat to the sentimentality of the season and the company I kept during the holidays. Christmas is special to me, as I know it is to you, and I don't mean in the traditional religious way. I mean in the drawn-together way which lessens the sting of winter frost. I do not follow any religious groups or their beliefs but I do know when people come together to eat, drink and make merry the world is better for a short while. I know the importance in spending time is not what it is spent on, more so who we spend it with.

Christmas emphasized this for me and became an exercise in embracing the human need to be social and committed to others regardless of any spiritual or ritualistic attachment to the season. Laughter in the hallways of my home was where the value was always found.

Now that I am old, I feel my time and how it was purposed made me wealthy beyond measure. Especially those times around the holidays, keep in mind this story is not about Christmas, but Christmas is where it started.

2. The last Christmas.

It was two days after Christmas, the year I turned six, so long ago. Christmas day had been a fine day and of all the gifts I received, there was none I wanted more than the new pair of skis. The skis were the last gift I unwrapped that season. This did not surprise me because mother and father were that way. They would overwhelm me and then, when I thought things couldn't get better, they always found a way to surprise me more.

On December 28th we rose early for our trip to the mountains. I was excited to be awake and it did not take long for us to load the car with supplies for my first ski trip.

There was a fresh layer of powder on the ground and the sun had just peeked over the horizon. It was a radiant new orange and the sky was blue. It was not just blue; it was what I call Connecticut blue. Connecticut blue is the kind of blue which swallows you when you stare up at it. The blue of the sky in Connecticut always felt that way to me. Maybe because Connecticut was home; it's where I was born. Maybe the sky of home always swallows us, I do not know.

Another important thing I can remember was the smell of the house when I left that morning. There was the faint smell of rum cake hanging in the air; rum cake mixed with peppermint and used pine from the dying tree. I still look for that smell every season but like petrichor before a storm, it remains elusive. I have only smelled it once since then. You might also know this smell. If you do, please understand, I know why you love it so much.

While my father warmed the car, we locked up the house and turned the heat down then we joined him. We pulled out of the driveway and drove across town toward the freeway. Mother and father were doing what they always did on trips, they were singing. I slept for the duration of the trip but the second my father cracked the window and let the mountain air in, I came to life. It was food for my lungs and it sparked my excitement.

Skiing is something I have carried with me my whole life. I love to ski and I owe it to that experience and those skis. Someday, again, I will thank the person who returned them to me.

My first experience with skiing made me love the mountains. Later in life I and Belle made a habit of traveling for the purpose of skiing. I have been many places but prefer those same mountains, the ones I learned on. The mountains in Connecticut are not big or majestic. They are relatively small, but on that day they were the largest mountains I had ever seen.

They were wrinkled with age and each crease was filled with liquid white. Smoke puffs burped from cottages into the Connecticut blue. People glided from lift to lift dressed in multicolored uniforms trailing left over Santa hats while cutting the snow. Their noses were frosty, their cheeks rosy and their ears pink. All across the slope the crystal white matched their beaming smiles. The lodges were occupied by non-skiing patrons keeping time with the cheer of those more skilled or motivated. My eyes were alight with excitement.

We drove by the ski slopes to a small group of cabins cradled in the trees beyond the lifts. Our cabin was a little crowded looking but otherwise cozy. It was made of log with a steep roof and a small garage. We pulled in and put the car away. It was still early but the sun was trekking up the sky quickly. We unloaded the car and had an even quicker breakfast.

I must have looked somewhat rude as I shoveled the food into my mouth. Under normal circumstances my parents would have told me manners mattered and scolded me, but not that day, that day they looked at me and smiled. They, however, took their time and made me wait while they finished breakfast.

As soon as the last bite was taken I leaned over and nudged father and then looked at my skis. He smiled and looked at mother who already had her ski jacket on and was zipping it up. With that, we left the ski lodge and hiked up to the resort in the crisp early air and the endless blue and white.

There is not much to describe about those three days and for brevity's sake I will skip most of the details. I have established the earliest memory of my parents which is the important part because it shaped my life with Belle.

Needless to say, spending my hours on the novice slope was anguishing and it made my first day skiing and arduous event. I fell a lot, failed a lot and got very frustrated with the process, especially when the skis decided my feet didn't know where I was going. The problem was the skis didn't know where they were going either.

It took patience to learn. Later in life, I discovered patience is one of life's great virtues. Also when you don't take the chances you miss opportunities.

I picked up skiing in a day or so and I learned to love it. From then on I skied every year. Later, when in foster care, I made the time and took every opportunity to go skiing. There was not a winter after I left the *Allotment* which I did not attend the season with a waiting sense of excitement. My skis are still tucked away in the closet of a house in northern Connecticut waiting to be found by another young boy who needs a thread to grasp.

In the evening, after skiing, we would soak in

the hot tub to sooth our bruises and sore joints. We would also drink hot chocolate, eat warm food, and watch movies while playing board games. Mother and father would listen to holiday music. They would laugh and joke while they sipped brandy and chocolate. Politics would somehow come up and they would make more jokes. They sang dirty songs and flirted with each other. I expected that kind of behavior and would wrinkle my nose at them and tell them to get a room.

I feel those early memories shaped me ever so subtly, sabotaging my ability to recognize the power in them and their influence over my dispositions.

However, it was not the experience of the first three days which was important. The night we drove home was more important. There is no secrecy in those memories. They too shaped me in obvious and profound ways, ways in which my recollection would have a hard time denying. They were the contrast to my bliss. They delivered a sharp message; life is not a happy place unless there are pitfalls which set up our appreciation. Appreciation and gratitude are important. I may be sad for some of the things that have happened to me, but I am also grateful for them. For all of it; that which I have had, that which I am, and all I will have in my few remaining days.

After we had our fun and the third day was at its end, we slowly packed the car stretching it out as long as we could. It made us a little late leaving the cottage. For many years I thought that delay was what caused the events which took place that night. Now that I am old I know the truth. I know it would not have mattered what time we left. We could have left the next day and it would still have happened the way it did.

It was just after dark when we started the trip home. The sky was clear but there were clouds on the horizon. They had not been there earlier and seemed to be moving in rapidly from all directions. My father suggested it was best to say goodbye to our vacation and start the trip home before the clouds overtook us. He did not want to be stuck in a snowstorm on the mountain. With caution we departed from the lodge and drove down the mountain to rejoin the noise of our everyday lives.

3. This magic moment. [1]

The drive was pleasant enough at first. The road was clear as it had been freshly plowed. Little mountainside farm houses were visible in the moonlight and their red barns were painted silver with a dusting of day-old snow. The eves were wet with dripping ice which formed long columns toward the ground. Lights in windows were dim orange while residents were settling in with their dinners and their TVs.

As we left the mountain road and pulled into the woods, the highway became a black and white snake

---

[1] "This magic moment" by Rachael Cantu ♬

winding along the river. Mother and father turned the radio on and started singing as they always did. I sat in the back seat breathing on the window and drawing animals in the fog. The drawings became a zoo as my fingers brushed the glass again and again. Dogs, cats, cows and all the things I imagined playing in the fields beyond the window.

As we looped into a hairpin turn the radio started a new song. To this day I won't listen to that song even though it was my mother and father's favorite song. The song I am referring to is *"This magic moment"*. At that point in my life, I had heard it many times and knew the words to it. Although the title was coincidence, it was still a macabre reminder that the universe has a sick sense of humor.

I looked at my parents in the front seat then back at my animals on the glass. That glance was all the time it took to change the world I lived in.

The snow had started to fall in sporadic patterns from newly formed clouds. They were rolling in quick and starting to mask the sky. Even though my father had slowed the car to take the corner, it was not enough. Someone was out on that road walking in the night, in the snow and the cold. As the clouds passed in front of the moon the light was snuffed and the shadowy figure of a man materialized out of the darkness in the headlights.

Coincidence needs no explanation and circumstance just waits to present itself when the right conditions are meant. He was just a man in the snow, an unknown face in the dark. I have often wondered what he was doing out there. For now, I will say he was going for a walk in the snow to wash bad dreams from his head. There are times when I go for walks to clear my mind. Sometimes I walk in the dark and in the cold, so I can make an assumption that I am not the person who does.

I will never fully understand that man's motives for why he was out there that night. However, I can understand my own and how he was linked with my life. I wanted to be mad at him for a long time, but that part of my life was just an accident without context. He was just a coincidence-manifest and a circumstance that was met.

Then I heard my mother cry out in reflex.

"Henry!" She shouted. It was the last thing I heard her say, the last sound which escaped her lips before the breaks guided the car sideways into the rail.

I saw the man for just a second as the car spun around him without touching him. As we went by he stood mortified with his hands in front of his face covering his head, afraid for his life. I wasn't able to formulate thoughts while this happened. This single event prostrated itself over my life and wrapped me inside of it. My mother's last word were its proclamation.

Time ran slow and I could see the physics being delivered in the car in front of me. Actions became chains of inertia happening in sequence of cause and effect. In my mind a recording started and every detail was etched eidetically into my memory with acid precision.

My father let the steering wheel go and threw his hand across my mother. She did not scream but instead she reached for me with a loose arm across the expanse of the back seat. I sat motionless watching her desperate hand coming through the darkness, suspended in space as the car spun.

A hollow sound reverberated through the car as metal bent. As the car struck the guard-rail, the front end began to deflate. Vibrations penetrated through its metal shell for a brief second until the chassis stopped the collapse. I still remember the sound- vivid, clear and defined by a lasting echo in my head and the jerk the sound delivered.

I felt acceleration pushing me into my seat. The car's back end lifted off the ground and arched. It pulled the rest of the car with it into the night. While the headlights passed over the railing I looked down through the front window. The road, white with new snow, faded into the winter emptiness. Objects which were stationed in the seat next to me were suddenly freed of their gravity and began to float in the car as it rotated around them.

I can remember a bottle of water spiraling through the void and my dad's briefcase refusing to move from its Central location hovering in the cabin

13

space. There was loose change scurrying through the open air, quarters chasing dimes, chasing nickels, chasing pennies in desperation.

My stomach became self-aware and pulled at my abdomen letting me know it was scared. My heart pounded frantically trying to drown the adrenal rush of panic and sooth the copper taste in my mouth.

Outside in the night, the rocks and bushes were distant and the ground was a soft white blanket smothered in darkness. It was unreal, non-threatening and far away. We spiraled and I could see everything the headlights touched. They illuminated the black water and ice. I could see the rocks and the still spots in the deep water. The radio was still playing the song as the car fell to the river some thirty feet below the road.

The cars sudden deceleration upon collision with the water pulled me tight in my seat belt. The air was forced from my lungs and I gasped unable to breathe in. My eyes shut instinctively and broken glass zipped by me stinging and cutting my face. There was a second when I lost consciousness. If I had known what the next few weeks would have been like, I don't think I would have come back but it was not a choice for me to make. I was roused when the frigid water touched my scalp. When I came around the song was still playing, but mother and father were not singing.

Mother was hanging from her seat belt upside-down, she was intact but her neck was crooked and her head was dangling in the ice. I heard my father choking

14

on water as he was reaching for me. His hand moved from the front to try and free me of the seat belt. He clasped frantically and jerked and tugged at the clip. When it was released, I fell into the current pouring through the shattered window.

"You have to leave!" My father said between gasps. "You have to go and swim as hard as you can!" I refused to go even though the water bit at my fingers and forced my lungs to seize. The car was being tugged by the current into the deep water and I could not bring myself to leave either of them. "Son, there is no time for this, your mother and I love you, now get out of the car!" He yelled.

I had never heard him talk the way he did that night. There was urgency in his timber I did not recognize.

"I have to free us, I will be right behind you, but you have to go now!" He said.

Reluctantly, I slid out through the broken window where my frosty animals had been playing. I could feel the glass shredding my knees and lower legs as I crawled into the fast moving water.

The current was so strong and the water was so cold. I could feel it burning the nerves in my fingers. As soon as I was in the river the current wrenched me from the car and pulled me away. My muscles were contracting and my lips were freezing as I swam for the shore. My legs kicked and I clawed through the water searching for something to grab, an anchor to hang on to. There was nothing until I felt frozen sand and mud in the webbing of my fingers. Pebbles bruised my fingertips as I tugged myself up on the bank.

I turned to look back at the car and pulled myself to my knees. The snow had started to fall harder and I could feel the wind picking up. The car clung to the black water and ice, it fought to stay above the surface. The world was silent while I waited. Even the faint sound of the radio was lost to my ears. In the stillness I wanted my father to come to me and bring my mother so she could comfort me. The blood started to run thin in my arms and legs. I lost the burning feeling in my fingers. Warmth leaked into them like a slow welcoming sedative.

I wish I could say my parents made it. That would be untrue. The truth is they died that night and left me alone in the drifting snow. They ceased to be a part of my world and I still miss what might have been. I do not think about it much because it does not help. As I sit here, I feel I did them justice in the way that I lived. They are the foundation of my being and all things they taught me comprise the stone on which I am built.

I sat frozen on the bank of the river, kneeling on bloody knees in the snow while I watched and waited. The car, with its lights weeping and its radio casting a soul shattering echo into the night, died as well. It eventually accepted the water as its new grave. The hollow crushing of metal signaled a giveaway and it slid under the ice taking my father and mother with it. As it did the music ended as well.

Yet I still waited. Hoping my father would surface. Watching intently for him to break the ice and claw his way to the riverbank.

While I waited I was dying in the soft white flakes doing nothing to save myself. Blood leaked like red angel wings from my shredded knees and legs into the pristine white and I felt my heart slowing. I never took my eyes off that liquid black mercury flowing in the shadow of that shallow canyon. I stared at its blackness until it was done.

That watery abyss has been the howling in my dreams. It is the desperation and it still comes for me when I am alone. Those dreams are the ones that force me out of bed to go walking in the dark and in the moonlight, and sometimes in the frozen snow.

The memory of this event does not define me and it does not influence my decisions. I do not let it overshadow my responsibility to be happy. I believe the accident happened because I needed to understand what risk means. Accidents happen and we have to remain bold if we are to claim all the positive things life has to offer. My mother and father knew this and because they were brave enough to take risks they were rewarded with happiness. Wherever they are I do not think they are disappointed with their choices and I hope they are not disappointed in me. I will cherish the days before I lost them as memory allows and know that I honored them by living to their standards.

I cannot remember all of the details after the car went under. At some point there were sirens and pulsing red and blue from the road above me. Those colors were splattered on the snowy evergreens on both sides of the river. There were shouts through the trees and the sound of a helicopter. Its light burst down from the sky spotlighting where the car had been. In contrast to the accident, those memories are like fog on my mind. Whether time has stolen their vividness or whether preference has selectively weeded them out I am not sure.

It was not long before I heard the hollow crunch of boots in freshly frozen snow behind me. Footfalls came at me with an empty ripping while they tore through the shrubbery. As they approached I gave the last of my consciousness away. I started to slouch from my knees into the snow but instead dropped into someone's arms.

He shouted for help and gripped me tight. Then my legs were lifted off the ground as he carried me. His walk was rough and I could feel him struggling up the slope to the road, or at least I think I did.

Snowflakes caressed my face while my legs swung. He held me and his warmth bled into my skin through wet cotton. It was that warmth, that thread of life, which my spirit held on to. It was a beacon in the dark; the glow that made me aware my heart was still beating and there was still breath in my lungs.

While my body struggled to keep me alive my

mind did not have such concern. I shrank into the recesses of my imagination. I was at home. I was warm in front of the fire drinking hot chocolate. Things were alright and mom and dad still sang somewhere in the distance. Maybe it was a Saturday and I was off for Christmas break watching cartoons or reading my favorite comics. Maybe I was napping on the couch in the living room. Time was endless and I was not aware of it in the capacity of memory but only in security and emotion. I felt wherever I went, I was home.

There were no time markers to tell me how long it took to get to the hospital. What I do know, was that I was revived by the medics at least once. I can remember the electric jerk that pulled me back convulsing my frame and forced my airways open. In denial I receded back to my place of rest but my heart continued to beat. Occasionally shouts and screams would bleed through as EMTs frantically tried to stabilize me. Needles were placed into me and thermal blankets were wrapped around me.

Of all the things keeping me connected to life it was a human hand holding mine that saved me. If it had not been for that hand, nothing on Earth could have kept me from joining my parents. Of all the technology the medics had, it was still human contact which possessed that power. Within the boundaries of hindsight, I am glad they we able to save me. So much good has happened since then.

I remember the smell of iodine and the heart

monitor's irregular beeping. It was a rhythm pinging in the dark with constant breaking in its hum. I woke just before we arrived at the hospital. It must have taken some time in the storm, minutes, maybe an hour, I do not know. My eyesight did not come right away. There was an awareness of people and sounds which came first. My senses slowly came back like volume being turned up. There was a flush of cold and hot as the blood flowed back into my extremities alerting my nerves. It was liquid hell burning in my fingers and toes.

I did not know who caught me in the snow and rode with me in the ambulance. I did not know who held my hand that night. Someone said it was a first responder, someone else said it was the man who had been in the road. Whoever it was I accredit them with my survival and given the chance I would thank them.

As I was removed from the ambulance the hand let me go of mine and I could feel the gurney being pushed across the loading bay. Snowflakes were hammering my face with the wind. They felt like drops of acid on my skin. There was a zipping sound as a door slid open. The warm air hit me as I was pushed through the inside doors to the hospital. Then there were lights, tarnished fixtures over my head, one after another while I was wheeled through the east wing of the hospital. They passed over me, my eyes dilated and I could see the filaments vibrating.

Shortly after that I heard the murmur of a doctor looking over charts and telling the nurse they would have to fix my collar bone, and cast my arm and fingers. I was too weak to fight or even worry about it. They gently placed the rubber respirator over my face. There was a whoosh and then a puff of something in my nostrils and I succumbed to a blacker kind of sleep. There were no dreams and there was no pain either.

I lingered momentary adrift while the surgeons worked. My mind was safe from the trauma. I appreciated that. It was a timeless void without sensation or noise, a quiet and neutral place.

I kept my eyes shut even after I came around. There was a weight in my chest which seemed to shift the more I lay in the hospital bed. There was also a silence in the air and I sensed someone was watching me or at the very least waiting for me. It was as if I could see them through my eyelids, a shapeless form that did not seem to move. I knew I would have to open my eyes sometime and accept the new world I was a part of.

When I did open my eyes they burned from the light and my pupils had a hard time adjusting to the hospital fluorescence.

There were shapes around the room which became more identifiable as my vision aligned and focused. I tried to lift myself up planting my hands on the mattress and pushing. It burned and the sensation made me retract my hand from the bed. The light was still blurry and I whimpered while my eyes strained to focus. I was scared and I felt small.

Finally, I could see a figure moving a chair

21

closer to the bed. It was a woman and as clarity drew up my eyelids she became a brilliant point in my world.

She was flawless in many aspects. I can remember her stony look of concern as she sat in the hospital chair at the foot of my bed. Her skin was like milk and her hair was auburn. It was pulled back in a style from a different decade. She appeared almost synthetic in her composure. She put her legs together and adjusted her skirt with lady-like precision then dusted its fabric.

Her hair almost looked like it was painted on porcelain and placed on her scalp. There was a mathematical and symmetrical equilibrium to her face which made it quite appealing and her white shirt was so clean it seemed to cast a glowing light into the room. I can remember her lips. They seemed out of place when contrasted to the color of her skin. There was a quiet grace captured in every movement she made and patience to her demeanor which was still like glass, smooth and tempered even across all parts perceivable. She folded her hands in her lap and leaned in close and waited for me to come around completely.

4. An Indigo greeting.

"Hello, and good morning," She said.

"Hello?" My mouth felt distant to me at first and my voice sounded hollow.

"Give it a minute… the anesthetic is still wearing off. You'll be yourself in a little while," She assured me.

"Where have I been, what happened?"

"You have been resting and healing. You were in an accident and almost died which would have been just tragic. I have been waiting at the diner for six hours since I got the call. You were here, you were hurt, and so you needed me, and here I am…" She paused and looked at her fingernails. "My name is Indigo."

Looking around the room I noticed it was just me and her in the empty space. Then I remembered the car accident and was filled with loneliness. All the events of the night before came flooding back into my life and I sniffled.

"My Mom and Dad?" I asked still clinging to hope that they had made it and were waiting in the next room.

Indigo looked down at the floor and didn't say anything. Her silence betrayed her though. It didn't matter, because I already knew the truth despite her being there. They were at the bottom of the river in the cold under the ice.

"They did not make it," She finally said in a solemn voice. My heart broke in my chest and I wished I hadn't asked. Hearing it from her made it absolute and that was a frightening thing to me. I started to cry. She came to the side of my bed and leaned over and held me. I couldn't stop the tears from falling and she did not back away. We were there a long time in a stalemate of grief and comfort until I regained my composure. She managed to console me and explained that it would take time before it would to hurt less. She finally stopped the embrace and leaned back in her chair, her white shirt damp from my tears.

"They were good people… I want you to understand, it is not your fault. There are things that happen and they don't have a reason, this was one of them," She paused. I did not understand this. "You will come to live with me soon, and that will make all the difference in your life," She said.

I nodded but it wasn't much of a comfort to me. The offer was all I had and there was no choice other than to accept it and get on with everything.

We spent a few hours together that night talking about them. She told me about her first skiing trip and how many times she fell. We carried on long into the evening, long after the orderly brought my hospital food and she helped me eat. I finished everything including my Jell-O. I did not mind her company. There was something calming about it. Before she left she came over to the bed and sat down next to me and placed a hand on my shoulder and looked me in the eye.

"Things will be okay, you'll see. Just hang on for the next few weeks and get through this. It's going to be tough but I know you can do it" She said. I nodded and looked up at her.

"You promise?" I asked.

"We'll shake on it," She said. I extended my casted arm and she took it and carefully shook it. "I will be back," She smiled and patted my shoulder then stood up. "Now you sleep tight, you need it," She said.

I watched her walk out of the room and then I was alone again with my thoughts.

5. The poisoned dream.

It was tough falling asleep that night. Horrible thoughts ran through my head and the accident kept replaying itself over and over again. Like a film stuck on repeat, circling from beginning to end and then back again in reverse. In every reiteration, I could see the chain of action, of cause and effect and then effect and cause. The whole event came in waves of slow motion in time with the music. Sleep did not come till late and it was sporadic.

Something happened that night I did not understand for many years. I had been trying to sleep for hours and I came to a state where I was not sure if I was asleep or awake. My eyes were open but the room felt clouded like a dream. Like a night terror, I couldn't move. I laid there in my bed alone. I was not focused on the room I was in, or the beeping machines watching over my vitals, there was something else there.

Everything went silent and I got the feeling something was watching me from the darkness in the corner of the room. The space was black and I couldn't see anything inside it. The silence and emptiness engulfed me. I cannot explain how I knew it was an artificial quiet, but I did, I sensed it.

I huddled in the dim orange and green bubble made by the machines as I searched the darkness straining to see what was there. There was a primal fear in my stomach. It was a fear that something was hidden outside the light shining on my little bed.

The room grew still. The silence became a shell around me and something in the corner stirred. It was just a shuffle to begin with, a quiet and methodical dragging of feet hailing from the vacancy of sound and noise. It was not just that there was something coming, but that it was coming from somewhere within the silence.

There was another foot fall, and then another and another. Out of the emptiness and shadow came a ticking sound which accompanied the shuffling, it was relentless, a clockwork pulse, slow and rhythmic. I shivered and tried to call for help but found my lips had no voice. Sound would not even leak from them. The figure came in closer and I could make out the shape of a man.

He was tall and lean with pale white skin. His features were masked in the dim light and he wore a pitch black three piece suit. I could only see the white collar standing out as if it was choking his neck. As he approached the ticking grew louder. Soon I could make out the crown of his bald head and his deep sunken eyes. They were only shiny pits in the gloom reflecting the green line from the monitor. His nose protruded from the center of his face and hung like a vulture's beak. I was terrified and felt a lump of fear growing in my throat.

He stopped at the foot of my bed and looked down on me. His eyes penetrated the little orange and green bubble I was trying to hide in. I could hear his breathing, but I could barely see him to put face to the sound. He paused and his stature became completely still hanging from the air. He became a solid unmoving mass for several minutes. I did not know why he stopped advancing. At that moment he was the only thing in the room and it did not feel like I was there with him. For many years I did not understand who he was or why he was there.

After a minute or so he twitched and then started to move again. The shuffling sounds returned as he rounded the bed and moved towards me. He stayed just outside of the light so I couldn't see his face, a face that was a pale shade with highlighted detail.

He stopped and slowly reached into the breast pocket of his suit. He reached across the bed with his other arm and grasped my wrist. The grip was cold and it felt like the moisture was being sucked from my skin. I was frantic and tried to break free from his grasp. He leaned closer and spoke in a soft voice that dug into the air. It was a harsh sound and carried with it a foreboding tone which infected my thoughts. It could be described as a slow voice. Yet, it was very articulate and dripping with strange proposal. It was as though it were a question without the inclination of tone required by a question.

"I am sorry for what I am about to do, but I must do it. You must forgive me, but this is necessary," He said with a hiss.

Adrenalin was pumping into my bloodstream and suddenly I started to struggle. It did no good because he was too strong. He removed the hand from his pocket and grasped in his fingers was a long, wicked looking syringe. His hand was like a swan's neck as glided over the sheets to my arm and placed it on my vein. I couldn't free myself and suddenly the point of the syringe was pushing through the tissue. He gritted between his cheekbones and his teeth flashed in the dark like flecks of ivory encased in a crooked half-moon. I was never sure if it was a grin or a grimace, either way I never forgot those pearls in the darkness.

"Someday, you will understand why this was done to you. I am sorry for this… " He said as he pushed the plunger down. I could feel the liquid surging out the end of the needle and into my arm. It was liquid gravity and it pulled my body to the mattress on the gurney.

It was warm and soft like cotton in my bloodstream. I could feel it crawling in my arm towards my neck with a slow burn. The strange liquid worked its way in between my muscles and fibrous tissues. As smoothly as he had injected it he pulled the needle out, capped it and placed in back in his breast pocket. The same shuffling leaked into the room as he backed away from the bed toward the door.

The ticking returned and became a furious drum

beat in my ears. He took his time leaving the room and never turned his back to me.

Suddenly there was sharp heat bursting in my head and nostrils. He opened the door and eclipsed the light bleeding into the room. The luminous ring around his silhouette blinded me as he disappeared into it.

I laid there in pain with heat coursing through my mind. The ticking grew louder and louder. My muscles started to contract and shake as it seeped deeper into my body pushing me into intermittent convulsions. They came in waves leading to a graduated buildup of noise in my mind. My body did what it was forced to do as the contents of that needle ate my insides. My skull was filled with the chatter of teeth as I bounced and trembled on the hospital mattress. There was a sensation, much like a thousand little spiders crawling into the cracks of my brain. It built until my senses gave in. My ability to control myself shut down completely. I had no choice, I laid there and submitted to it.

The pain and confusion continued for many hours, then, it abruptly stopped and I went limp. In my head the tramping sound of little feet was gone and I was alone with my thoughts and my exhaustion. The terror no longer mattered and I succumbed to sleep. I slept until late in the morning without waking or incident.

The next day I said nothing to the nurses. I figured they did not need to know about what had happened. I suspected it was most likely a dream and dismissed it.

The Nurses and doctors came and went all morning checking my vitals and looking at charts. The pain was gone, I seemed to be alright and there were no side effects at the time but I was still confused.

Indigo came back that morning and we talked for a while. We watched some TV and she played games with me. She did not stay very long but while she was there she told me it would be the last time I saw her until I came to live with her at what she called the *Allotment* with the other children. It did not make me happy but it gave me a little hope, and hope was what I needed.

She said that some people would be coming to sort out the details my father's estate and I needed to be honest with them about how I was feeling.

One was a Mr. Black, the executor and the other was a Mr. Vincent. One was a lawyer and the other was a social worker with child services. They needed to do their job so I could go live with Indigo. She left around eleven and I spent the rest of the morning waiting for them to show up.

6. Mr. Black.

It was not long before the arrival of Mr. Black. He was a dreary looking man with a balding scalp and thin, clean-cut hair around his crown. It was silver and peppered with spots of dark grey. His spectacles were thick and sat on the end of his nose. His job was to be the executor of my dad's will. I didn't know what that

30

meant and didn't care, but I had no other relatives. I was the only one it could be read to.

He showed himself in and sat next to the bed. He was a nervous man with little grace about him. He adjusted his gray suit, checked his cuff-links, opened a small leather briefcase and retracted some worn paper with quivering fingertips. There were no pleasantries with him. He was simple and straightforward. His greeting was one of the only courteous actions he displayed during that meeting.

"Let's get started," He said as he began to explain why he was there. "This is the last will and testament of your father," He held up the paper. "Do you know what that is? He asked. I nodded my head and he rested the paper on his lap and adjusted his glasses.

He continued to read the papers and ask me questions about my comprehension of the document. I would nod or shake my head no and he would explain. The truth of the matter was I really did not care and just wanted to get it over with. Mr. Black, despite his lack of courteousness was quick.

What it broke down to was that my father had left me only one thing- a trust worth four million dollars to be stipend when I turned twenty-one. This did not matter to me at that time and I would have given every penny of it back just to see them again. Later in my life I forgot about it completely. I never actually collected the money, it became lost to bureaucracy and I was doing so well I never pursued its where-abouts. That money is a different story for a different time and thinking back on it- I don't think Mr. Black should have been there without a legal representative for me. Most people would be concerned about the loss of four million dollars but money was never important to Indigo's Children.

Mr. Black's process did not take very long. When he had finished he put the papers in his briefcase and stood. He looked down on me in the bed and drew a thin smile. "You are definitely your father's son, you have his constitution. Mr. Vincent will see you now. Thank you for your time," He said coldly. He left the room as quickly as he had come in. On the way out he greeted someone. It was Mr. Vincent. Mr. Black showed him in and then left.

Mr. Black was not a part of my life from that point on, but the trust my father left me is important even though I never used it. I should have kept tabs on Mr. Black, but I was too young to really understand those things.

7. Mr. Vincent and me.

Mr. Vincent was even colder than Mr. Black had been. He was also taller and thinner too, but he was not nervous at all, his calm demeanor was like a salamander in cold water. He glided into the room with calculated movement and dusted off his suit and carefully sat then adjusted himself in the chair. He produced a clip board from his attaché and set it on his lap. He looked about the room nonchalantly until his eyes came to rest on me.

They were the color of gray skies and penetrated me, reading my behavior. He paused and wet his lips then introduced himself.

"My name, is Mr. Vincent, I am your case worker," His voice was thick and dripping with articulation. "Do you know what I do?" He asked. I shook my head no and he continued. "I help people who have been through traumatic events, I help them to understand how they feel and provide tools to cope with those feelings. I provide relief and resources to all kinds of people. You are one of those people," He finished.

The session with Mr. Vincent was long and arduous. He asked a lot of questions and made sure I understood a lot of things which were already apparent to me. I took batteries of tests for him. Among them were word association tests, imagery tests, reaction tests, and one which confused me called an ink blot test. My answers were short and lacked investment. Every inkblot he showed me was a simple object such as a clock, a robot, a mushroom, a treasure chest, a pretty lady, an old house and so on. He did this through a stack of ink blots and continued with his verbal tests. He was there all afternoon and I got a little frustrated because he would not leave.

When we were done it was late and the sun was fading. He carefully filed all of his findings away in a manila folder with my name on it, then tucked them into his attaché and stood. He dusted off his jacket and took his case under his arm while he slid his gloves slowly over his fingers and then picked up his umbrella.

"You will see me again in a few days for the funeral, I will have the nurses keep this in mind and I will drop in with your suit and tie before we check you out of the hospital," He said. "I must go now, but I wish you a good night and hope that your injuries heal fast, please let me know if you have any other things you would like to talk about or need. The nurse has been instructed to contact me," He turned and walked to the door. "Good bye and good night," He said softly from the doorway in his smooth voice.

I looked down at the bed and the cast on my arm. I felt incomplete and decided Mr. Vincent was not there to help in the same way Indigo was. After he left I was alone with my grief.

This is one of my first impressions of life; sadness must be dealt with silently and alone because, no matter what someone says, it is rarely enough. It is something I have fought very hard to change in myself while I strove to be a functioning part of the world I live in. That impression led me to conclude that most of the really important things we do in life, we will do alone.

I have, through the course of my life, learned we are alone only in perception, and other people can understand our unique situations, but not how we feel. Feelings are as unique as finger prints or sense of taste. At the time I believed myself to be utterly alone because I lacked coping skills and the ability to understand empathy.

I did not sleep well that night or for the next few nights. I had more headaches and some nausea which seemed to come and go. I refused to tell the nurses about them because I did not think anything could be done for them. I wondered if the nightmare in my room had something to do with the headaches. They lasted about half an hour and would disappear almost as fast as they had come. Often times they would be accompanied by unusual feelings of disassociation as though my body were somewhere else.

The throbbing in my skull was a rhythmic pain stuck between my ears. Over and over again it would beat to the sound of my heart and pull my senses in multiple directions. It was a disorienting experience and it seemed to happen at the same time every morning, just before the sun would come up. The headaches came and went for many weeks. However, after I left the hospital they happened much less frequently and slowly as I grew older, they were replaced by something else.

The days passed and turned to a couple of weeks. Soon my cast was removed and my arm was placed in a sling. The drip was taken out and the color returned to my skin. I was getting tired of hospital food and just wanted to leave. I looked forward to seeing Indigo again and I wanted my own bed to sleep in. I would have been glad to sleep on a stranger's couch over the stiff hospital mattress. I craved the company of other children and was feeling older by the day. Even though I didn't really like Mr. Vincent at the time, I eagerly awaited his return so I could move on with my life.

When he finally did come back, it was a rainy Wednesday. I had just finished eating when he entered the room with a black garment bag. He laid it at the foot of my bed and instructed me to get dressed. He wanted me ready for the funeral. I hesitated and he repeated himself in a less friendly voice instructing me to go into the bathroom and get dressed. I did not want to but I also did not want to hear his voice again, so I did. I took the bag into the bathroom and unzipped it. Inside were my *formal clothes* as my father had called them.

With some difficulty I took my hospital gown off and slipped into the black slacks and put my belt on. It was hard with the sling on but I managed. Pain shot up and down my arm when I had to put my shirt on. I draped the white dress shirt over my torso and tucked it in making sure the creases were in the back. I buttoned it up and slid the tie over my head. I tied it in a double Windsor just as my father had instructed me. This took some time with my hand in a sling but it looked nice, even and tight.

I creased it, put the loose end in the tie clip and pinned it to my shirt. I put on my black socks. To this day, I think I was the only six year old in existence who could tie a double Windsor, a fact my father was very proud of.

I paused and made sure my dress shoes were

completely shiny. Then I slid them on and tied them making sure the laces hung at even lengths. Before I came out with the garment bag I stopped and looked myself up and down in the mirror.

My father had always taught me that looking rugged was only acceptable if there was sophistication underneath. Sophistication was apparent when a person cared about how they looked, how they groomed and how they spoke. I was dressed well and had my father's words in my head. It was what I needed to get me through the day. However, I swore I would never wear that suit again. The only reason I did what Mr. Vincent asked was because my father would have insisted and he would have insisted it was done right.

I came out of the bathroom to where Mr. Vincent was waiting. He was tapping his feet impatiently and drumming his fingers on the counter top under the television. He looked me up and down then spoke.

"Impressive," He said. He smiled a crooked smile then cocked an eyebrow and told me, "At least you know how to dress and how to present yourself," As I got to know Mr. Vincent I discovered, to him, this was the highest compliment and as long as I knew him, his compliments were short, simple and not very obvious.

He beckoned for me to follow. We left the room and headed out and down the hall to the elevator. We filed in and went to the first floor then checked out and walked the long path down to the front entry way. I stood just for a second bathing in the fluorescent lighting and then caught up to Mr. Vincent. A cold gust of wind blew through me as we exited and made our way to the black sedan waiting for us.

Mr. Vincent opened the back door and told me to get in. I did so and he got in the front passenger side. He told the driver to head to the cemetery in a very casual manner. It was then I understood why he was so dry and did not seem to care. He must have done the same thing hundreds of times with different people. I think it was a matter of habit for him and every time he dealt with it, he lost a little more of who he was. It must have been a tough job.

He nonchalantly took his paper and started reading as we pulled away from the hospital and moved out onto the main arterial running parallel to the hospital. I watched through the back window as it grew distant. There was no denying it, I was scared.

8. The funeral. [2]

The snow had turned to rain and all the white had wilted to brown slush in the streets. The trees, still naked, were a thick skeleton army on either side of the road and the clouds hung low in the sky. I watched them go by as we made our way across town. I tried not to think much about the future because at that point, living was a day to day process. Getting through the funeral

---

[2] "Hide and Seek" by Imogen Heap ♫

was the first task I had to accomplish, after that, I did not know what to expect. My thoughts were not those a child should have concern them self with.

We pulled into the cemetery and up to my parents plot. I couldn't understand why they wanted to be buried in such a place but as I have stated already-they could have starved happy and content, as long as they were in each other's reach. It made sense to me that this fact had not changed in death.

As we approached I could see people standing around two boxes suspended over two holes. The holes were black cracks in the mess of slush and I knew that below them was the abyss, waiting to consume them leaving only my memory as a record of their time together.

The car stopped and Mr. Vincent got out, he carefully opened my door and motioned for me to get out as well. I stood in the cold and forbidding wind looking over the group of people. I waited until Mr. Vincent motioned to me then I started to walk to the service across the sloppy grass.

There was a preacher standing in front of the caskets waiting with his book in his hands. People said things to me but I was not listening because no words could comfort me. I walked between the two groups of people to the front where Mr. Vincent had instructed me to go. I stopped and stood there with all the people. People I didn't know.

When they had all arrived the preacher started

his service. His words were just words with no soothing qualities. Because they were empty, I did not feel obligated to listen. I was looking at the two boxes as he talked about man's belief in heaven and how there was always room for good people. I did not believe it and I still don't, but my spiritual beliefs are not the focus of this story. He, being a preacher was obligated by his ideology to talk about it.

To me, at my age, it was all a meaningless ceremony strictly for the living. It was a way to politely hide the bodies and mortality of loved ones so we can forget them because, for most people, this is how we heal. Later I learned it was called closure. Even wounds change to scars when our bodies forget how to remember the pain. At least that was what I thought. My approach has changed dramatically since then.

Inside those boxes were the shells of my parents. There was no meaning to it, live or dead, I hurt for them. The people standing around me sniffling and crying did not know them the way I did. It didn't matter though because they knew them in some other way and this was as important as my perspective. As I sat on time, waiting for the ceremony to end, the preacher's voice raised and lowered. This was all I heard from him, the pitch and inflection of his voice which became a droning sound in the background of my mind.

9. The first encounter.

A short time after the service started I felt

someone else watching the graveside service. I couldn't place it but I could feel eyes burrowing into my back. I looked down either side of the group but did not see anything. I tried to ignore it but it became overpowering. It was a curious feeling and the hairs on my arms stood on end. There was a soft sound accompanying the feeling.

It was the sound of a man's whisper. It was too quiet to distinguish words within it as the cold wind carried the sound to my ears. I couldn't make out the sounds as they mingled with the preacher. I looked around to see if anyone else heard it. No one seemed to notice. They all continued to stand motionless and unaware.

I listened closer trying to catch where the sound was coming from. My ears perked and I cocked my head to each side trying to pinpoint it. Then my eyes caught a jerk of something behind the shrubbery across from the plot and behind the accompanying hedge.

I looked closer and saw a person standing away from the group masked by the wall of neatly trimmed bushes. I could only make out the tan of a coat and a hand resting though part of the shrubbery. He kept quiet and continued to whisper almost as if he were in distress.

My head was throbbing and pulsing. My heart beat had started beating in time with the incoherent muttering. Pain gripped my skull and ran the length of my spine. It was like bleach burning in my head, neck and back. It drilled into my eyes and the light of the gray sky became too much.

Still, I looked into the hedge to try and see who was watching. I adjusted myself by stepping to the left slowly and looking deeper. I made eye contact with his blue-gray eyes and he noticed me. He locked his them and continued to mumble under his breath as the pain built in my mind. I did not know who the man was and I could not pull myself away or say anything. I only stared. Even though his words had no language behind them, I felt he said more than the preacher, and he understood more on the subject of death than any preacher. It seemed that he knew more about the human condition and the sorrow we skirt our whole lives. It seemed that he understood me.

It was the first time I felt like I was not alone in my own life.

Then, it was too much. I was too raw and I became fatigued by the encounter. Overwhelmed, my peripheral vision started to go black and fade into paisley stars while my eyesight started to narrow. I bent over and felt my stomach convulse as my food came up.

I made it a couple of steps and then collapsed onto the wet green and thinning white. There was an icy dampness between my fingers as I held myself above the ground trying to avoid getting the suit wet or landing on my arm. It was only a few seconds before someone was there to help.

They pulled me up and when I was on my feet

the pain was gone. My head was fine except for some mild dizziness. Someone was dabbing the corner of my mouth with a handkerchief and speaking softly to me making sure I was alright. I was, but I was also confused.

The man was gone and so was the gibberish. I looked and looked but I couldn't find him as my eyes darted around the cemetery. I lied and told all the concerned people standing that I had not been feeling good and it was only some stomach issues.

The preacher came over and looked down at me. He said it was okay, things would get better and that I was grieving. It was a natural part of the process of loss. There was a short recess and then the service continued despite my fit.

The sermon was very generic and no names were mentioned except that of my parents. I did not speak of the man I had seen to anyone. I am glad I didn't because Mr. Vincent was there watching me. He was judging my emotional stability and I wanted to stay with Indigo, I wasn't going to risk the only option I really had. As long as he was watching me I wasn't going to say anything because I did not trust him. I did not want to take more tests and I certainly did not want to go back to the hospital or to adoption services.

For years I thought the mystery men who appeared that day, and earlier in the hospital were symptoms of mental illness.

As I grew older I discovered craziness was really

a relative term. There are, and were, bigger things in my life which could be construed as symptoms of mental illness. As an old man I learned to submit to these things and embrace them with an open mind. I do not label myself mad for all I have been through. Crazy is just a word people came up with to cope with their own feelings of discomfort around people who are different. I do not like labels and I will claim none. I was, and am different. Indigo knew this and made sure all of the children at the Allotment were well trained to hide in plain sight. We were all normal, to other people's eyes, and we liked it that way.

As the feeling settled the preacher finished and Mr. Vincent was at my side. He handed me two roses. Everyone else had two as well. When the preacher closed his book he called a moment of silence and then said a prayer. It was short moment and as soon as it was done the coffins were lowered into the ground. We all started to walk single file to the two holes. Each person threw the roses into the ground on top of the coffins and slowly walked away.

When it was my turn, I walked up to the graveside and looked down at the two roses and the two graves. Somewhere inside I became acutely aware of how short life was. It took me a long time to complete the ritual but reluctantly I committed and dropped the roses into the ground. Mr. Vincent ushered me away and back to the sedan.

I would never see them again, I would never

hear them sing again, and I would never again be held by them. Only in memory would I have access to them. Somehow I had to be okay with that and not allow it to break me.

The wind was starting to blow harder when I got into the car. It was crisp and cut through my suit and into flesh. It tugged at my clothes and bit my bones. Mr. Vincent shut the door behind me then got in the front seat and told the driver to go to my old house. We pulled away but I did not take my eyes off the small group of people still lingering around the site.

I kept looking through them and the surroundings, searching for the man I had seen. Hoping I could recognize him in the crowd. I suspected he had long since left.

I watched as we pulled further and further away. Then onto the main road which lead back towards the downtown area. Soon I could no longer see the cemetery or the parade of cars leaving the lifeless parcel of land with all the stones.

They had gathered their memories just as I had and were moving on. Mr. Vincent did not ask any questions about what had happened in the cemetery. He did not seem interested. I never went back to that cemetery to see them; I prefer the way they were to the way they are.

10. My old house.

It was not long until we arrived at my old house.

A duffel-bag was given to me and I was told to go and get only what I needed. This meant only clothing and a couple of items which were important to me such as photographs or small things of sentimental value. Mr. Vincent gave me the keys and I got out of the car.

My old house was a slightly smaller red brick house. I loved that house, every inch of it was familiar to me. It was a two level with bay windows on the two front corners and heavy hardwood beams supporting a spacious front porch. There was a lot of character in the woodwork which was mostly hand-hewn. The floorboards were not completely even or smooth, but they retained character, some of them squeaked and some were always quiet.

It was home. It was the place we my family listened to old vinyl records and played board games around the dining room table. The place we ate and slept. It was the place we dreamed and dared. We teased each other there and told stories and watched movies there, and I missed it then, as I do now.

The left over love was fading, I could feel it, and soon the house would be a shell. I sighed, walked up to the house and unlocked the door then stepped in.

It was darker inside and my breath echoed without any words to project. I turned the lights on and the smell of home hit my nostrils. I breathed it deep. It was not the smell we left. It was not a Christmas smell, but it was the smell of home. The house was clean and all the appliances were unplugged.

The Christmas decorations in the living room were still up and the lights were on. Reds, greens and blues hung on its bows and spiraled around the room. It was exactly as we had left it except the Christmas lights. I didn't remember leaving them on, nonetheless, they were comforting and added some warmth to my old home. I thought maybe my mother had left them as friendly ghosts representing the jubilee of the season. It was our residue left in its bones. It was our settling dust in the living room, and it was our remnants of laughter in the kitchen.

I remember, and still can remember, all the fun we had. All the soft Christmas specials we had watched together and the heaps of wrapping paper which littered the space on Christmas morning. Those memories were still fresh in my mind. I looked over at the tree which was losing its needles and was on the verge of turning brown. For the most part its smell had gone away.

Beneath it was a scrap of golden wrapping paper. I took it from the floor and put it in my pocket. It was one of the only things I took. I have kept it my whole life. I still have it and there were many Christmases where I put it on the tree as an ornament just to remember.

I crept up the stairs listening to every squeak and I ran my hand along the banister trying to burn its feeling into my head. It was the feeling of rough wood grain which had been saddled by many palms and smoothed with use. It was the banister's finger print and

47

it was unique to that house.

In my room on my bed was my pair of skis. I was thankful someone had found them and returned them. I suspected they were returned when the car was pulled from the river. They had been maintained and waxed which was nice. Next to them was their carrying case, it was water damaged but still in usable shape. Mr. Vincent had told me to take only what I needed, I decided I needed them and he would have to let me have them. I placed them inside their case and packed my clothing. I could think of nothing else I wanted, at least nothing which could be taken.

I paused at the door and looked back at my room. It had been my sanctuary and safe heaven. My father had always told me to leave things orderly. I made sure everything was neat and perfect. The bed was made and the clothes were folded. There was nothing on the floor, no clothes, no toys and my books were all on the shelves in order. This had been the way my father had taught me to be. I had grown to like the order. Looking back I feel this was a strange thing for a six year old to be concerned with but at the time it didn't seem strange. But in part, as I soon learned, Indigo did not seek out normal children to share the allotment with.

I shut my bedroom door behind me and started down the stairs. I hoped Indigo would be the same way. I hoped she would be a good parent as mine had been. Even if that were the case, my mother and my father were both irreplaceable.

I walked across the landing to the stairs and then down to the front door. Next to the door was a small stand and on it was a solitary picture of our family. I picked up the antique wood frame and removed the backing then took the picture out. It was the only picture I took. I have kept it with me always. I have it here with me as I write this, it is old and it is worn, but it is not faded. I laminated it and kept it protected. I tried not to fold it or pack it wrong. It has a special tube I put it in when I travel to keep it safe.

I locked the front door and walked down the walkway to the black sedan where Mr. Vincent was waiting. He was tapping his fingers again showing his impatience. To my surprise he did not comment on my skis. I got in and Mr. Vincent motioned for the driver to leave.

There was no looking back because it was too painful. It wouldn't have done me any good to look back. There was nothing I could do to change any of it. Instead I decided to forget about it until it could be processed and I knew some night it would find me and I would face it, however, it was not the time.

The sky was starting to clear as we drove up the ramp to the freeway. It was the same ramp, which had brought me such joy a few weeks earlier.

I watched the gray and pink bands shed beams of light across the farm fields. There were pastures dotted with barns and open expanses where cattle were statues in the melting snow, motionless and still. Among the fields were little houses covered in rain-washed icicles and bleeding lines of wood smoke which brushed the horizon. I could see lights coming on as workmen returned home to their wives, their diners and their televisions.

Soon we left the fields and traveled into the woods along the river moving through the broad leaf trees stationed along the sides of the road. I could see the colors of the setting sun through the empty frames while the sky became damp with night and it reminded me of death. In a certain way it framed my situation well. It was a long skeletal tunnel of lifeless trees leading to an unfamiliar place.

To this point I have only spoken of death and pain, this story is not about those things. A person, especially a child does not get over them fast. I was no different as I assume you are not either. I assure you, even with how the story of my life started there was also much joy in it.

11. The Allotment. [3]

It was almost five when we pulled up to the driveway of the Allotment. It was a quiet estate miles from any neighbor. There was a mailbox hanging at the end of the driveway on a stout piece of oak and off in either direction extended a stone wall which disappeared

---

[3] "Lost Boy" by Ruth B ♫

into along the main road. Just behind the mailbox the large wrought iron gate anchored into heavy stone pillars. The driver stopped the car and got out. He slid the gate open and drove the car in then closed it.

The road was paved and it was free of ice and snow. My eyes followed the black stripe into the distance along its winding route. On either side there were tall and naked walnut, maple, and cherry trees. Between them were blocks of land in neat little squares which were partially fenced. The car drove along the asphalt twisting its way to the main house.

I had arrived at what Indigo had referred to as the *Allotment*. On the top of a small rise I could see the house sitting alone on a bald patch above the trees.

As we approached it occurred to me just how big the estate was. It was at least a mile from the road to the main house and the out buildings. The land was covered with ancient trees draped in moss. I saw horses and some cows as well as deer and elk in the distance along the tree break.

The house was a large Victorian style home with Grecian pillars holding up the front. There were grape vines growing on trellises at the corners of the home and a wide and expansive lawn extending down from the front porch which wrapped around both corners of the house. The paved driveway cut through the grass in a circular shape which rested at the door so visitors would not have to back out, instead they could drive through.

The house had many windows and many doors.

It was four floors counting the basement. The windows were starting to frost as the temperature dropped.

Children looked out through the spiraling frost to see who was coming. Their faces pressed to the glass in curiosity. Behind them, in the living space I could see the dim glow of a warm fire. It lit the icy panes in a shimmering orange. My eyes followed the chimney up to white smoke oozing from the top and across the tall gables of the house.

Although the home's style was somewhat old, the construction was not, or it had been very well maintained over the years. Everything was in immaculate order.

I could see the out buildings and the red barn behind them tucked in the folds of land. The paint was new and even in the failing light I could see how well each structure was built. There was a second when I felt it was too splendid a place for me to live.

Mr. Vincent had the driver pull the car to a stop at the mouth of the front porch next to the steps. He took a brief look back at me, then forced a smile and announced we had arrived. This was my new home. I took my skis and the duffel-bag from the car, got out and looked up at the New England home.

There was still some Connecticut Blue above me, but it was disappearing fast and I was getting tired. My bag was heavy and my mind was numb but the fire behind the large icy windows looked inviting. More so, my heart felt the warmth inside, behind those doors.

Mr. Vincent told me to go up to the door and knock. I broke my self away and walked up the walkway to the house. I grasped the knocker, lifted it, and let it drop. There was a hollow thump from the inside and some chatter from the living room. It was not long before I heard the deep growl of the hinges. The door swung open and Indigo peered out from the orange glow and then down at me. Behind her I saw the shadows of three dogs sitting in a perfect line at the bottom of a large staircase. She turned and excused them, then returned her eyes to me.

"There you are," She said with smile. She waved to Mr. Vincent so he could leave. He quickly said goodbye then got into the car and pulled away. This was not the last I saw of Mr. Vincent. I would see him on a regular basis until his death, which in a roundabout way I am also responsible for.

I watched the sedan glide down the driveway into the distance then I turned to Indigo.

"Well don't stand out there on the porch freezing, come in, come in," She motioned me inside.

It was very warm in the house. I was standing in the open foyer in front of the old oak staircase leading to the second and third floors. To the right there was a large living space with leather furniture and an exposed fireplace where flames licked the stone behind a heavy fire screen. Five children sat in front of the fire laughing and talking with each other. The other side of the room was all bookshelves. On either side of the stairs were hallways leading back into the houses darkened corners. Indigo stood next to me and looked with me.

In every shelf there were ancient hand bound books sandwiched together and I detected the faint smell of old parchment and leather in the air.

"It's quite a house isn't it?" She asked. I nodded and she reached down and took my duffel-bag. "I am sure you will like it here, I will show you your room... it's got a view…" She smiled and her ivory teeth formed a big grin in the dim light.

I nodded again and we started the hike to the third floor. The stairs were old and each step told a story. Like Braille, the worn wood sung in squeaks and creeks. There was mystery in that house and the steps themselves were only superficial to the journey.

The wood banisters were all hand carved giving it an old world feel. On the walls hung old pictures of people doing amazing things and other pictures of people traveling to fantastic places. Some were photographs and some were hand painted.

One thing I noted was that there were no pictures of children anywhere along the walls.

I also noticed a lot of old maps. They were yellow with age and in many places there were spots and water stains. It seemed that they had been well used as if someone had traveled the world with them. There were technical maps and there were framed newspaper clippings as well. While staying at the Allotment, I never took the time to read them. They seemed to be more decorative, as though they were details to fill the atmosphere.

The ceilings were high giving the house an open feel. Despite the size and high ceiling I felt no drafts. The rooms were quite warm and alive.

We went up two flights. There was a sharp turn and we went to the front of the house. Indigo told me to follow her down a hallway along the outside wall. After a few steps we came to an oak door. She opened it and let me in to my new room, which was mostly empty. I walked over and put my duffel-bag and skis on the bed. She came over, sat down next to my stuff and motioned for me to sit next to her.

"I know it's been hard for you, and I can never take any of that away but this is your home now and there are plenty of kids just like you here. You are all special. You are my children and I will take care of you," She said. "Unpack your clothes and then come down and meet as many people as you can. We are having dinner in an hour and I am sure you will love it," She said.

I was hungry and it had been almost three weeks since I had eaten a real meal. She stood up from the bed and gracefully slid out of the room so I could get changed.

My new room had two huge windows overlooking the grounds. There was a large wooden desk in front of the window with a lamp squared in the corner. There was also a portable computer placed on the desk top. The bed rested along the inside wall. It was made and the sheets were all tucked in. Next to the bed was the closet and next to the door sat a bureau, which was also hand crafted.

I quickly unpacked my duffel-bag and neatly put the clothes into the chest of drawers. I took the sling off because I was tired of its awkwardness. I had a little trouble because of the pain in my arm, but I managed, it did not hurt as much.

I changed out of my stuffy suit and put on my jeans and a t-shirt. I hung the suit neatly in the bag and swore I would never again wear it.

When I was done I left the room and came down to the top of the first flight of stairs. I stopped and listened to all the people below talking and laughing in the living room. Their conversations were carried up on warm currents of air from the main floor. I heard a lot of different voices but couldn't discern how many children were there. I did not really want to meet them but I knew my interactions with them would be inevitable. I slowly crept down the stairs but the old steps gave me up. I was on the third step from the top when she rounded the corner and looked up at me.

She was a little girl, about my age, wearing sweatpants and a blue shirt. I froze and she looked up at me in the darkened staircase. Her eyes were sharp and she gazed at me with curiosity. Her hair was dark brown and it framed her cherubs face like a picture frame. I could see her small hands and little toes glued to her bare feet.

I did not say anything. She held my stare for a while then she smiled. There was a sparkle about her I had not seen in any child I had known. It was painted in the expression on her face.

"Hey," She said waving her hand at me.

"Hi," I whispered as I placed my hands into my pockets. She said nothing more, rather she turned and motioned for me to follow. Stepping down the last steps, I followed her to the living room where about ten children were talking, playing and laughing. They were sitting slouched in various chairs and bean bags around the room. There were also larger chairs, bound in Corinthian leather occupied by some of the older children. They were reading as they basked in the warmth from the glowing flames. Some of the children were playing board games while others used their personal computers. Two boys were wrestling on the floor.

I would eventually come to know the last two very well. They would become two of my best friends, Clark and Clyde.

The thick smell of roast beef was lingering in the hallway to the kitchen. Instantly my mouth began to water. The air was heavy with chives, garlic, rosemary and thyme. It was accented with the smell of freshly baked rolls.

I followed the girl down the second hallway behind the living room which lead to the kitchen where there were more children helping Indigo make dinner. There was a very large pot simmering on an oven island and freshly chopped veggies were stacked in neat little piles next to it. Two boys and two girls hovered over the pot adding the ingredients. Indigo looked over her shoulder at me and smiled.

"Dinner will be ready in about half an hour," She looked at the girl next to me, and smiled a little. "Belle why don't you show him around..." She quartered a potato and tossed it into the pot. I looked over at the girl. She nodded then motioned for me to follow her as she left the kitchen. I walked just behind her down the hallway. She talked over her shoulder to me as she took me from room to room.

The house seemed to be larger on the inside and I found myself being more and more impressed with the craftsmanship. It was something my father taught me to appreciate. He had always said quality was more important than quantity because value was established in quality and value was important. The quality of craftsmanship in that house was, for lack of better words, impeccable.

Belle explained that there were thirty children in all, and three dogs. She told me they were service dogs but they were to be treated as family. She showed me each floor.

The layout was simple and functional. On each floor there were ten rooms, two large hallway storage rooms, three bathrooms, a broom closet and a study room. It was very ordered and all the children were accommodated. It was a short tour of the house and we did not see the basement because Indigo's living space was down stairs. Belle made it very clear none of the children were allowed down stairs. As far as I understood it was a full residence apartment complete with a lower entrance from the back.

After the tour I met the three dogs, Loki, Odin, and Thor. They were large and obedient German shepherds. All were well trained and came and lined up in a row when Belle called them with a whistle. She told me their duty was to watch over the children and make sure the house was secure. It did not take me long to become accustomed to Loki. He was always sleeping at the top of the third floor stairs. If I had to go to the bathroom he was there and would walk down the hall with me in the dark. I loved that dog.

It came time for dinner and we returned and filed into the back room off the kitchen. It was the dining room. There were three large tables which sat ten people each. The dogs came as well and sat just off the end of each table and waiting patiently.

The places were set for thirty children and three large stew pots were brought in and placed in the center of each table. All the bowls were filled, Indigo sat in an extra chair at a smaller table in the front of the room. She had one of the children from each table pass out the freshly baked and buttered bread. She watched patiently observing to make sure all of the children were fed. She was always that way; putting the children first in all things. I never saw her eat that night. She just watched the children eat. That first night, about half way through the meal she stopped everyone and made my introduction.

"Children, we have a new room-mate," She announced. All the kids put their utensils down and greeted me in unison. "Why don't you introduce yourself?" She asked. "Go ahead, stand up and say hi," She said. I did not have much to say but I reluctantly stood and bid everyone hello. It had been a long time since I had used my voice for anything but grief and it felt strange to speak for other reasons. It came out as a whisper. My introduction was short and shy, and I quickly sat down and started to eat my food. They all said hello then went back to eating as well.

The roast beef was good and I was glad to have it. I was impressed that dinner was made by the children, but came to learn it was that way at the Allotment. We made our own food, grew our own vegetables, collected our own fruit, roasted our own nuts and rarely ventured off the establishment for supplies. The Allotment was designed to be self-sustaining. Later we made many trips to town, but not for the purpose of getting food.

I got to know a few people that night. I meant two of the first children Clark and Clyde. I met Ralph and Susan who were both newcomers. I met Frank and Alley and most important I met Belle. I did not know it at the time but she was my perfect match, I will never find another like her. She is the reason I put this on paper and sent it to you. If you know about Belle than this is in the right hands and you might have had a recent experience which would resonate with this.

I went up to my room early that first night and crawled into bed. At some point I woke up to Loki licking my face. He seemed to know how I felt. He was soft and warm and crawled into bed with me for a brief time to comfort me. I did not wake for the rest of the night. Loki made a habit of crawling in bed with me and I made a habit of leaving my door open a crack so he could slip in.

I slept deep and my mind took a rest for the first time since the accident. I do not mean sleep, I mean rest, there is a difference, rest comes when one feels secure, and sleep comes from exhaustion.

12. My first day.

The next day I started my adjustment period. It was early in the morning and I could hear noises stirring in the house. I opened my eyes and saw the light bleeding from the window. Beyond it was the familiar blue. It was crisp, new and cold. It ushered in my new life, new habits and perspectives. It was sharp in my eyes and to a certain extent I welcomed it after the weeks of darkness and rain. Loki whimpered at my open door and I pulled myself out of bed and told him to come in. He greeted me by licking my palm and nuzzling my face. Then he sat and waited because he knew I needed to go down stairs. I got dressed in the same clothes from the night before and left my little upstairs room.

Loki walked me down the flights to the main foyer and to the kitchen where a breakfast was being prepared. Indigo and four different children stood in the kitchen frying eggs and making toast. She looked over at me and motioned for Loki to return to his duties. I walked over to the stove where the children were preparing breakfast and felt the stoves warmth. Indigo handed me a spatula and told me to flip the pancakes. I did so while I watched the eggs sizzle.

"There are some things I need to go over with you as soon as we finish breakfast," She said with a smile. "We have a very balanced life here, and I will show you how it works," I looked up at her and nodded as I turned a pancake. The smell of dough hit me and I became hungry. The tables were set and we all ate.

When we finished, Indigo told me to follow the other children and wash my plate, my silverware and my glass. Water was already drawn and we were fast, in a few moments all the dishes were done. I was impressed with the order and speed in which things were completed. In time I would discover just how organized the group was. I would also get used to it and become a part of it. We supported each other's function. This was important to our purpose and it was one of the reasons we were selected by Indigo. She knew what kind of people we were going to be, and she fostered certain behaviors to get us there.

When the washing was completed Indigo told me to walk with her and she handed me a coat. It was comfortable and very warm. "We have some things to discuss," She said in a very casual manner.

I followed her and we went to the front door where some boots were waiting. We went out into the winter air and down to the barn where she started to feed the livestock.

"I hope you like it here, you will find I expect much and I provide much. This is just a formality and I already know you will exceed my expectations. Everything will be provided here and you may find some of my children are quite remarkable, but then again, so are you... Always remember that. All of you are remarkable. Here you will be a part of something amazing and as long as you participate and function as a part it, you will always have a place here," She handed me some chicken feed and told me to give it a try.

I tossed the food to them and watched their heads go up and down as they collected it in their beaks.

She talked to me as she would have an adult. I did not understand some of it, but I remembered it, and over time I began to comprehend it.

"Here, there are no bullies, there are no non-valuable people or ideas, there is no name calling or teasing and there is no judgment or reason for it. This will lead to harmony. This makes us different in the world. Each of the thirty children I have selected have specific qualities making them unique. Those qualities also make them important to the group and a valuable part of the whole. Without any one of you the group is incomplete. You do not realize it yet but the outside world is a place where these qualities do not exist in the same capacity. Cooperation and tolerance are not taught well or held as standards. People, for the most part, do not value them anymore. They have been replaced with more material values. There is a great deal of misery outside these walls because of it. Here, those qualities are special. They are manifestations of a person's character and are important. There are very few things you can take with you through life, character is one of them. This group has great character and can achieve so much," She smiled took some chicken feed and joined me feeding the hens.

"See these chickens, they would not eat if we did not feed them, and the eggs we ate this morning would not have been laid. In other words, we would not eat if they were not fed. This is very much the way I want things to be here. Once again, I already know you won't have a problem with this but I want you to remember it as well. Here you will get fed, you will have friends and you will be loved and valued for your character. You will be schooled in all aspects of life and I will provide an education for you- beyond that of the schools out there… beyond that of most colleges. You will learn just like in public school but you will know more truth, and you will learn how to teach yourself. Teaching yourself and learning to learn are far more important than knowing things. You will learn how to search out answers and discover. And your aptitudes will be exercised," She said as she put the chicken feed up.

"It will not be hard or easy. It will be natural. Another thing I want you to remember is there is always time for fun, I know given the circumstances, fun is the last thing on your mind but nonetheless, there is always time for it and eventually you will learn it. When you do, you will exercise it as well. Everything here is important especially your classmates because they are, and always will be your family... And the dogs, they are people too," She smiled and looked down at me. "You have met them?" she asked.

"Yes. I met all three of them," I confirmed.

"Good. They are important to us. They are all still young and somewhat unruly but I finally got them trained well. I hope they provide you with comfort. We have a lot to do here, but as long as everybody participates the whole thing works,"

She took some hay and gave it to the animals in the stalls. She finished and walked up to me and knelt down and looked me in the eye gently placing her hands on my shoulders.

"I am sorry for what happened to you but I am glad you are here. I cannot think of a better place for you to be. You are the last of the children I plan to take in. I have thirty children here and all of them have similar stories to yours, you will discover all of them have been through great tragedy and tragedy can make a difference in understanding," She hugged me and I went loose in her arms. It was the first time anyone had touched me since the accident.

I spent a good deal of time in the barn with her tending to the livestock. I thought it was strange the other children stayed in the house all day. Indigo told me they were working on projects. She explained I would learn very fast and my schooling would start the following week.

We finished the chores for the morning, ate lunch and continued with our day. Most of the afternoon was spent touring the grounds before we returned to the house. When we got back the children were all in the main room and the dining hall. They had their laptops open and were typing. It made me feel a little inadequate. I had no idea how to use a computer let alone type on one. They all knew how.

I sat in the chair by the fire and took one of the books off the shelf. It was a hard bound book, an Atlas. I opened it and pretended to read it just to try and fit in. I wished I had my comics and I felt awkward sitting there with nothing to do.

At three in the afternoon the clock chimed and I looked up. All the children were closing the computers. I looked at the nearest boy and asked what was happening.

"Schools over for the day," He answered simply.
"You guys do school on a computer?" I asked.

"Yeah, I like it much better than regular school,"
He said. He put the laptop in his bag.

"And it goes faster too, so I can get to the fun stuff- like playing with the other kids. A couple days a week we get lectures from Indigo, but they are way better than the teacher I used to have in school…" He paused and looked at me and I recognized him as being one of the kids who had been wrestling the night before, his name was Clark.

His face was long and his nose was large. His hair was short and brown. There was a heart shaped birthmark on his neck. I can recall liking him right away.

Clark spent the rest of the day showing me how the Allotment worked. He showed me how all the children alternated chores and everyone did them, there were no exceptions. Maintenance of the Allotment was crucial and participation was required. He told me it would not take me very long to get the hang of it. He was right, it was a simple system and all the tasks were on a very large whiteboard in the kitchen. Although trying to remember things still gave me headaches, so chores were a painful task at first.

Over the next few days my headaches came and went. Indigo told me this was to be expected and my body still needed to heal.

The pulsing would creep up my back in the early morning and wake me. I would feel the paralysis and lay in bed struggling with my inability to move. There were times when the sound in my head got so loud I couldn't hear myself breathing. I would silently convulse and thrash in my sheets. My muscles would misfire and my heart would palpitate but I could do nothing to stop it.

Certain nights, when I had worked hard all day, I came to expect them. I would submit to the seizures and be tossed about by bursts of electricity surging through my body.

The first week went by quick and I started my schooling the following week. As Clark had indicated it was not typical school. I was the only one who did not know how to read and write which was my first task, to learn to read, write and comprehend. I got a few private lectures for this from indigo. She started by asking me what I liked. This was hard for me because I did not have much experience. I thought about it and answered that I liked to ski. She explained we would start there because it would be pointless to teach me to read something I was not interested in and doing so would teach me to dislike reading.

She told me to get my laptop and bring it down to the living room. She turned it on and showed me how to access the learning program she called *Prometheus*. I was surprised to see there were no words when it first opened, just pictures and small icons. She explained I needed to go through them until I found one which interested me. So I scrolled down through hundreds of simple icons and selected the picture of a mountain. Then I scrolled through the icons until I found a snowflake and lastly I scrolled to a picture of a ski. This was how I learned to read. The screen would flash a series of objects and the phonic symbols or letters would accompany them.

After some orientation, it would add the symbols together and flash the object then the word. Next it would flash the word, sound and then the object. Lastly it would only show the word and we would have to select the object and say it or spell it out loud. I started slow, and every time I would complete and refresh the lesson it would unlock more complicated icons. By the end of that first day I knew almost everything there was to know about skiing. I now understand that most children do not learn by this method.

I learned to write much the same way. It was harder because my coordination was not developed. I used a little track pad and a stylus. When I could write a word and the computer could recognize it, the computer would move me on to the next one. Each time it would fine tune its recognition and I would have to improve my handwriting. The first week was long and I went through hundreds of icons. But at the end of the first week I could read and I could write at a basic level.

It surprised me how fast I learned. We studied all the basics, math, science, history, grammar, English, and so on. For every subject a similar system had been set up so we could do our work. It was striking that I didn't seem to forget anything. It was also interesting that it felt very natural.

13. My education and new friends.

Those first two weeks I learned the fundamentals of my education. Everything except Math was built on this kind of learning method. My mind soaked it up so fast I don't think I could have stopped the process even if I had wanted to.

The more I learned the more frequent and intense the headaches were, as though the knowledge was being forced into me and making its own room in my mind.

It was not long before the screens with the icons were flickering so quickly it was hard to keep up. I was having difficulty comprehending the amount of information I was absorbing. I seemed to be drawn into the process. In just a couple of months I was reading and writing at a middle school level. I was running out of icons in my lessons and it wasn't just the reading and the writing, but all the lessons.

I developed several interests in my studies. I loved history, biology, chemistry and most importantly math.

Indigo told us we were lucky because not everyone got to pick what they studied. She explained that public schools had to study the same things over and over again for twelve years. She wanted us to be functioning in our aptitudes after three years. Our aptitudes however, did not excuse us in our other studies and we were expected to keep up on them and be well rounded.

As a group we also learned to play. It was as Indigo told us we would. Clyde, Clark and I excelled at playing. There was never a day after our studies that we couldn't be found running around the house, chasing each other.

Even though I had not fully regained my sense of humor I found it was easy to enjoy myself. In the evenings before bed we would play all kinds of board games and word games. My favorite was Risk. Clyde and I were really good at this game and spent a great deal of time running the board on our classmates.

In the early morning we tended the livestock and the chores, this was how we got our exercise. We alternated out and I learned how to take care of cows, chickens, sheep, and how to tend to the garden and make sure it got prepped for the spring and the growing season.

The garden was just behind the house in a small ravine and once the snow had melted there was a lot of soil to turn and there was mulch to spread. It was an acre plot of land with a red-washed cedar fence about six feet tall. It ran around the acre to keep the animals out. I loved the garden, it and the small adjacent lake became my two favorite places.

14. Working with Mr. Vincent.

Those first few months I saw Mr. Vincent again. I was informed he would come and do assessments on all of the children to see how we were coming along. He was the state's liaison with Indigo. Someone said he was paid very well to keep an eye on us, and despite his somewhat aloof personality I became very used to him. His job on each visit was to council a different child to find out how they were progressing through Indigo's program. He said he was impressed with the academic progress she had made but he was concerned with our mental health and I suppose this was because he was a social worker. It was his job to care about us and report to the state.

When he visited, he would take me to the study with the big windows in the back of the house and close the door.

As usual his grooming was immaculate and his expressionless face never gave away his emotions. I would have a seat and he would take out my file and set it on the desk in front of him. He would proceed to look it over for a minute or two and re-familiarize himself with the details. Each time I saw him he asked more personal questions. I assumed this was his way of testing me and gaining trust. I was as honest as I needed to be and I gave him the information he wanted because there really was nothing to hide.

After each session he would leave me in the study and then go talk to Indigo about my *status* as he called it. None of the students were allowed to know the details of those meetings but again, I assumed they went well because no one ever left the Allotment or needed additional visits from Mr. Vincent. I believed his assessments were all positive experiences until Clyde was caught with the red notebook. The red notebook changed everything.

His face became a regular around the Allotment. I became quite aware of his mannerisms and what they meant. His raised eyebrow meant that he was skeptical, his twitching eyelids affirmed he was impatient and the effeminate way he crossed his legs meant he was preparing to build trust and so on.

I learned to read his tells and provided the answers he was searching for. Every time he visited, my file became thicker and the papers started to leaf out the sides. I cannot imagine what all that information told him but I was glad he came to meet with me sometimes. During his visits I was able to work out some of my emotions and come to grips with the death of my mother and father. As time went by there were other things I was thankful for. He had a way of making me see why I did the things I did and showed me better ways of coping. I do not think he knew I was studying and learning about him more than he was learning about me. He taught me a great deal about how people deceive each other and themselves. Also how people sometimes need the illusion to see around themselves. Sometimes a person can only start healing from behind the memories, and getting behind them is the real trick.

15. Days, nights and fireflies. [4]

The spring came and went. We prepared the garden, we planted, we tended, and cared for our harvest. It was part of our education in sustainability. I loved it because I could watch the progression of my work. I also learned about what Indigo called *farmer's wisdom* which in many ways I found to be a more useful type of knowledge. As the plants grew I watched the spring unfold into warmth and sunshine.

Summer was no different. The days were long and lazy and our studies shifted to the outdoors. We learned herbology, horticulture and botany alongside our daily studies. It was also that first summer I learned about bee-keeping which became another enjoyable part of my life. The honey was not bad either.

Summer evenings were one of my favorite learning experiences. We would watch the fireflies churning in the cool air and they would turn to glowing beads roiling in the early night along thermal currents. Indigo told us they were helpless to each other, only following pheromones while they chased each other in desperation. They were desperate because their lives were short. They had little time to burn, so they burned bright. The little lights in the night would soon die, but they would be back next year. They made me happy and sad all at the same time.

---

[4] "Made of light" by Mikky Ekko ♫

Indigo would take us into one of the meadows away from the light pollution and we would learn about the patterns of stars and how to navigate by them. We never asked why it was important to learn this. As children it was obvious, all the technology and GPS could never match the excitement of learning what explorers did for thousands of years.

Each night was an adventure with the greatest explorers in history. We were taught the myths behind the constellations and what times of the year they were visible.

Indigo told stories about them as she explained the navigation process. She made me feel like I was a part of history and connected to the ancient world somehow. Those late night lessons infused me with a profound thirst for discovery, adventure and learning. Seeing into the dark of night is a lot like discovery and if you are too scared to look you will never see the magic which hides among the dying fire flies.

As the late summer nights progressed my headaches came fewer and further between. They still occurred, especially after particularly grueling days of learning and exploration. I was not afraid of them as I had been. They were a relief. As if all the pent up energy and emotion suddenly had a vent to escape through. I would have them, which was uncomfortable, but when they were over I would sleep well.

It was also that summer, in July, when I found out I was not the only one who suffered headaches.

On Independence day Indigo rented a charter bus that took us to the fireworks show in the nearby town next to the river. It was the only time we left the Allotment that year.

We spent the day eating junk food and playing. Indigo told us about the American Revolution, why we celebrated it, and she shared details including dirty little secrets left out of the history books.

That night we sat in the park across the river from the display with hundreds of other people looking up in unison at the sky. The fireworks burst like multicolored blossoms across the heavens and the delayed echoes rang in our ears. We gazed at the incandescent light with childish amazement and enjoyed every moment as the sky was painted with a pallet of fire. It was, after all, a grand New England show.

It stayed warm until late. The crickets started to sing as Indigo gathered us up and loaded us onto the bus to head home.

When we arrived back at the Allotment Clark mentioned he was going to have a headache. He said he got them all the time and they were caused by intense flickering lights. Sometimes he got them when he studied too much or looked at the flashing screen on the laptop too long. I asked him what they were like and he told me.

"I usually get them when I am sleeping, early in the morning. A lot of us get them," He said. I asked him to describe them. "They start in the back of my head and move up and down my back. I can't move when they happen. I am not scared of them anymore," He said.

"Yeah?" I asked.

"I had this thing happen to me when I was younger and I was in the hospital for a long time. As far as I can tell that was when they started," He said.

I did not ask him what he was talking about until later. Over the next few weeks I asked some of the other children if they had headaches and all the children told me the same thing.

I did not understand what the headaches were or their connection the children but I was sure there was one.

I was very busy with things that summer so I let it sit as days passed. The season slid through autumn, with its oranges and reds, to the white ice of winter. I kept up on studies and I kept up on the chores. I made more friends and learned much more about the world and did not ask any more questions about the headaches.

I thought very little about them until one winter night while playing chess with Clark. He brought up the headaches again so I asked him what happened. He told me after his house had burned down he was in hospital with smoke inhalation and he had what he thought might have been a dream. He mentioned there was a tall dark man who injected him with something. He wasn't sure if it was real; he referred to him as the tall man who sounded like a clock. He said he used to be afraid of him, afraid he would come back.

Over the course of the next year I got to know other children. I found we all had similar situations. We all had our parents taken from us at early ages, usually the age of six or seven. We were all stricken with terrible headaches. Each one of us had seen the tall man although by that time I had heard him called other things such as the clockwork man, the skinny man, and the dark man.

I would later discover the contents of the syringe were not biological or chemical in nature. I did not learn anymore about it from the other children.

I studied hard and I played harder. Just as Indigo had told me, I eventually made it through the grieving process. I went skiing my first few winters at the Allotment. It was hard the first time without my parents but I enjoyed it nonetheless. I felt bad that they were not there to see how good I had become. Mr. Vincent played a crucial role in this with his weekly visits and he helped me to understand a few things about how I was feeling. With his help I managed to turn my ski trips into a cathartic experience. I out grew those skis and was lucky enough to get a new pair from Indigo my third Christmas at the Allotment.

Another year passed and I had more visits with Mr. Vincent. I thought about the tall man and the syringe often but we never talked about it. My studies became more comprehensive and I discovered I liked the subject of math. In fact it was my strongest aptitude. I would hesitate in my studies just so I could spend more time on it and enjoy myself while I studied.

It was at this point my perception of the world changed rather profoundly. Maybe this had something to do with my human development and puberty. Maybe it had something to do with the amount of information I had taken in. It was a very sudden change and it foreshadowed the end of my headaches. I have only had a few since that day.

16. My aptitude. [5]

I was alone in the study, sitting in a chair at one of the desks looking at my laptop. There was a fire blazing in the fireplace and the crackling sound was soothing. It was early March. I was studying my high-level trigonometry. The screen was flitting images so fast I could hardly read all the problems.

I heard a snapping sound in my head and pain shot up and down my spine. I felt my arms start to twitch but I did not stop typing. The headache came with a wave of nausea but I maintained my focus on the keys, and my fingers danced with the clicking rhythm. I became my hands and nothing mattered but the completion of the problems. Micro seizures started in my arms but they did not affect my hands or my ability to move them. They traveled up and down from my wrists.

---

[5] "What Pi sounds like" by Michael John Blake ♫

The cords of sinew were pulled tight in my shoulders and a vibration went through my body. I did not fight it I simply pushed myself faster and faster through it. Moving the angle marks and the degree numbers on the screens, working out the tangents and cosines and where to put them.

The pain circled up to the base of my skull and still I did not stop. I don't think I could have at that point; something other than myself was driving me.

The sensation stayed in my head building into a pressure at the back of my brain. Mad fingers ran away from it across the keyboard desperately trying to stay ahead of the sharp stabbing. My skull was in a vice and the ants were making noises in my ears but I maintained focus and did not let it distract me.

Whatever it was building inside me finally burst and numbers flooded my mind. They overwhelmed me. I did not just see them in my head I visualized them in the real world. The screen turned into floating points and the keys became integer input. I did not turn away I solved the problem I was working on. When I looked up I had a sudden new understanding of the language of math and my surroundings.

It was everywhere and my mind was drawing in information from my environment and setting up equations for unknown integers. Every floorboard, every corner angle, the distance between objects, every nail in the house became part of a problem with an answer which plugged into another equation. Each of those then became a part of something else in a cascade of information that flowed through my world like a river.

When I looked at the fire in the fireplace my mind drew in the information and assimilated it into thermal equations and spit out temperature and temperature dissipation, oxygen consumption, energy use, and BTU output.

I did not move for a while because it was too overwhelming. The equations manipulated through time frames and faded into each other seamlessly. It was a breach in the universe where I could look through and perceive the rules of the construct. I could see the universal mandates which governed action and reaction, cause and effect, and so on.

I was eventually able to wrench myself from the chair and head upstairs. I left the study with a sense of amazement. It was hard to find my way back to my room. I decided it was the only place I would feel comfortable until diner.

When I emerged for the evening meal the house was bleeding numbers which flowed down the stairs through the living room and into the kitchen. There were times when I forgot to breathe. I was seeing the tiny nuances which stitched reality together and I could feel my mind accepting them as truths- as matters of fact, or maybe the facts of matter, I do not know.

No one talked to me during the meal, which was a good thing because I most likely couldn't have responded with anything but gibberish. Clyde said hello to me and all I could muster was a simple head nod. After it was over I washed my bowl and went directly up to my room where I sat for hours trying to wash the math-syrup from my mind so I could sleep. For a while I was afraid I wouldn't be able too. If it had not been for the tall man I most likely would have been driven mad as well, but then again I would have never been in that position if it weren't for him. The effect lasted a couple of weeks before I got it under control.

I learned to count myself to sleep. Counting deadened the running script and created a rhythm of numbers to lull me. I rocked when I did this, back and forth with the clutter of numbers. This seemed to shake the numbers into repeating patterns which helped. Patterns are soothing to me.

The rocking helped me to create circles of numbers in my head.

Slowly it went away and I was able to sleep without the rocking but it took me a long time to learn focus. When the numbers were ordered they fell naturally into my subconscious and I was free of them. It was then that I could sleep.

Weeks passed and my understanding and scope of what was happening to me expanded but only as fast as I could re-order it.

I watched the days in patterns. It became easier to function and I found I would turn it down and dim the intensity by engaging in conversation or doing other tasks. I hid it very well and avoided being singled out.

I became more attracted to solitary activity because it made things easier and less overwhelming. People were an interruption and caused chaos in my thoughts. Although I could still understand them, I found our interactions were more convoluted. They seemed to add a certain disorder to the running math in my head. It took me a long time to learn that chaos and disorder were as important as order and control.

My favorite things to apply my aptitude to were the bees and the garden. There was a call and response to the behavior of the plants and the bees. I saw it as a sublime communion.

I was happiest that year when I was tending to them- the bees and the plants. Each plant was mathematically tracking the sun day after day, and each movement of each bee could be predicted simply by factoring the movement of the other bees. They corresponded and responded to all things around them in a methodology which can only be described as perfect.

I felt connected to something bigger when I watched them because I could see how I directly affected their behavior by being there and observing them. I learned that observation is interaction- therefore every living thing, big or small, was important.

Indigo took notice of my skills and she presented me with advanced calculus problems. I spent a little time learning the symbolic language and then pretended to have difficulty with it. I took my time and day dreamed a little in between problems but the truth was I had finished the problem once I learned the language. This gave me some free time. I was still studying other things so I caught up on those subjects in my ongoing schooling.

Indigo was pleased and told Mr. Vincent how well I was doing. It was not long before he became curious about my aptitude. He would try and sway the conversation to the subject during our sessions but I would refrain from talking about it and move back into the standard routine of Q and A.

There was a tension in the meetings which had not been there before and each time he would pick for a little more information. The more I resisted the more he pushed. I found this very uncomfortable and started to dislike our conversations, yet there was nothing I could do to avoid him. He would fidget and fumble with his pen on the desk in some of our meetings. I wondered what was on his mind and what made him so nervous. Before then I had never seen him lose any composure.

He would come around twice a month and sit in the chair behind the desk looking over his glasses at me with an eyebrow cocked.

Eventually I caved and told him about my skill with numbers. He was not surprised but as expected he rewarded me for my honesty with complements then probed deeper. He asked me to show him. He wrote a simple equation on a piece of paper and passed it across the desk. I solved it without any trouble and gave him the paper back. He wrote another more complicated problem and we repeated the process.

We went this way for a while and then he had nothing he could give me. I had exhausted his knowledge of the subject. He sat back and placed the pen on the desk. He looked down his nose at me and then raised his hands locked them, then rested his chin on the backs of his hands. He was silent for a minute.

"Impressive." He said with a fixed stare. I had known him long enough to know this was his tick and it meant he was contemplating his questions. He would continue with the same train of thought until he got to the root of his curiosity. It was unfortunate because it was that same curiosity which eventually got him killed. I knew he would pursue it until he had the answers he wanted.

He paused and took out a legal pad and began to jot notes on it. I couldn't read his tiny script from my side of the desk. It was impeccable writing and he compartmentalized it with a most precise structure. He stopped for a second and looked up at me and smiled. It was a grim and somewhat fraudulent smile which told me to hold on for just a minute.

I can remember the sound of the pen on the legal pad as it scratched out the words. I waited patiently and watched him take notes.

When he finished he looked up from his pad and placed his pen on the desk again.

"Let's continue," He said. "When did you become aware of this?" He asked. I told him about the day I was studying and he continued listen. I left out the details about how vivid it actually was and how it affected me. As I went on he would occasionally seize his pen to take notes.

When the session was finished he took the folder and placed it into his attaché, then carefully put the pen into the breast pocket of his overcoat. He placed the case on the table and stood. He turned and looked out the window.

"You know this is quite a gift you have. There are a lot people who would love to see you develop it," I nodded and told him I understood. "Those people want see this aptitude of yours, and I want you to know it can open doors for you. We will talk about this more when I visit again. You are progressing well, and I want to keep it that way. But I also want to provide some opportunities for your future," He said as he collected his things.

He bid me goodbye and left the study. I followed him to the front door as I always did showing him out. He came and went over the next few weeks, but he did not come to talk to me again for quite a while. He left me with his last words in my ears.

17. Clyde's mistake.

My relationship with Mr. Vincent changed dramatically a few weeks later. I was playing with Clyde that day. We were out in one of the far meadows after our early studies. It was just before mid-day and we were climbing logs and playing in one of the gullies, exploring the woods and enjoying the morning before afternoon studies.

It was Clyde's day to meet with Mr. Vincent so we headed back early. On the way back from the woods Clyde noticed the daylight door to the basement was open.

Indigo did not have many rules. One of her only ones was that we never went into the basement. All of the children were curious about it but none of us challenged her rules. I was curious but not curious enough to trespass. Clyde, on the other hand, had no problems bending the rules. He looked at me mischievously. I shook my head to say no, but he crept into the basement anyway and I reluctantly followed him.

"We shouldn't be here," I said.

"Stop being a wuss. It'll be okay. I just want to look," He said.

We crept in quietly and hushed our voices to a whisper. The main room was vacant of furniture except for a desk, chair and a book shelf. I kept suggesting we leave. Clyde would not consider it and continued to look through all of Indigo's things.

She had many books laid out across her desk. We judged by the shape of the dog-eared pages, that she was a person who loved to read. There were volumes of old journals and paperbacks scattered everywhere. They were not just on the desk but in neat little stacks all around it. There was also a shelf with nothing but hand written notebooks in it. We assumed that they were her diaries. The shelves trailed down the hall and along each side to the back room.

Her desk was a large vintage desk and it had several folders on it and a stack of neatly written pages which we did not bother to read. There was also a pendaflex and an old rotary telephone on the left side of the desk.

On the corner was a book which caught my eye. It was a notebook with a rust red cover and worn pages. Clyde grabbed it and opened it. It was handwritten in the same simple and meticulous writing. Clyde took it and slipped it under his shirt. I told him he should put it back.

"I will, but I'm going to read it first," He said with a smile. This was Clyde's biggest mistake and it ultimately cost Mr. Vincent his life.

His curiosity was never ending. Ironically this downfall made him an asset as an adult allowing him to reverse engineer just about anything. But as a child it created more trouble than it solved.

More than the things we saw in the basement that day, it was this simple act of taking the notebook that changed everything.

Clyde strolled about Indigo's space for a minute looking at stuff and flipping over folders, poking in drawers and fingering books in shelves. Clyde opened the closet and looked inside.

"Whoa, you gotta' check this out," He said. I came over to the closet.

There were three steamer trunks. They looked old, like they had come from a 1920s train station, as though they were stolen from history. Clyde tipped one over and undid the latch.

When Clyde opened it I saw why Indigo did not want us in the basement. It was filled with money; hundreds upon hundreds of thousands of dollars. All in neat little stacks of fresh new bills with little numbered bands around them. As a young boy I wasn't as worried as I should have been, although I later learned it was not obtained from criminal activity, but in a roundabout way it was still stolen.

18. Indigo's packing crate.

Tucked on one side of the other trunk, with some clothes and trinkets, were old film reels and a projector. The film spindles were in projector cans and looked as if they had come from the forties and fifties. These too, I would later come to know and they would become part of my daily life.

The third trunk was different. It looked newer and I did not recognize the lock type on it. Clyde tried to unlock but it would not budge. The trunk was slightly larger than the others and it was a deep blue-purple color with carbon-brass bindings and ornate hinges. It was not made with wood, metal or plastic and neither of us could identify what the material was. The only markings it had on it were on a small bronze plate directly in the middle of the top under the handle. Engraved in a simple font and centered on the plaque was printed:

"Indigo-8.1.50"

Printed in smaller print under it on the same plaque was:

"Steam Trunk model-16"

We did not say anything to each other. We just looked at it for a minute. Clyde quickly shut the trunks and we lifted them back up, trying to put them exactly where we had found them. We left the basement as quickly as possible. Clyde did not put the book back as I had recommended. We went to the front of the house not saying anything.

As we came around the corner we saw Mr. Vincent on the front porch ringing the doorbell. He was there to meet with Clyde, and tucked in Clyde's pocket was the notebook.

For all of his shortcomings, Mr. Vincent was anything but unobservant.

"Clyde," He said tipping his hat. "Did you forget about our appointment?" He asked.

"No, I just… was out playing," Clyde said.

"Well, I am ready for our session, so we can start now. I have another appointment in town so we will have to be quick," He said as Indigo opened the door. Mr. Vincent motioned Clyde in with one hand and said hello to Indigo at the same time. Clyde looked and me but did not say anything.

He followed Mr. Vincent into the house and back to the study. I went into the living room and sat down on one of the large leather chairs to wait for Clyde. Normally the sessions would last about half an hour, but Clyde was in the study for well over an hour, even though Mr. Vincent had said he was in a hurry. I waited patiently listening to the ticking of the grandfather clock. I could hear the soft murmur of voices behind the heavy oak door and the back and forth questioning which was characteristic of Mr. Vincent. Then I heard the crack of the door and the growl of it swinging open.

There were no farewells bid, Clyde came out to the living room and sat down while Mr. Vincent let himself out.

As Mr. Vincent opened the door I noticed the red notebook protruding from his coat pocket. Years later I would find out what was written in the pages of the journal and why the little book was so dangerous to the Allotment. There was a very real reason Indigo did not want anyone in the basement. I thought it was the trunk full of money, but I was wrong. When I eventually did find out what was written in it, I was an old man and the consequences of trespassing that day became very clear.

For Mr. Vincent, it was far more dangerous and

it cost him his life. If Clyde had not taken the book, Mr. Vincent would have never started asking questions and he would have lived. The Allotment would have eventually been shut down and all of Indigo's children would have been adopted out to foster homes.

19. Mr. Vincent's death.

Two days later he showed up for my session. The black sedan pulled up and circled the driveway coming to rest in front of the house. I watched from the living room window as he got out of the car and walked up the front steps to ring the doorbell. I knew something was wrong by the look on his face. The doorbell buzzed and I opened it and looked up at him.

"Is Indigo here?" He asked.

I looked at him and then glanced behind me to the Kitchen.

"I'll go get her," I said.

I went back to the Kitchen and told Indigo that Mr. Vincent wanted to talk to her. She took off her apron and came to the front door.

"Can I help you Mr. Vincent?" She asked. Mr. Vincent handed her a piece of paper. She took it and looked at it briefly. Her face dropped and she told me to go in the house and shut the door. She had never talked to me in such an abrupt manner. I did so and went to the front window and watched while they argued next to the car. She did not yell and her body language did not give much up but I could tell she was angry. They argued for a little while and then she came back to the house. She called the children together and announced that the counseling sessions would no longer take place at the Allotment. Instead they would be moved to Mr. Vincent's office in town.

"The state says I have to let Mr. Vincent do your assessments at his office. I don't like it, but I must comply with it," She said. There was a collective groan from all of the children. She looked at me. "I am sorry you will have to go with Mr. Vincent today," She told me. "Get your things and go with him, he will drop you off when the session is done," She said.

I did so and came to the door with my coat then went outside. He was there tapping his foot and waiting for me on the porch swing. We went to the car and then to his office in town. The session was not too much different but I was not at home. I knew it was his way of bringing my guard down. I do not know what he hoped to ascertain from this tactic but I suspected it had something to do with the red notebook. As far as I was concerned everything was going well but nonetheless it made me a little uncomfortable.

Over the next few weeks his attitude changed. He would ask questions which were uncharacteristic and I would not have the answers for him. He seemed to be perturbed with my lack of engagement in this matter.

Then one day I went to his office and he was different. His demeanor had changed and he seemed to be more human, more involved and more talkative, not just business and therapy. It was as if he was letting me see who he really was. He started the session off in a different way. He opened the door and let me into his small office and told me to sit down. I did so and he sat across the desk from me. We sat in silence for a minute. He looked at me and asked nothing, he waited and then sighed.

"I am sorry," He apologized. I looked at him confused.

"For what?" I asked.

"For your situation. It is partly my fault," He answered. I did not know what he meant. As far as I was concerned, my predicament was perfect. "During these sessions we always talk about you, I feel that is unfair. You are a young man of exceptional talent and strength. I think it is fair that you know the truth. My colleagues might call me out on this one if they knew I was talking to you about this, but I believe you are old enough and smart enough to understand. We state workers have confidentiality to uphold..." He laughed nervously and rolled his eyes. "So I will talk to you about me and what I do, the whole story or what I know about it," He rotated slightly in his chair. "It seems you know very little about your situation and that is okay, but I cannot proceed until we are completely honest with each other," He paused and unlocked his desk and took the small red notebook out and placed it in the center of the desk. "You have seen this before?" He asked. I hesitated and nodded slowly.

"I have," I confirmed rubbing my nose. He did not open it. He just continued to talk as it sat there between us, like it was a barrier to mediate our discussion.

"I do not know if the contents of this notebook are truthful but it got me asking some questions. It is not the content per say but the fact, as far as I can tell, that someone believes it. What is written in it is... fantastic, yet it is also disturbing. I was told that this red notebook was Indigo's and I can only infer she wrote it," He paused and reached over to the corner of the desk to get his coffee. He looked at me and then took a sip and continued.

"When I agreed to facilitate Indigo's project I was not sure what to expect. After reading this, I started digging. I did not find what I should have. There is no paperwork behind her, there are no records of Indigo being registered with the state adoption agency, or any agency for that matter. Even the title of the house you live is not registered to a person, but rather a corporation. Indigo has no records. I could understand not having credit or not having banking records and so on. But Indigo has no records, no medical records, not even a birth certificate. It's unsettling. So I started to dig further and look for anything about her. To shorten this story I found absolutely nothing. If there were any records on her they have been destroyed or they never existed," He paused. "I know you know nothing about this. What mystified me is how 30 state-wards were handed over to a person who legally doesn't exist who lives on a very large and expensive estate which no one seems to own," He looked down at the notebook.

"This notebook tells a horrible story of manipulation and I think you and the other children are victims of it as well," He said focusing his eyes on me. "And that is something I cannot in good conscious allow," He said.

I looked across at the notebook curious to see what was inside it. I wanted to know what had gotten him so agitated. He stood up and turned and looked out the window overlooking the small Connecticut town.

"I got into Social work to make a difference in people's lives, especially children as I cannot have any of my own. I have not lived up to that mission. In my field we call it an ethical dilemma," He faced me and looked down across his desk at me. "Do you know what that means?" he asked.

"Yes," I said.

"Despite what people say, ethics are still important. They separate us, good from bad. Clyde came to me and tried to hide this book. It was obvious he was not supposed to have it and did not want to get in trouble. He left it with me, and I read it," Mr. Vincent stopped and rubbed the bridge of his nose.

"If what is written in it is true, then it is my duty to tell you and the authorities. If it is not true, then Indigo is a dangerous woman who is suffering from some serious mental issues and you children should be removed from her care as soon as possible, and I alert the authorities. In other words I have to tell the authorities. The ethical dilemma I have is this... In all the times I have visited you and your foster siblings, that's hundreds of sessions, and all the notes I have taken, all the words I've had with you children, I've never found anything unhealthy about your situation. You will be removed when she is investigated," He said.

I felt a lump in my throat. The Allotment was home, my friends, my family were there. I couldn't bear to lose them again.

He stood up and walked over to the filing cabinet and removed my file, came back and moved the notebook aside. He took a pen from the holder on his desk and opened the file.

"I have known you for a while and I can honestly say I like you. You are a good kid. I have to ask you to be honest with me," He opened his yellow legal pad to a new page and hung the pen above the first line. "Since I read that..." He said gesturing at the notebook. "I have been asking your friends and discovered all is not what it seems. What do you know about this? The red note book mentions all of you... I need to know what you are aware of."

He paused and lifted his head. He was not looking for me to answer, he was listening to something. I felt it too. It was something in the room, something else watching and waiting. There was an accompanying high pitched sound almost too faint to hear. I could taste the atmosphere and the humidity.

My vision went red and blurred. I felt the familiar feeling. It was just like my parent's funeral. The ticking and marching ants filled my mind and I heard the sound of a man shouting in unfamiliar language, muffled as if he were yelling from a closet. The room started to spin and my head began to hurt as I slouched back in my chair. I couldn't focus and my eyes dilated and contracted.

Mr. Vincent looked at me.

"Are you okay?" He asked.

The light that poured through the large window in the room seared my irises. Just before I covered them I caught a glimpse of the building across the narrow street. There was a figure on top of the building adjacent to us. The figure was just a shadow in the light, and there was also a man in the window directly below him banging on the glass. I assumed he was the one yelling. The light became too bright and painful. I shielded my eyes by throwing my hands up.

I watched through the cracks in my fingers. Mr. Vincent stood and was said something to me but I couldn't hear his words.

There was a muffled *pop* followed by a shattering sound. A hole appeared in the glass behind him and little shards sprayed across the room. Then there was a zipping sound and a bullet penetrated the room pushing shock waves with it. With a hollow thump the bullet burrowed into Mr. Vincent's back. He stood there for a second while the sound in my head continued. I lowered my hands and stared at the little red spot on his white shirt. The red was just a pen point at first. He did not seem to notice until he looked down. Then the crimson wicked into the cotton, the pinpoint became a spot and then grew into a large stain.

He wavered and then fell forward on top of the desktop. His hands stretched out and scattered pencils from the little cup sweeping his coffee onto the floor. He grasped the red book and fell back into his chair quivering.

I have never seen a person clutch something as he did the notebook.

Knowing what I know now, I suspect there was a dawning epiphany in his mind about the nature of his situation. Like the man on the road that winter night when my parents died. It was sick realization painted on his face and I saw it spread as he fell. It was the overwhelming fear of comprehending one's own end. He was scared as a child would have been. I think most of us are children when facing death. Infants in front of it because it is the only truth all things share, an absolute to all living beings. And that scares the hell out of most of us. Mr. Vincent was no different.

Dizziness made it hard for me to stand. I tried and toppled onto the floor as my knees gave way to disorientation and vertigo pulling me down.

From the floor I could see Mr. Vincent's legs kicking under his desk. He was convulsing in his chair.

The spasms were not sharp or strong, they were weak kicks to the underside of his desk. I threw my hand up and grasped the edge of the desk. I struggled to pull myself level with it.

There was a small trickle of blood at the corner of his mouth. His eyes bulged and his muscles tensed.

I crawled around the desk to look up at him. He was panting and trying to reach around with one of his arms so he could get to the bullet. His arm reminded me of a loose wing, as he did this, his feet continued to kick.

I pulled myself up the desk as the ticking sound in my head faded and my balance started to return. It was replaced with an equally uncomfortable feeling, panic. I turned my head around and looked out the window as I steadied myself. My eyesight was still pulsing but I caught fragments of what was happening.

The figure in the window was gone and as my eyes climbed to the roof of the building, I saw the second figure running across it to the opposite side and then it disappeared over the back end of the building.

Mr. Vincent was arching in the seat and trying to say something. His mouth was opening and closing like a fish removed from its aquarium. There was also a deep wet and raspy breath leaking from his lips. He was hissing wildly and trying to form words. I could see the light in his eyes and it was flickering with his slow convulsions. He let go of the notebook and it fell to the desk. He reached up and grasped my collar and pulled me close.

"Pen…!" He sputtered reaching out over the desk with his shaking hand. I was frozen with fear, but he persisted. I grabbed his pen and placed it into his grasp.

He immediately began to spin it wildly in the air trying to write something. I pushed his hand down onto the pad and the pen moved in jerking leaps. It took him a second to get the strokes down. He finished, dropped the pen, shuttered and fell forward onto the desk and then off the side falling back into his chair.

Across the paper was scrawled, *"don't go back"*. The letters were not neat; the phrase was hidden in the jerked loops of his penmanship. I will never forget that little phrase. For a second I considered that I shouldn't return to the Allotment that night. I have often wondered about my choices at that moment. I have difficulty understanding that phrase even today.

In the second it took me to read what was written Mr. Vincent died. Life was gone and I was alone in a room with my dead social worker. He was slouched back in his chair, contorted upward with an arched back.

I did not know what to do so I stood looking at him, unable to move. I was paralyzed and my mind was screeching to me telling me to do something. There was reluctance when I picked up the phone. I called the only person I knew could help, despite Mr. Vincent's warning. I raised the receiver to my ear and made the call. My fingers dialed her number for me because I was too distraught to think.

Indigo answered the phone and all I could say was, "He is dead, Mr. Vincent is dead…" My voice sounded unfamiliar to me. It was small and weak. I was a child calling home for help.

"I'll be right there," She said without asking who it was or where I was.

She hung up leaving me motionless, in waiting. I turned away from the corpse and looked directly at Mr. Vincent's book shelves trying to avoid the cold stare of his sideways eyes which had become greasy with death.

I watched the clock above the shelf as it ticked slower and slower. The more I watched it the slower it moved. I tried to do equations in my head to take me away from the empty room and the dead man, but my thoughts were scrambled. I tried counting to keep myself from hysteria, but the quiet was penetrating. I silently repeated patterns and sequences under my breath while the clock slowed.

19. Upon arrival.

Minutes later I was pulled from my concentration. The door opened and Indigo came in and hugged me. I was so distraught I couldn't say anything. When I finally stopped shaking she drew away and asked me what happened.

"He was shot. He died..." I answered in shock. Indigo walked over to the phone and looked at his body. For a second she hesitated and then she saw the notebook in his hand. Her face was troubled as she removed it and put it in her purse.

"This does not belong here," She said under her breath. She picked up the phone and dialed 911. "Yes, I need police assistance. Right, at 221 main, second floor, suite 21. I will be here when you arrive," She said then hung up the phone.

She came over to me and leaned down.

"It's going to be okay, it really will, but you have to go now and wait in the car. I will take care of this," She said.

I looked up at her. She told me again and I turned and left the room. I ran down the stairs and out to the car. I climbed in and waited.

I could hear the police sirens as cars pulled up in front of the building. The police rushed in the door and an ambulance skidded to a stop in front of the building. It was not long after the second group went in with a stretcher that Indigo and one of the first responders came out. She was talking with him and he was writing on a small notepad. She pointed at the car and then she walked over and opened the door. She told me to come out and tell the police what I had seen. I scooted out of the seat and followed her to the police car where they took my statement and provided Indigo with some service information.

I told them everything I knew and had seen. I was sure I had seen multiple people, but I did not tell them that. I did not mention the notebook to the police. I decided to omit it because at the time I could see no clear connection. Many years later the notebook would find its way into my hands and I would know the truth.

We were there for some time and one of the officers told me everything would be okay. He seemed to be respectable and he assured me it was not my fault. Then one of the other officers handed him a cup and he gave it to me. I was still shaking when I took the cup from his hand. It was hot chocolate from the bistro around the corner. He told me not to worry and just have a sip. Before we left he told Indigo he would have to stop by later and check in on some things. She told him that would be fine.

Indigo finished her statement and the policeman excused us. We got into the car and started the drive home. She did not say anything just let the silence bleed in the cab as she looked forward with glassy eyes.

"This was an interruption," She finally said.

"A what?" I asked.

"It was a minor setback. I didn't want anything to happen to Mr. Vincent but I knew something was going to… although he had a good heart, he had untrustworthy associates..." She said. She looked at me across the front seat and became very serious. "Did you read any of the notebook?" She asked. I looked back at her.

"No," I said.

"Good. When you age and leave home, it will not matter if you read it. Sometimes the things we don't know are the things that give us freedom. What is written in the notebook is not for your eyes, at least not yet..." She paused for a moment and then continued. "Do you know what the difference between a deception and an illusion is?" She asked me.

I shook my head no, it was a confusing question and did not appear relevant.

"An illusion can look like something wonderful, a deception rarely does, by definition they are almost identical but in understanding and context they are very different. The notebook would take something away from your life if you read it. This is very much the way children are raised. Parents take care of the things which are unpleasant so that they can afford their children an illusion until they are ready for understanding. The notebook is important to me, it keeps me on track. It reminds me of things I must do and how I must do them. Your life and the happiness you have come to know at the Allotment are all dependent on that illusion and although I cannot stop you from investigating, I would ask that you don't until you are sure you can understand. I assure you, someday, you will know what it says. However, for now you should spend your time being young. I cannot undo what has happened, but I will make sure that no more tragedy comes to you. For now, forget about it, this is one of those things which is better left uninvestigated," She said nervously as we approached the front gate of the Allotment. "Home again," She said under her breath and she turned onto the driveway and started the drive to the house.

Indigo stopped the car before we climbed the hill.

"I am sorry you went through that," She said looking at me and putting a hand on my shoulder. "Sometimes things happen, I will not tell you they happen for a reason but I will say that they will give you unique perspectives on things even if they are sad. Events do not have meaning per say, but people can choose to make what they will out of them," She paused and repeated her empathy to me.

I sat in the car looking at her sad eyes and wondering if I would ever really understand what she meant. She sighed and continued.

"Tomorrow, I have something to tell everyone and I will excuse your studies for the day. I have an announcement for all of you. But tonight I want you to sleep well and be rested. That might be difficult, but please try," She said with a crisp and gentle articulation. She returned her hand to the steering wheel and looked forward and accelerated the car up the hill.

We pulled up to the house and into the garage. I got out for the last time as a boy. The next day her announcement would change my life forever. We would start new studies and become new people. I would move on to adolescence.

There was not much to say to anyone at the Allotment when I came through the door. I took my shoes off and went upstairs to get in bed early. I undressed quickly, wrapped up in my blanket and shut the light off. Sleep did not come and I curled up in the corner to look out the window at my lonely little world.

My fingers tapped a rhythmic math as I laid there. A digit abacus ticking on the wall, they sang an escalating song as I tried to soothe myself and scrub the image of Mr. Vincent from my head. Although I had experienced death before, it had not been that way. I rocked in time with the finger movements counting in my head as I went. Colors flashing in the dark with each connection as the math rolled back and forth between my fingers. I called on it to take me away, to show me a larger pattern, something bigger than death, something wonderful and invigorating. I wanted to see something still growing, something more than entropy. I closed my eyes and counted, then gave up and opened them, my eyelids were restless.

I watched the ice form on my bedroom window as concentric crystalline structures featuring Mandelbrot sets and fractals. The crystals traveled along the temperature variances in the glass. I predicted the patterns in my head and watched them unfold while I relived the events of the day. I had done this so many times before to get to sleep when I had first arrived but it had been a long time since I had needed it. Many hours later I eventually drifted off to sleep.

20. The end of my childhood[6]

As you can see my life as a child began with tragedy and ended in the same manner. This was the summary of my childhood. It set the pace for my life. It was born with the death of my parents and ended with the death of Mr. Vincent. An end begetting more ends is the cycle of my life and with every new end there is another more important beginning, around and around, energy recycling. I came to realize as I aged, even life itself is an act of recycling. Your body, your mind, and all that you are is owned by the universe. The price for having them is that one day you will have to give them back. This is apparent to those still around, to the older generation and the acolytes of the old world. There are not many of them left.

To Mr. Vincent I would offer an apology that he became collateral damage to the affairs of my world. Even though he is dead I feel compelled to get this out there and make sure someone knows there is regret in his sacrifice. Hind sight is sometimes cruel and it directs us to our own regret.

Weather I am responsible or not, his passing weighs on me. Mr. Vincent's death opened doors for the students. Without Mr. Vincent in the way, the next step in our development would free us of any state investigations. But I still feel guilt for his death, and all

---

[6] "Childhoods End" by Pink Floyd ♫

the other people who lost their lives as well. I am sorry to all of them and I hope wherever they are they can accept my apology.

ACT II: The Youth I want to be again.

1. Youth.

I had a good youth, it took place in simple times and although it was not as innocent as my childhood, it was still a time of personal growth and enrichment. There was much learning and development during the years of my adolescence. I cultivated my understanding of the world and learned to plan for my future.

My friends grew and fell in love; we became adults together, and moved forward to meet our purpose. We became our own individuals and re-purposed our skills to make sure we were ready for adulthood. It would be an adulthood we couldn't even imagine.

My adolescence started the day after Mr. Vincent was shot. I suppose the timing of his death was predicted. What I gathered was that Indigo had been waiting for it but I had no proof of her involvement in the actual event.

The next day yielded some insight as to why. Mr. Vincent was our last attachment to the state. He was what had prevented her from delving into our extended education. If Mr. Vincent had found out about her education plan, through our weekly assessments, the state would have removed us and dispersed us into foster care. Not only would that have been a tragedy, most of us would have been lost to each other.

Mr. Vincent's death was tracked to a gambling habit although most of us suspected there was something else going on. We speculated about it, as kids do. He

111

was a gambler and he was, most likely by his own admission and diagnosis, an addict. His preferred addictions were playing cards and high risk, which got him into some trouble with bad crowds. This was not any reason to judge him. For all the counseling I had received, he really had helped me to get through my loss and the grieving process. I would still consider him a good person at his core. Even though he had done bad things to good people to cover his debts, I still hold that he helped people more than he hurt them.

Mr. Vincent had payoffs to make for his losses at the card tabled and I suppose that is why he was singled out to be our lesion with the state. He was easy to control and he was expendable. He had no family to come looking for him, no next of ken, and no close friends. When the police eventually came to talk to Indigo and the children, all fingers pointed to his gambling habit. All paper trails led to shady and dubious places where identification was a process shrouded in deception.

There were so many dead ends in the case that it was eventually lost to time and a lack of manpower. It wound up on a shelf in a storage unit somewhere when the investigator on the case retired. He had no regrets about letting it go cold, and as with so many things in my life I dealt with the effects and learned the cause later.

The reasons did not concern me and would not for many years. My primary concern was a daily investment in my activities and I never thought long term until I grew older and developed more patience and consideration.

When I had aged, I discovered his death was not related to gambling at all. He was killed because he was Indigo's last connection to the state. Without him, Indigos children would be forgotten by those who came to check on us, we would fall into obscurity. Those who watched would eventually lose interest.

As a child, it was time for adventure and discovery. It was time I expanded my skills and learned more about who I was. I owe who I am to this time in my life. Most importantly, it is when I fell in love with Belle.

2. Clark's gift.

The next day Loki came and licked my hand as I lay in bed. The sun was coming up and I was listening to the sounds of the house settling. There was still frost on the window. The horizon was just starting to light up in different shades of orange as the sun rose behind the house. I scratched Loki's ears, and rose from the bed and put my jeans and shirt on to prepare for the morning chores.

As I left my room, the house came alive with the sounds of young teens racing up and down the stairs as they brushed their teeth and showered. Loki followed me out of the room and to the top of the stairs. I stood for a minute watching the controlled confusion and then

Loki nuzzled my hand. It was his way of telling me to go down to the kitchen and eat breakfast with the rest of the children because he would not be allowed to eat until we had all eaten. So I hopped down the stairs and made my way to the kitchen.

The dining quarters were full, and there was warm oatmeal dished up in bowls. There were fresh cinnamon rolls and there were bacon and eggs along the center of the tables in skillets.

We all took our time eating while Indigo sat at the head of the tables watching. She was reading a book, in her perfect posture. She was methodically and rhythmically turning the pages.

She never ate with us. This was just part of who she was. She did not like people watching her do things and for the most part she managed to avoid it. She believed in being both involved and removed at the same time. She was flawless in her approach and interaction. I could never tell how she got so close yet stayed so far away all at the same time.

To the best of my knowledge I do not recall ever seeing her eat or sleep. I believed she displayed this behavior intentionally and everything she did was calculated to help her interact in just the right way. She sat proper at all times, lady like and vigilant over her children. She did not speak to us until every child had finished.

When the last spoon was put down she quietly closed the book and placed it on the small table in front of her squaring it in the corner. We anticipated she would speak right away, she did not. She let us sit in a silent purgatory of curiosity. Our little minds toiling with anticipation as she let hear the quiet.

It must have been five minutes and she made sure to make eye contact with each and every one of us as she waited. This was to let us know and reaffirm how important that day really was. There was no discernible emotion on her face.

That was the day we learned how differences can fit together to construct something beautiful. We learned how diversity can create a patchwork of innovation. Without the pieces, the whole would not function or make sense. Each and every one of us would be a part of something, a terrible and wondrous picture.

When she finally spoke it cut the silence in a way none of us expected. It was cold and reflexive with a touch of seriousness. It caught us off guard and sat us up in our chairs.

"It's time children," She said as she stood and walked around the small table to face all of us. "Clark?" she said looking next to me at Clark.

"Yes ma'am," He affirmed.

"Could you please come and sit at this table?" She said.

He nodded, nervously came forward and planted himself in Indigo's chair. She picked the book up and walked out of the dining room area to the kitchen. She placed the book on the counter and reached up into the

115

cabinet and retrieved some toothpicks, then returned through the large open archway to the dining hall. There was still an ominous quiet in the room as she glided across the floor to Clark.

She opened the box of toothpicks and dumped them in front of Clark. Clark seemed to be a little confused. "I want you to move a tooth pick," He reached across the table and pulled a toothpick out of the pile and placed it to the side. "Okay," She said. She looked at all of us and paused. "This is an act of will Children, Clark wanted to move the toothpick and used his hands to make that thought happen. We all do this every day, in fact since you became old enough to move, you have trained yourself to take this for granted. In this case, there was a great deal of work required to move the toothpick. I told Clark, he heard me, interpreted the sound as a command and then recoded the output to his nervous system and sent it as an impulse along bundles of nerves to his hand. As his hand moved he had to constantly adjust that impulse and correct movements to seize the tooth pick. A series of feedback, response, and adjustment corrections from his brain to his hand were required to move the toothpick and place it off to the side. If a person were to strip away everything but this impulse there would be a line of electricity from his brain to the toothpick. This is how we operate. Our mind does it with ease. It is nothing to us. Yet it is an amazing process. It does more complicated things than we can understand. In fact it is so good at it, it does these things even while we sleep. We function this way, like a machine. These operations happen in the background and we give very little thought to them," She stopped and reached into her apron pocket and pulled out a single red toothpick. She placed it in the pile with the regular toothpicks and smiled at us then turned to Clark.

She knelt down next to him and looked into his eyes.

"Now, move the red toothpick, without using your hand. Cut out the middle man Clark," She said sternly. Clark smiled inquisitively.

"How can I move it without touching it?" He asked as though he already knew the answer. Indigo looked back at him and grinned.

"Clark, you have to feel it as though you were moving it with your hands. This begins with the realization that hands are only tools. You and all the other children have been given additional tools. It all begins with this realization and breakthrough," She looked at all of us and stood up. "Everybody, gather around, this is your first demonstration and the first lesson in your new education," She gestured for all the students to gather round and then turned back to Clark.

"Am I going to do that?" He asked.

"Yes, but only if you want it to happen," She said. Her voice became smooth and unwavering and there was a hypnotic undertone to it which was very compelling. "Concentrate on the red toothpick. Block out the rest of the pile and feel it in your mind. It's

117

texture, its shape, its points and color. Know these things with your perception. Imagine that you are picking it up out of the stack… now, shut your eyes but do not lose the image of the red toothpick. Move it with a different set of tools," She told him.

Clark was staring at the table, his eyes dilated and his body relaxed, but they did not shut.

"Stretch out, feel it in your fingers but do not move your hands. Lift it slowly from the pile and move it," She said again.

A few seconds passed. No one said anything or moved. We stared transfixed on the small table and Clark. A minute passed as we watched and then there was a shutter in the table. It was faint but we all heard it. Clark however did not move. Our eyes widened as the single red toothpick began to vibrate. It freed itself from the pile and glided vertically above the table. We could feel the vibrations in the air as it hung there suspended by Clark's imagination.

The other children stared in amazement at the frozen image before them. Clark was motionless. The toothpick started to spin as if invisible hands were manipulating it. Indigo watched for a minute and turned to us.

"This is possible not only because Clark believes it is but because he has an ability new to humans. He is using his mind at a level most humans can't. He is harnessing the electrical fields his brain produces and forcing them to interact with the fields of the red toothpick... Because the toothpick has an electrical field, a kind of subatomic glue, and his brain also has this same glue, he can interface with it. All things in the universe have these fields and all things, given the right circumstances, can be interfaced with in some way. He does not need his hands because his sets of tools are more advanced than his ancestors were. He is an improvement on the generations which came before him. So are all of you. It is why you were chosen to come and stay with me. I hand selected you on this premise and someday all of you will learn to understand this sort of gift," She smiled at us and turned back to Clark, who was still sitting at the table.

There was another jolt and another toothpick trailed up into the air and touched tip to tip with the first one. They started to rotate and soon a third joined them. It was not long before there was a geodesic shape rotating above the table. No one said anything. Clark manipulated the wooden picks in a number of patterns cascading above the table. He did not appear to strain as he held the shapes together and transformed them.

"Thank you Clark," Indigo said softly. "You can put them down now," She turned to all of the children. Slowly and methodically she began to walk around the students. "This is Clark's gift. Since every person is different all of your gifts will manifest differently. Each and every one of you will, if you haven't already, discover there is something different about you. There is no telling what will set you aside. This is the part of your education which is unique to you. I have taken you through your schooling and all of you far surpass most public educations. Now you must discover how to teach your selves. I have no frame of reference to help you. I am only here to guide you. In this part of your development, I cannot help you. Although I can give you advice on life, I have no firsthand knowledge of what you are going to go through. No one does, you are pioneers, fireflies in the dark. As you grow and change through adolescence you will change more than the average youth," She paused as she walked around the group and looked out the back window in the dinner hall. "There is much to learn, there is much to explore, and there is much to develop. As I said, I can help you but this is your journey now," She finished.

She said this knowing all of us had already noticed our abilities. We hadn't exposed each other to them yet, but we have discovered them. I suppose this is why she picked Clark for the example. He was the first to figure it out, he was also the oldest. For quite a while, a number of us had operated on the suspicion our burgeoning abilities would single us out to be ostracized. As we discovered, each and every one of us was a part of a larger plan, and those abilities were all part of it, yet the whole picture was still hidden.

She paced around the class letting us sit and think about it in silence. She did this to let us digest it before she spoke again. Her next point was crucial.

"This is the only place you should ever practice

these gifts. The world outside of the Allotment does not understand and most likely never will. It is imperative you use them sparingly or in the company of people you know and trust. Children, do you understand?" She asked.

All of the children shook their heads. "All right then, your next task is to figure it out, I have some further lessons which we will indulge in but they are not school lessons per say. They are more for adult survival-Social acclimation for when you go out into the world. From now on academic lessons will be maintenance only..." She slowly walked back to the small table and excused Clark. "For now, you are all dismissed. There will be no further discussing this for the day. You are to think deeply on the matter, and let it sink in. I cannot show you the gravity of this responsibility now, but some day each and every one of you will understand," She said. With that our lecture was over.

We stood and left the room, one by one. There was silence on our lips as we thought about it. We shuffled out to do our chores and remain in our thoughts for the duration of the day as Indigo had instructed. Each of us would have a gift and there was no knowing what it would be.

The day was silent and slow. We took our time with our chores and we were quiet as the sun tracked its way towards bedtime. Our lips sat rested while our minds mulled over the day and what would come next. This was how Indigo had wanted us to treat the matter.

3. Metamorphosis. [7]

I was not prepared for the next few weeks. The changes I saw were surreal. It occurred to me, had I not understood certain concepts everything could have been construed as magic for its absurdity. One by one, like flowers the other student's talents opened, and the skills were vast and varied.

At first it was small. We were not open about it and we remained timid with what we learned. Slowly, one at a time we came forward and let people see the splendid things we could do. At the Allotment there was no judgment for who we were, and there was no envy either. There came an awareness of each other's capabilities and a respect for them.

The twins had a full understanding of the movement of molecules under pressure and found they could control gasses and liquids. A couple of the students started to absorb linguistics- between them they could speak 51 different languages and 40 or so dialects. Paul, one of the youngest could phase through some solid objects and his best friend could change the perception people had of him and look inside their minds. Jim, one of the students on the second floor was unaffected by weather and climate of any kind. He would never freeze or suffer heat exhaustion- to our knowledge he was not affected by temperature at all. It

---

[7] "Byegone" by Volcano Choir ♫

was in that same year that he stopped eating completely. Another student was a human lie detector and emotional regulator. Belle was an empath and thought reader. Given my affinity, I assumed I was a human calculator as no math was too hard for me.

It was not long after we discovered our gifts that we started what was called "our socializing education". We took frequent trips to the nearby towns and attended all sorts of events. While we were there it was our duty to observe behavior. Then we had to implement our observations to create communication personas. Our communication personas were to hide our invisible selves from the world. That is to say the truest versions of us, Indigo had made it very clear it was not safe to show people what we could do and who we really were.

The personas we developed were the ones we were expected to present to the world. They were designed to hide ourselves when we eventually left the Allotment. Indigo insisted that we would be able to sell ourselves in any situation. It was a much harder act of study than the academics had been and required a larger amount of energy and observation.

Indigo informed us only through interaction could we use the skills and learn to hone them the ways we needed. We were intended to use them, but we were also expected not to compromise people's ignorance of us. Our task was to quietly hide in the folds of the populace and be inconspicuous.

I remember the numerous lessons on self-marketing, or "personality presentation" as she had referred to it.

Let me reiterate here, I do not believe that Indigo had anything nefarious in mind when she showed us these things. I think she had a keen understanding that it was the best way to make sure we were safe. She knew the only way that would be possible was to make sure we were able to hide. The rest was up to us.

Another thing we started that year was a class she called "Our history in black and white", which consisted of strange black and white films. I could see no purpose for it then, but I trusted there was a reason for it.

Every week we would sit in the study hall as a class and watch a series of films. We were told they were extremely important and someday they would make sense. At first they were very hard to understand but as we watched them more and more and they became routine we accepted them as a part of study. We were not supposed to understand them. We were supposed to watch them and like food they would become useful when digested.

The films themselves were not really anything but a string of black and white news clips put together in a rhythmic pattern on repeat. Each clip was a series of events which led to war somewhere. I was not sure if they were fiction or fact and I couldn't place the geography either. They had a purpose but I also think they were to help us understand what war was. To comprehend how it starts and to equip us as we journeyed out into the world. Most of us would travel and we would need to recognize and develop situational and political awareness.

We watched with no explanation and were given instructions not to discuss them but to let them soak in silently. Of course being children we did talk about them but only on a superficial level.

During this time we also learned many other skills, some were obvious skills, some were not. They were geared to teach us how to function in a modern world. We learned how to finance our lives and how to adhere to laws and rules if we needed, also how to navigate them.

Indigo told us that by the time we left the Allotment she wanted us to be prepared, if need be, to act as our own representatives in court. We all learned how to drive and had our licenses earlier than most- as age permitted. We all learned self-defense, as well as dancing. To me there was not much difference, they were very similar to each other, I picked them up right away. Although, being the lover of music I am, I preferred dance. When I looked at the movement I was reminded of the honey bees, they danced too but for different reasons.

Aside from the formalities we learned survival skills, one day a week we were led out into the woods, whether it was sunny or rainy or snowy or windy. We were shown techniques and methods of survival. We were taught to avoid panic and fortify our mental constitution, to protect our attitude because it was our most important asset. We were taught to use what we had around us to survive. This was standard every week during those years.

4. Growing pains.

I was entering into adolescence and things were changing. Along with the physical changes I was going through, my mind became a jumbled cascade of uncontrolled thoughts and feelings. Puberty was both complicated and difficult and there were no guidelines to get through it. Thankfully we had just enough occupation to keep us out of trouble.

Many of us tried all the natural pitfalls of growing up. Some of us tried smoking, others drank a little bit and some experimented with sex, but none of us were habitual for very long. None of us remained delinquent for anything other than a fleeting moment, a summer or a winter, just the turning of a season.

The only one I ever partook of was smoking behind the barn. Incidentally it was the only time anyone was ever caught by Indigo. I can remember how I felt when Indigo came around the corner and found me and three other kids puffing away on chesterfields. She did not become angry, she did not guilt us.

She took a milk crate and sat down, straightened her skirt and made sure she was sitting properly.

"Can I have one of those?" She asked. We did

not know what to say. Clark reached into his jacket pocket and took the pack and handed it to her. She smiled and looked at the pack then flipped it open. Very carefully she removed one and placed it in her mouth. We did not say anything; we were not sure how much trouble we were really in. She fidgeted a minute patting her pockets for a lighter.

I realize now that she was fully aware that nowhere in any of her pockets was a lighter. Instead she looked at Ron.

"Could you do me the favor?" She asked. Ron nodded and stepped forward. He reached up and flicked his fingers and sparks ignited his fingernails. She leaned in and put the cigarette into the fire. We all looked at her sheepishly holding our cigarettes. There was another moment of silence and a look she gave us which would forever affect our decision making process. Then she spoke.

"How is it going boys?" She asked as she inhaled the cigarette.

We did not know what to say. She sat there for a minute. "Well?" She asked. Clark quietly answered.

"Alright I guess…" We followed suit and nodded and muttered while we smoked. She did not seem mad, but her demeanor was deceiving and we all knew she was sitting there smoking and talking to us just to make us uncomfortable. She smoked that cigarette down, letting us watch it and think about it as she did.

When she finished she rolled the ash out of the

end of the cigarette and took the butt and placed it in her apron pocket. Then she spoke again.

"Boys, I want you to listen carefully, time is precious, and smoking is not. Now think about this and decide if this is really a good investment of your time," She said. It was not necessarily what she said that affected us; it was how she said it. The message was clear and after a moment of quiet, we dispersed. That was the last time we smoked behind the barn.

Indigo always had that effect on us. It was in her presentation and in the tone of her voice. She was quiet, but when she spoke people listened. In many ways she reminded me of my own mother and the way that she spoke. It had occurred to me that all of us at the Allotment were the same and maybe she reminded each and every one of us of our parents.

Life was pretty regimented and we fell into patterns which were dictated to us through the phases of our growth. We all knew through the process of growing that there were bigger changes coming. Several weeks after Clark's demonstration, a stranger was brought to the Allotment. His name was Eric.

5. Introducing Eric. [8]

I have mentioned I was the last child to come to the Allotment; I still maintain the truth in that. Eric was

---

[8] "I am only Joking" by KONGOS ♫

not a child. He was something else completely. Most of the kids at the Allotment ignored him. He was in all manners unfamiliar and somewhat unsettling but Indigo had a very strong attachment to him and she made sure everyone knew it. It was not that she was playing favorites; it was as though she knew him, and more importantly he knew her.

He was not like any of the other children. He appeared much younger than the rest of us. His skin was a pale white and his hair was a jet black. There was emptiness in his hollow amber eyes that made us very uncomfortable. We would grow to disregard this quality with time but it was still unnerving when we first met him. His white skin was always a curiosity and his small stature was striking, almost skeletal.

I can still remember how he never seemed to change his clothes, yet they were always clean. This might have been because of his meticulous nature. Everything about him was not only clean, it was sterile. Even the way he moved was unique. He glided around almost as though he were on rails. He seemed to always know where he was going. There were mannerisms about him he seemed to have no control over. These were very faint and hard to notice. One of his most unusual ones was a twitch in the corner of his mouth. It was always there, barely noticeable, but if we looked close we could see the tremble. There was also a hiccup in his shoulders when he would change directions as he walked.

Indigo and Eric did not say anything to each other, the two of them seemed to get along just fine without any sort of outward communication. Their relationship was like the relationship of a sibling rather than a parent.

He would sit with her on the stoop out the back door. They would not speak to each other. In fact none of us heard him speak for quite some time, but Indigo seemed to understand his solitude and she also seemed to be allowed inside of the stillness which surrounded him.

He attended all the classes and lectures. Eventually, he was welcomed and we became comfortable with him but he was never interested in interacting with the group. He kept his distance as if he was observing us and seemed to self-regulate his participation.

Of his many strange habits the one I found the most intriguing was his constant diagramming. It did not matter where he was or what was going on, he always had a drafting pencil and a sketchbook with him. He was constantly drawing in it.

He would sketch throughout the day. It would start at the breakfast table while his food sat untouched. His little balled up fists would work furiously around each leaflet of paper until it was covered in meticulous diagrams, blueprints, and tiny handwriting.

He would not let us look at it and we respected his wishes, but we would occasionally catch glimpses of it. It was so orderly and technically pretty that if we had not seen him drawing it, we would have assumed it was printed. The drawings were confined to little boxes and ordered around the page. Within the boxes were all kinds of mechanical devices- cogs, gears, reduction boxes, springs, on so on. I assumed they were a type of schematic but without any decipherable engineering language.

I will admit he was the most brilliant person at the Allotment and his gift, like mine, was not a tangible one. He had a way of seeing the bigger picture and the evolution of that picture, more so becoming an integral part of its construction. He was also very private about his gift even among those who were also gifted.

His day to day existence with us was troubled at first. A lot of the kids shunned him right away. There were whispers about him from some of the children but most of it was just ill placed curiosity.

He was never made fun of directly- the taunts were quiet whispers and I got the feeling he knew about them but didn't care. Some of the children tried to access the small room off the study which was given to him, but discovered it had been locked and it could not be penetrated with any of our aptitudes. Having short attention spans we eventually gave up and pursued more rewarding endeavors, like the opposite sex. In turn the rumors died down as he became more and more a part of our lives.

He kept up on all his chores. He never fell

behind in studies and his cold and mysterious demeanor slowly turned to a shadow in our peripheral vision.

As we grew, he did not seem to grow with us. He changed his hairdo and sometimes he wore a hat, but it seemed his size and shape shifted very little. I asked Indigo about it once and she said it was because he was a late bloomer, which made sense.

This contrasted with some of the other kids who had already started to mature. They were all getting taller, their voices were cracking and they were developing breasts, facial hair and starting their cycles. Eric did not change much, and I kind of felt sorry for him. It felt as though he was always left out of things. The truth was I don't think he wanted to be included. Eventually even my eye turned to more interesting things- such as girls.

And of course, as nature would have it, it was during those years I fell in love. It was not exactly what I had expected. For most people, falling in love is an act of tolerance and private exploration of another person's inner identity. Sometimes it's when two people provide comfortable allowance and access to each other, and then discover that they like what they see. Lovers usually derive meaning from it and build a shared familiarity. This kind of love lasts as long as it is still interesting, honest and respectful.

However, as anyone who has ever been in love knows, words, literature and music sometimes do not capture feelings adequately.

Love takes us for a ride and makes us stupid for a while; it is only when our heads clear that we know if we invested wisely. So many have said, love is like falling, and I would agree with them. It might hurt when you land, or you might find yourself out of breath looking up at the vast open heaven and the beauty of the stars, the moon, or sun.

My exposure to love was sudden, shocking, and stopped my ability to function correctly, as it does with most. I suppose it had to be that way. Indigo didn't teach us much about love. She did tell us to expect emotions which are inherently unchained, irrational, and raw. She also told us that those emotions were young and strong, but ultimately lacked wisdom.

I will sum it up as best as I can: my brain was castrated and its decision making processes were spread elsewhere. Its critical thinking skills were relocated to my neither's. It left me with nothing but visceral, guttural, primal and possessive feelings in my head. It was the same physiology we had been taught about in our human growth and development class. Even though I knew the science of human change, nothing could prepare me for how it felt. No teacher, regardless of how good they are, can teach someone how feelings feel.

My raw and unfettered experience was Belle.

I had known her for some time. She was the little girl who stood at the bottom of the stairs beckoning me to join the others in the kitchen that first night at the Allotment. She was the first child I had seen when I came to live there, and I had always seen her as ordinary in most aspects. That was until the day I realized she was not a child anymore. That sudden, catastrophically wonderful event is one of the fixed points in my life which all things orbit around.

6. Falling with Belle. [9]

It was early June and all the kids were out in the garden tending to the leaf-lings and the new veggies. We were weeding the damp soil in the evening air and churning it for more plants. The sky was spotted with white clouds and there was a light breeze in the air. It carried the nectar of the fruit blossoms with it making the wind sweet.

I had taken my shoes off to feel the warm black soil between my toes and watch the bees on the flowers. Each was a little algorithm while they danced their way from flower to flower. I could hear the buzzing of each individual bee and see its path as it lit from plant to plant.

As I watched I heard their buzzing grow louder and louder. I realized it was not the bees which were buzzing. It was the same buzzing I had heard from the funeral and when Mr. Vincent had been shot. But unlike the past it did not bother me. There was no dislocation or confusion in it.

---

[9] "Like real people do" by Hozier ♫

It soaked into me and I felt my limbs begin to vibrate. The sound became a harmonic resonance inside me. I didn't feel compelled to fight it or be afraid. In fact I would say it felt completely natural. The world around me started to cease its state of frantic disorder. It became a smooth, slow-motion symphony of coordinated movement around me.

Once again I felt the presence of someone watching me from outside my world. I could sense eyes on me from somewhere nearby and I could hear the dis-conjoined sound of quiet muttering. It was the same muttering I had heard at the graveside of my parents. It had felt sad before, it did not when I heard it in the garden that day. It felt comforting and joyous. It felt as if someone were rejoicing for me and with me. I slowly looked up from the soil and turned my head to see where it came from.

When I did, I was allowed a separate space to exist in. It was only a millisecond but a millisecond was all I needed to see her in a different light. It was like someone grasped my head and directed my attention to the girl next to me, and furthermore helped me understand what it meant to feel the importance of the moment.

I saw Belle. She was barefoot, just like I was, on her hands and knees in the dirt planting food for the fall and the winter. Her hair was about her face and she looked at peace. She had a trowel in her hand and her fingers in the Earth. She was digging.

The meaning I found in the moment was only equal to the magnitude of my submission within it. My breath was non-existent in my lungs and my senses were rooted in the endless oceans of perception. Nothing in my life before or after has carried as much meaning as that small millisecond. It was not that she was beautiful, although she was. It was not that she was smart or funny, it was not any of those things. It was a connection to an unfathomable current in my life, a universal mandate of attraction. It was an undeniable, immutable truth. Our relationship would be a fixed event from that point forward. I did not know there was more to it than that at the time.

Belle was no longer a girl. She was a woman. I watched her in my small pocket of reality taking it in. Every aspect of her small frame was the essence of appealing. Every facet of what I already knew about her became fascination. Every mannerism she had was a comfort to me.

All the while a third party was participating in my life, watching me, and reveling in my realization. His muttering seemed to have laughter and excitement in it even though it was just a quiet whisper in my ears. Although I couldn't identify his speech, I could feel his congratulations speaking beautiful nonsense to me. He was happy for me.

I knew the three of us were connected, but I did not know how and in the moment I did not care. Belle must have felt me watching her because the second she noticed me, was the second everything returned to continuity. The feeling of being watched vanished and the buzzing disappeared. The insects started moving again and the world seemed to skip back into a place I was more familiar with.

Belle's gift was empathy; she felt things and had the ability to truly know what someone else was feeling. It has dawned on me since then that she might not have experienced the perfection I did, but she had most certainly felt it. As long as I knew Belle, I always wondered if the reason she was with me was the power of that moment. Was it she who had captivated me, or was she the one who had been captivated? I don't think I will ever know the answer to that question.

For a second we just looked at each other. Then we smiled at the same time. Like magic and without communication we started to work our way together while tilling the soil with our trowels. And a minute later we crouched next to each other. Just like the bees on the flowers. From that point on everything was different. We never spent more than a few hours apart and when we eventually left the Allotment, we left together, hand in hand, side by side.

I was sixteen that summer, the summer I found love. That is what my story is ultimately about. I emphasize this now for a reason, because the opportunity is one you have, or have already had.

For ten years I was never unhappy or regretful. I had a bliss which has overshadowed all the tragedy of

137

the past. Indeed, Belle is the reason I am still around to write this story. She is the reason, even though she couldn't have children, I still managed to. If not for her this story would be a different tale and would have ended much sooner in more violent ways.

I might not have noticed it then, because the isolation of the Allotment, but I was not the only one who paired off with someone so easily.

Looking back I can see how some of it was engineered. Other members of the class soon started pairing just like I and Belle had. If I had not been raised in isolation, I might have noticed how unusual it really was. Looking back on it, my younger self might have commented he did not care because he was in love. My younger self most likely would have insisted that the end of the world couldn't have stopped him from being with her. I would have agreed with him too. As my memory recalls, I could have died happy as long as she was in my reach.

We spent the rest of the day together. After we finished our chores in the garden we had the last few hours of the day off. So the two of us left and went across the Allotment to be alone together. We made love in the woods. Without fear or hesitation, without worry or nervousness or any stigmas, there was no fear we would lose each other or fall apart. I suppose that lack of fear is why we were so successful at being together. Fear has a tendency to ruin people.

I will reiterate, this is not how relationships

usually work; things do not grow so fast and time is how most people become attached.

Our relationship was no secret to any of the other kids. Eventually we, all of us, found someone. There was, after all, the same number of girls as there were boys and pairing seemed logical. Even with two of the guys pairing together, and two of the girls paring together. The young men and women at the Allotment established mates in a seamless way, without complication, without competition, and without trial. Like I have mentioned, it was engineered. Later, when we returned, those couples who had paired with the same sex managed to come back with children, I never inquired how but I assumed they did it through in vitro fertilization. Their children were genetic matches and carried their traits on.

Days passed, June turned to July, and then to August. We harvested the best crop in years from the Allotment garden. We gathered all the fruits and veggies and canned them for the winter. We prepped the out buildings, kept the shelves stocked and the wood chopped as we went into winter. All the while Indigo kept us under her tutelage. We kept up on the routine training and classes. Even when it was coldest, the Allotment was always warm in both spirit and temperature.

Indigo watched us grow and as we neared our adulthood she slowly separated herself from us. We were starting to master our gifts and I think she figured it was best to avoid interference. She was still there for us when we needed her, but she was more distant and spent more time in her quarters in the basement.

Eric also continued to exist. He went about his day the same as always, diagramming and drawing in his little sketch book, never saying a word to anyone. Eric was the only person at the Allotment who never paired with anyone. He was a puzzle to me and something told me not to dig too deep. When I looked at his place in the Allotment, nothing added up. He did not seem to have a function. He watched us, he monitored us, he never engaged not even in body language. Not even Belle could tell what he was feeling. But he seemed benign enough and exerted very little influence, so we let him be as he was.

Months and years passed in that wonderful holding pattern and winter gave way to the spring of my eighteenth year. My eighteenth year was the year we left the Allotment with all of the other children. We became dandelion fluff in the wind, and it took us to the furthest corners of the world.

One day in early April Indigo suddenly started scaled down our studies and withdrew nearly completely from us. For a few weeks we only saw her once or twice a week and it was only in passing. Of course she said hello to us and was cordial but it was almost an empty and vacant interaction and every time she seemed to distance herself more from us. The house still maintained itself well. We took care of everything and made sure it was all in order.

We noticed Eric was the only one who had any contact with Indigo, though sometimes she also avoided him. There was a concern among the students that she was sick. We discovered the truth about her that spring.

7. Fragments of Indigo. [10]

It was early in the year and all of the students were out on the Allotment grounds doing the chores and keeping the house up. It was our policy that someone would be back at the house keeping the kitchen ready but it was early in the season and we needed all hands to help get the grounds ready.

We had just finished planting the crops for the year and trimmed back the grape vines and the fruit trees. Mist was drifting up from the ground and embracing the trees as the sun warmed the fresh leaves. There was new life in the air. Even at the shore of the small lake in back of the house the ducks, geese, and waterfowl had returned.

Belle was tending to the birds and bees. She was helping them to pollinate the apple blossoms. I loved watching her do this. Her gift was not confined to interaction with just humans. She could influence the ways in which animals behaved. She understood them. She would orchestrate them across the orchard. It was

---

[10] "Where is my mind?" by Storm Large ♫

like watching a puppet master perform.

She would stand in the center of the orchard with her arms out and guide them in an even spread from one end to the other until she was sure all the plant flowers had been fertilized.

When she had finished she returned to helping the rest of us pruning the trees. She picked up her sheers and on the first pass pinched her hand.

She told me she was going back to the house for some bandages. I stayed in the orchard trimming the branches and getting the starters ready to be planted.

I was kneeling in the dirt when I started to hear the ticking sound in my head, then came the mumbling and whispering. It coursed through my body. It was hard to fight and it penetrated me as it had in the past, crippling all my senses. I could feel it in the ground and there was a faint smell of ozone in the air. My fingers started convulsing in the wet soil. I barely managed to turn my head enough to catch a glimpse. Although blurry, I saw the figure standing in the garden a few rows away. It was clear he was talking at me. He seemed desperate about something.

The buzzing and ticking increased in volume and I felt myself weaken. It was surging through my bones at an ever increasing intensity. My joints were burning under the sensation and my vision flickered in and out rapidly. My arms gave way and I fell face-down in the soil.

I awoke to the sound of a scream from the house.

It was deep and guttural and it resonated across the grounds. There was fear in it and all the birds became a black cloud as they sprayed into the sky. It pierced deep into my ears and I too felt fear in my stomach. I wanted to run from the sound. Then I realized it was Belle who had screamed. I found myself running toward it. Dazed and dizzy I groped my way through the orchard to towards the house, the buzzing growing faint in my ears as the vertigo left me. Other students were running through the Orchard toward the house as well.

There was another scream as one of the other students arrived and came through the front door. I was leaving the woods and sprinting for the house when Belle came out. She was crying and holding her stomach. I rushed to her and grasped her.

"What happened?" I asked frantically.

"I felt him, I felt his feelings, and I know what it is like inside him. I had no idea... She's dead, she's dead. Indigo is dead... I think. She is in pieces on the floor of the study. I don't know what is going on... Eric is in there with her... I looked into him..." She gasped through hyperventilation. "It was like nothing I have ever felt before. He's inhuman..." Belle muttered.

"Let me go check, you stay out here," I said. Belle would not let me go in and she tugged at me to stay outside with her. I had to reassure her before I and Clark went into the house. We followed the hallway back to the cracked study door. A few other students joined us and we all stood in front of it holding ourselves back. Clark reached out and pushed the door open.

It was hard to understand what we saw on the other side of the door, hard to fully comprehend without any frame of reference. The room was only lit by the natural light coming through the window.

Eric was in the room with his back to the door. We could see his small frame in front of the table. He was bent over something on the table which we couldn't see from the doorway. The sunlight was shining off his jet black hair as we worked. He seemed very unaffected by our presence and didn't turn around to confront us. Clark leaned into the room and spoke.

"Eric?" He said. "What are doing?"

There was no response.

"Eric?!" He repeated a little louder in a more harsh tone. Eric paused for a second and tilted his head to one shoulder without turning it.

"Can't you see, I am busy?" He said sternly and in a low tone. We had never heard his voice before. It was like slow ice chiseling into our ears. Clark walked into the room and I followed while the others stayed at the door jam on the other side. Across the table were strewn a number of tools; hammers, screw drivers, wrenches and several other wedges and mallets.

As our eyes adjusted and the table came into view we saw Indigo's head sitting flush on the walnut slab in front of Eric. Across the table were strewn the parts of her body. They were neatly lined up from her

144

toes to her fingers, in dichotomized organization, as if they were being scientifically cataloged.

There were also a number of other things set up in rows next to her parts. Little sprockets and cogs were arranged by size from smallest to largest. We saw no blood; we saw no tissue or other stains. Then the eyes in Indigo's head started to blink independently and her mouth started to open a little and close as it was trying to mouth something but no sound came out. Like a fish trying to breathe.

This seemed to annoy Eric, he reached up and carefully turned the head around to face the wall. Shock was on our faces and neither one of us moved. Eric carefully put the screwdriver down and turned around to our interruption.

"You two always have a habit of upsetting work, don't you? This was supposed to be done by now," He said as he glared at us. "Let me explain this before you ask. She was malfunctioning, I have to take her apart and fix her so she can be put to use at a later time," Clark started towards him. "I wouldn't do that if I were you, without me, there is no way she will ever be put together again, and besides I would not want to hurt either of you. She worked so hard to make you into descent human beings, don't take that from her. Like I said I can put her back together again, but not if you do anything irrational. And trust me, she means more to me than she does to you," He said as he turned back to his work. "Now go, leave me alone and let me finish my work," He said picking up a screw driver and rotating back.

"Malfunctioning?!" Clark shouted. "What the hell does that mean?!"

"It means she had some anomalies which were stopping her from doing what she was designed to do. She was either finished doing it or she is broken. I will know as soon as I take a closer look, which is what you are preventing me from doing. Now go away," He said disdainfully.

Clark started to move towards him with his fist balled up. Eric turned and calmly placed his hand around Clark's neck and lifted him off the ground. Despite his stature he still managed to get his feet a couple of inches off the ground.

"What did I say?" Clark's face was starting to turn red and his feet were starting to twitch. I moved into the room and spoke.

"Eric, just put him down. Please. You don't want to do this!" I insisted.

"I suppose you are right. It would be a waste of Indigo's purpose. But he will have to calm down or I will have to make him," Eric replied as he slowly set Clark down and unlocked his hand from his throat. Clark slouched over gasping for air.

Eric looked at him and spoke a little softer. "I do not want to hurt you, please leave. I will call you when I am done here. I will call all of you and your questions will be addressed then," He said.

I helped Clark up and we backed out of the room slowly together. We joined the other students and shut the door.

We all left the house and congregated on the front lawn. Only a few of us had seen what Eric had done and we had no explanation for it. There was a lot of confusion. Clark kept asking "Did you see her? Did you…"

I could only answer with short monosyllabic words. I had no explanation, and I knew he didn't either.

I found Belle and held her. She was still crying and scared. After a moment people gathered around and started asking what had happened. The few of us that had seen it tried to explain it, but there was too much confusion and fear to get out the words. And even if we were able to tell them, they wouldn't have believed us.

We milled around on the front lawn for a little while in silence and confusion. Clark was still rubbing his neck and shaking his head. We had one of the students who could heal check his neck, but there was no permanent damage.

After a half hour or so there was a groaning sound and the front door slowly opened. Eric stood there looking down the steps at us. His eyes went back and forth across the group. He did not speak; he simply raised his hand and motioned for us to follow him.

We shuffled in silently behind him. He did not lead us to the study. He led us to the common room off the kitchen and told us to take our seats at the tables. We

147

felt we had no choice so we all sat down at our places. He told us to wait and said he would be right back. We sat in silence and waited in the thick tension hanging in the air.

When he returned he was carrying a box which he placed on Indigo's table in front of us. He carefully reached into the box and extracted her head and a small stand. Half of her face was missing and there were exposed sprockets and gears packed neatly inside of her. The other half was still as perfect as when I had met her. One of her eyes sat perched in the nest of metal and the other seemed to possess life, wet shiny life. One seemed lifeless and without any anima. With great caution he placed the head on the stand and adjusted it to face the students.

He gently reached into her hair and touched something at the base of her skull. For a second nothing happened, and then the eyelids began to rapidly blink at different speeds independent of each other. The cogs began to turn and there was a low pitched whirring sound. Light returned to her eyes and they moved slowly back and forth from one side of the room to the other like a printer, in lines from the floor to the ceiling. Eric stood next to her while this took place.

Then she spoke. At first her voice was randomly pitched and full of static. The tone was off but she kept readjusting it like she was tuning a radio. Then her voice became clear.

8. Indigo bids farewell.

"My children please allow me to explain," She paused and looked across us again. "It was not supposed to be this way. I was supposed to deliver this in full… and by that I mean in one piece," She said as her eyes flitted around the room. "I am Indigo, version number eight-point-one-point-five-zero, my model number is sixteen…" she said.

I felt a cold draft on my spine and I suddenly remembered the packing crate Clyde and I had found in basement *(8.1.50 Version 16.)*.

It was her packing crate. Not a packing crate she owned and kept things in, but the packing crate her body was shipped in.

She paused for a little longer then spoke again.

"I am sorry for the deception, it was never easy to hide this but it was felt the form given to me would be soothing only if you remained ignorant of its inner workings. I had no choice in this matter, ever since I was unpacked and assembled. As with you, my knowledge was and still is limited. I came with only the knowledge of what I was, what I had to do, and how to do it. Despite this, I have loved each and every one of you and I have always known you are special. It must be a shock to see me this way and I am sorry. Please do not be frightened," She paused and her eyelids blinked rapidly.

"I have always known this day would come and that my functions would wind down. This means my job is done. Eric was kind enough to finish my diagnostics and determined I had indeed completed what I was purposed for. I cannot argue with his skill in this matter," She twitched and smiled a warm toothy grin from the table.

As she did so I could see the inner workings of her face. Little cogs and gears pulled half her mouth into a crescent shape while the other half was pulled up by synthetic skin.

"I was purposed for raising you. I was designed to ensure you all became leaders, innovators, dreamers, inventors, spiritualists and so much more. You were raised to make the world a better place. You will be there to pick up the reins and lead those willing to follow in a new world. You are seeds which will grow into something wonderful and great. I cannot tell you who wanted it this way, I cannot tell you where I come from and I cannot recall how I came to be here, because I do not know. There is nothing before my assembly. I was only given guidelines, and instructions, I have no past. It was never written into my performance and is limited to a couple of years before the Allotment was started. An extensive past does not serve my function. What I do know is that I have fulfilled my purpose… To love you, to raise you, and to make sure you were prepared for the future. I have been very blessed in this because not many can claim to have shared a life with such very special individuals," Her face scrunched for a second and the corner of her mouth vibrated.

"Let me explain what I know so you can move on. Your lives began with tragedy, and I am sorry for that. It was not orchestrated, it was coincidence and misfortune. It was necessary to pick children who knew loss and understood it, because knowing loss will help to understand the nature of taking and giving. This is fundamental to being a good person. It teaches value. I was made to ensure you became good people, educated people, kind people, and you are. It just takes a nudge, one way or the other. I was designed to nudge you the right direction. In this aspect, I am so very proud of all of you. What we do with value is empty without choice, so as you grew, I allowed you all to choose more and more. A peaceful society needs a few things to thrive. Choice is primary to humans… You needed to be educated in many ways. This was hard to overcome because there was so much to learn, and humans forget so much along the way. You, all of you, were given a small injection of little machines to help you with this. Nano-machines were used to accelerate your learning. The machines will keep you healthy, they will keep you from being sick, and they will make sure that you never stop learning. They will gift you with so many things. Sometimes it will be hard because they will give you things you may not want, but the things you truly need. They will not keep you from aging and dying, mortality is necessary to all people. Your gifts stem from the way they interact with you. It is because of them that you are above average in your aptitudes and skill sets. The

151

things you can do have never been seen before, they will be in every generation after you. Your children will carry the changes in their own way.

"Secondly, you needed to be both unique as well as be a part of a collective. This was also done for you here at the Allotment. You have become part of each other's lives, and that will never change… You are family, together you are whole. The Allotment has provided an isolated and somewhat self-reliant environment for you to mature in. A small contained group of people who have grown to need each other in a benevolent way. This was the goal of the project; as I said you are the seeds which needed to be planted so a new world could be grown from changes you will bring. It will take time because true change does. It also takes patience, sacrifice and perseverance, little changes happening on top of each other over many years to make a bigger change…"

"Third, you all have been imbued with the qualities of stewardship, meaning you have been taught to think of commerce as an act of giving rather than getting or receiving. You have fostered within you characteristics of peace, meaning, value, love, kindness, empathy, leadership, harmony, compassion, and understanding to name a few. These things, in conjunction with education and intellect, are the things which make peace work. Above all you were provided common sense and wisdom to know and also feel what is right. To know when a bad thing truly is the only option, and when a good thing is self-serving.

"Lastly, you were paired off with the perfect match. The person you came to love. You were provided with suitable options, opportunity was opened, and you were given the chance to experience choice. This last one is the one I have enjoyed watching the most. Watching you find the person who complements you so completely. We left everything else up to nature. I can truly say my job is done. You have reached the age of legality and you are equipped to discover the world and experience it and spread what you have learned. Indeed, you need to know the world to be whole. You need to know it before it changes, the way it is now so you can remember the pitfalls and miracles it holds. It can be dangerous, perilous at times, even sad and helpless but it can also be exhilarating and wondrous...

"I am experiencing that moment every parent must face. You must leave and find your own ways together and this is bittersweet for me. I am both happy and sad all at the same time... I have never experienced this feeling," She paused and it almost looked as though she would cry. Her eyes fluttered again and she spoke for the last time.

"In each of your rooms is a small envelope with a sum of money, this is to get you wherever you want to go together. There is also a letter I have written to each and every one of you. This is why I have been so distant and withdrawn recently. I needed to say goodbye to each of you and I did not know how to do it. So I wrote letters

153

to you. Included in the envelopes is a passport, driver's license, your birth certificate and information. On that letter is a special email setup just for you. There is a list of everyone else's email, so you can keep in contact with one another. I have provided your information to companies around the world. You will receive job offers. But for now, I want you to see the world, it is special, it is unique and it needs to be seen and appreciated. Travel is something missing from the world out there. The people out there do not explore anymore. They have such contained minds because they choose to limit the scope of their world and thus their perspective," She twitched again and continued with her train of thought.

"The next part of your education is to see the world, experience it and see how it needs you. Meet people, make friends, be fearless, try new things, be hopeful and be amazing. Never lose contact with those people you shared your childhood with. Someday you will all meet again and when you do I would hope you have enough stories about your life to chronicle for many generations. Your children will need those stories as an example. I will miss each and every one of you, at least I hope I will, I do not know where I am going. This will have to be good bye. I want you to go to your rooms and pack all the things truly important to you, and then I want you to leave in all directions," She stopped for a minute and looked across us, her cheek was twitching and one of her eyelids was flickering open and closed, then movement started to cease and her porcelain demeanor turned her face to glass, but she said one last thing.

"Good bye… children, students… it has been a pleasure and a joy, thank you…" She finished as her eyes shut. Then there was nothing. Her disembodied head was idle and motionless. The silence was so loud it penetrated our minds.

9. Leaving the Allotment. [11]

We left the main hall and made our way back to our rooms. Our world was shaken and while, in most ways, there was a disbelief in our mind and hearts. There was also an exhilarating sense of freedom in the air. It was not odd that she was some sort of machine, we were used to the strange and impossible, it was that we were free. There was no yoke of guidance on us. We were free to achieve, free to leave the Allotment, free to explore and in a way we realized Indigo had done a superb job preparing us for the world. We were everything she had told us we could be. Deep down all of us craved adventure and travel.

There had been so much joy on the Allotment with our friends and even though we would see them and could contact them whenever we needed, they would not be next door. I don't think any of us knew

---

[11] "Doors to heaven" by Shake Shake Go ♫

how to feel about that part.

I went up to my room and got my pack out then looked around slowly. It was not the first time I had left home. The difference was I was doing it with someone I loved and cared about. It did not take me long to decide what I wanted to bring with me. I went to my desk and took the laptop from the drawer and I took the photo of my parents from the window above the desk. I found the envelope on my pillow, but I did not open it. I took my clothes from the closet and packed them into the bag making sure they were all tightly folded as my father had showed me when I was a boy.

I double checked the drawers and the shelves but there was nothing irreplaceable to take with me. The skis my parents had given to me leaned behind the door and for a moment I thought that I might take them, but I had long since outgrown them. I would buy a new pair anyway but I would never forget them. I breathed in deeply and felt nervousness coursing through my veins in a pattern of uncertainty.

I took the envelope from the bed and opened it. Inside was a passport, which was odd because it had my picture and don't ever recall having my picture taken for the passport. There was a new driver's license, my birth certificate, some other forms of ID, and four neatly banded bundles of hundred dollar bills.

It was then I realized the money we had found in the basement was not intended for Indigo, but the children at the Allotment. There was also a black debit card with my name on it. I was not really interested in those things. I was more interested in the letter from Indigo. At the bottom of the large manila envelope I found a second smaller envelope. I hastily opened it and started to read the letter inside.

10. Indigo's letter.

Here is what it said:

My child,

Ever since you came to my door I have known your life would be different than the others. I am sorry for what you have been through, and will have to go through. You of all my students have suffered. Just know with Belle you will find satisfaction most of the children will only know part of. She is the only one who can know you in your entirety. The next period of your life, I am sure, will be the best. I can see a bright future for both of you, but do not forget to stop and enjoy each other. Life moves fast when you are not looking. I once said you would have the answers to your questions- this is still true. That illusion I spoke of in the car the day Mr. Vincent was shot will be clear someday. Like I said sometimes the illusion, although mysterious, has more value and lessons than the truth. Please stay the course no matter what happens, our future is dependent on the choices you make, not all of them are easy to make and sometimes the hardest ones we face are the ones that

bring the most happiness and peace. Stay in love, enjoy
life, and when the veil is lifted, know that every decision
whether hard or easy carries ripples which affect the
world, maybe the universe, in ways you cannot imagine.

Yours truly, Indigo.
P.S. Don't forget to keep skiing.

I folded it and placed it into the manila envelope.
Then I put the envelope in my pack and left the room. At
the door I stopped and thought of the loyal German
shepherd who had once greeted me every morning. Loki
had long since passed, but none of us had forgotten him.
As I walked toward Belle's room every crack oozed with
memories and the creaking floorboards gave way to an
honest representation of my life to that point, a temporal
finger-print of my time at the Allotment. I could
remember all the nuances of every season. The pictures
on the wall with only adults in blacks and whites
watched me as I moved to the top of the stairs.

I went down the stairs and around the corner to
Belle's room. The door was cracked and I pushed it
open. Belle stood in the middle of the room with her
arms attached to her bags handle. The bag was resting
on the floor as she held it upright. She was motionless
and there were tears in her eyes.

"I don't know how to be with this," She said. "I
feel like everything's falling apart and I cannot fix it," I
put my bag down and came over to her.

"It's going to be okay, Belle," I said as I hugged her.

"But this is home. This is where I want to be, with you, and the others. I don't want to be away, and the worst part of it is, I only feel this way because I am scared and confused and don't understand. I am so used to understanding how everyone else feels, I don't know how I feel," She said with a whimper.

"We are not leaving them love; we are going out into the world so we can see it and share it. This is what Indigo wanted. Everything she taught us was so we could one day leave. I will be with you and we will see all of the things we always wanted to. You know... All the places we have seen in movies and magazines. We will take pictures and have memories. We will share our experiences with each other and visit our friends all the time. This is how I want to see it. We are not losing something. We are discovering the world and we are doing it with our friends," I said wiping a tear from her cheek.

"I know, but I am frightened," She said. I held her and she cried for quite some time. I didn't tell her I was just as scared and confused as she was, though I suspect she felt it. Then, finally, she pulled away and nodded. "Okay, Okay... I am ready, I think," She said.

"Do you have everything you need?" I asked.

"Yes, and I got the letter," She whispered. "She really did care, didn't she?"

"Yes she did," I said softly. I wasn't sure she

159

did though. She was a machine and my mind was having difficulty with that.

I took Belle's hand and we left the room and went down to the foyer where several students were gathering.

The door was open and there were other students on the front porch. We all waited until the last of us made their way down and joined the group. We made sure to say goodbye to everyone. We shook hands and hugged all the while a melancholy cloud over us.

Looking back, I could never understand why we just left. We didn't question it, we were not defiant. We just did what she wanted without questioning it. We did not even stop to consider staying; it was as if we were programmed to leave.

Clark and Susan left first. They were always leaders and although I knew he was scared too, he was the best at handling it, and he showed the others the way.

Soon we were all leaving, one at a time the couples found their way down the paved driveway leading away from the Allotment. It was not long before I found myself, hand in hand walking with Belle down the winding paved road, our bags on our backs.

It was a clear day in early June when I took Belle's hand and walked away from the Allotment. Other couples were filing out behind us with their partners by their sides. They were spreading like dandelion fluff on the wind. We did not look back. We just kept walking until each and every one of us was out of sight.

And then we were gone into the world.

My life as a youth was a good time and although it did not end the way I thought it would, it ended with something new and unexpected.

This was the summary of my youth. In it I found friends, I found family and I found a lover. I matured and came to see how life could be a wondrous experience. True, there were parts of it which defied my logic and things I didn't think could ever be explained. I lost my home and my only semblance of a parent figure. I gained so much more important things, the knowledge and wisdom that come with growth and aging.

My youth was a blessing and I am grateful it happened the way it did.

ACT III: The Adult I was.

1. Adulthood. [12]

It was a beautiful adulthood, full of the adventure I always wanted. It took place in exciting times and wild places. It was a time for enjoyment, exploration and travel. I was still learning and creating during that time in my life. I had a brilliant woman with me and a whole world to see. I learned what life was supposed to be about and how to enjoy it. I learned how adults play. Indeed it was the future I had cultivated and planned for.

With Belle we were never out of a purpose, that is to say spiritually lost. We were never unfamiliar with whom we were. Our rhythms seemed to be endless and perfectly synchronized with happiness. We had become one unit and the skills we had we re-purposed making them a part of our everyday lives. We used them to make a living.

We had learned so much about the outside world but we were still missing the experience. As we traveled I learned that experience makes a difference.

The affairs of the world when we started our journey were calm; I say calm because the world is never really at peace. There were always conflicts. At any given time dozens of countries were fighting with each other. Sometimes they would flare up and become more than a localized event- but I will get to that.

---

[12]"Bonfire Heart" by James Blunt ♫

The world was a safer place then and we took advantage of that and went places we could not go even just a few years later. It started that day we left.

2. And we were off.

After leaving the Allotment we found our way to the nearest town. We bought a map of the United States. It was the first thing we did in our new lives. We could have bought a GPS system to use, but something felt right about an old paper map.

We found a local diner and sat down with our bags at our feet. We ordered a couple scones and a cup of coffee then spread the map out on the table in front of us.

We could have gone anywhere. We had enough money to go around the world a couple of times but we felt starting locally would be a good idea. We had never been outside of Connecticut.

I went up to the counter, took one of the pens and came back and sat down next to Belle. Our coffee and scones were brought to us and we began the selection process, all the while keeping in mind Indigos directive to explore and enjoy the world.

I looked at her small frame sitting on the bench across from me. I smiled at her. There were so many places we had talked about visiting when we got older. It was time to stop talking about them and start seeing them. She smiled back and took a sip of her coffee. I could see her big eyes looking over the rim of the cup at me.

"I want to see the redwoods in California," She said bluntly.

"Alright, let's go there," I said and circled Northern California. "And I want to see the everglades," I said as I circled part of Florida. "Your turn," I said handing her the pen. She took it and circled Chicago. We went back and forth this way until the whole map was covered in small circles. I looked closely at it and started to draw a line from circle to circle, I made sure not to loop back too much and follow the interstates. I knew along the way we would find many places we did not know existed. I was sure things would change as we traveled. For the first time in our life there was nothing we had to be doing, there were no chores, there were no mandates, no requirements or lessons, just unfettered time with no constraints and no conditions.

When we were done we paid up the tab and cashed out ready to leave. Before we left the diner, I reached into my bag, pulled out my small pocket knife and flipped it open. I scratched our initials gently into the corner of the table.

I don't know why I did this. I think it was just to leave a mark, an etching next to the other etchings. They were worn and old, collected in the shadows of the corner booth. Names, hearts with arrows through them and sayings scratched into the wood with pockets knives just like mine. I noticed among the names, and the obscenities a phrase that seemed *a per pro*.

It read: *"Go forth and be"*.

It made me smile and realize I had opportunity and I should be grateful for it and honor it by not wasting it. Belle smiled, she saw it too and I know it had the same meaning for her. We stood, grabbed our bags and went across the street to the bus terminal.

Together we bought our first ticket to get us lost, to go somewhere where we could be without knowing where we were. Somewhere so lost that the only thing we could find was ourselves. We had never been lost before. Our whole life we had always known exactly where everything was. We had studied the world from the books at the Allotment but experiencing it was going to be truly different.

We boarded the bus a little scared and anxious. As soon as the bus started to move our hearts were throbbing with energy. Excitement was coursing through us and our knees were shaking in anticipation. Our hearts were ready. Belle and I were going to see the world.

3. Across the United States. [15]

It did not take us long to figure out buses can get you to where you need to go but they won't do it comfortably.

Right after the first leg of our journey we bought

---

[13] "House of gold" by 21 Pilots ♫

166

an old truck which became our vehicle to get us to the west coast. I loved that old truck and all of the memories we had in it. It did not run exceptionally well, but it never quit. It took me some time to learn how to shift it because the transmission was old. My screaming and fumbling with the shifter gave us some good laughs. When I figured it out, it became second nature. We chased the sunset as we moved westward and we saw unbelievable things.

We saw the night lights of New York City as I had wanted to. It was a million electric bulbs lighting the waterfront along the shores of a seemingly endless ocean. We saw Boston and its historic harbor where men had thrown tea because of taxes. We traveled to the capital and saw our forefather's monuments, reminders of what our country used to be. We saw the battlefields of the civil war and walked with ghosts on the hallowed ground paying homage to their pain and sacrifice. We got to see the Everglades and it was all I thought it would be, if not a little swampy. Its inlets were filled with a unique dichotomy of animals. We saw New Orleans, ate Cajun food and danced on river boats with French boat masters. We smoked hand rolled cigars on outdoor patios on bourbon street. We roamed the muddy Mississippi, our pant legs rolled up, and nothing but a melody to show us the way.

In the great interior, the heartland, we slept in the back of our truck under a crystal sky and beaming stars. In the back of the truck we held each other with the dying fireflies.

We traveled through the cowboy states and saw the vast expanses of emptiness and blue where livestock stomped their feet in the same rhythm with the oil wells bobbing up and down. There were plenty of small restaurants and hotels to stop at along the way. We ate a lot of burgers and homemade apple pie. We slept in many beds in small rooms where the walls were paper thin. There was plenty of dancing too, and singing to songs to the radio just as my mother and father had done.

We were awed by the Rockies and their splendor, and the sheer magnitude and force with which they pushed skyward stretching to meet the havens. For several days we followed the Earth's elevated rock-spine through the center of the country. At the top of the great divide we looked down on the west as eager children.

Every night we would listen to the cricket song invade the dark summer silence. We would start a fire where ever we slept and warm our bones by it. It took us till early September to get to highway 101 in northern California. Our zigzagging path had touched all of the circles on our map. It was a lot of traveling and most people would have considered it exhausting but I would argue that with little worries, a person is rarely exhausted.

As we rolled our old truck up to the beach head in northern California, I knew, there was no going back. That was the moment I realized I was grown. I was an adult and there was something sad about it even though I had Belle next to me. Almost like losing a friend or a sibling, or watching as a lover grows apart. Maybe it was arriving at the destination to find the most important and exciting part of the trip is over. It was then I realized the journey was so much more important than the destination.

The Pacific, which contrasted the way I felt, was so blue and endless I could not find myself in it. We found a beach and drove the truck out on to the sand and parked.

We got out and walked to the edge where the sand met the lapping of the ocean. The sun was bright and sparkled on the water bringing it to life, making it dance with the light. Orange was playing like crystal off into the horizon where the sky touched it. We stood together in the sand letting the waves tug at our toes and the cold salty spray permeate our clothing. Northern California was nice. It was beautiful, it seemed wild.

4. Finding a place. [14]

Highway 101, as you may know, is one of the most amazing and beautiful places in the world. It is a winding strip of asphalt placed on the edge of the world where the giant redwoods wage battle with the Pacific. The road itself can be treacherous but the scenic and

---

[14] "Free the mind" by Johann Johannsson ♪

meandering highway is, I would say with no other way to explain it, spectacular. We instantly fell in love with it. It was also the first place we lived after leaving the Allotment.

As we drove we kept seeing more and more places we wanted to stop and stay the night. It was September and some of them were closed as they were seasonal but nonetheless, northern California struck our interest and we wanted to spend a little time there.

The small town of Elk is where we finally decided to root for a while. As an old man I know why that town was so attractive, but then it was different. I was more spontaneous and it was whim which brought us to Elk. Even though we had no attachment to it, we decided to stay for a while, at least for the winter. As it turned out we spent a little more time than just the winter in Elk. It was a place to rest our feet as we explored.

Elk was a sleepy little town nestled close to the Redwoods. When we first arrived we were welcomed by jagged cliffs descending to the ocean and small cottages across the smattering of rock outcroppings. Along the left side of the road as we drove southward the hills rose to open meadows dotted by trees and houses and split by glacial streams which tumbled over granite cliffs to the ocean.

The first thing we did was pick up a paper and start going through it looking for apartments. Indigo had done a very thorough job at making sure we were prepared to obtain what we wanted or needed. Within three days we had secured a place, had our services hooked up, had furniture delivered and set up. Of course it was not much to deliver. All of Indigo's children had been taught to live light.

Our place was nice. It was almost on the edge of the cliff, set back just a little. If we left the window open at night we could hear the surf and catch the wind blowing in from the ocean. It was the ocean which put us to sleep at night and I was able to substitute its sound for my obnoxious counting.

In the morning the sound of seagulls would wake us up. Our little balcony was filled with plants and from it we could see across the *inner reach* where all the boats were moored. Our place was behind a small bead shop and was adjoined with another place, a duplex we shared with another person.

The real estate agent told us an old man lived there and we needed to keep the volume down and be mindful. We tried to respect his request, but we were young and still liked noise. We made our place sing with joy. We bought an old record player the first year and filled the house with music and dancing. The old man never complained, I know he liked the music and the noise because he was all alone and everyone needs company, it just how humans are.

We were within walking distance of a little path which would take us down the rocky cliffs to a small beach. We spent a good deal of time there. We also spent a good deal of time hiking in the hills above town and along the grassy pastures. We used to borrow a neighbor's horses and disappear into the redwoods together. There were also times when we would take day trips down to San Francisco and although I liked it, I found it too crowded. To this day, I would never want to live there, but it was fun to visit.

5. Making a living.

After we had settled in and made a temporary home in Elk we began the process of communicating with our friends who had also left the Allotment and re-established connections. We also received a single job offer each to get us started. This was a good thing because we knew the money Indigo had left us would not last forever. I was amazed at how easy the offer came, and how quickly an email was returned when I applied for it. After I filled out the information packet and emailed it back, the company did a background check, a security check, and a day later they had accepted my offer. The same happened with Belle. Whatever Indigo had done aligned us as prime job candidates.

It was my first job. It was a consultant job which paid well and guaranteed work for me. My official title was *engineering consultant*. I checked calculations for a development firm called *Origin Incorporated*. They specialized in structural integrity for buildings, and large and small machinery, as well as a number of other

172

services. From radiation decay problems to environment and carbon control, I consulted on them.

I double checked the engineer's work, and solved mathematical dilemmas from weight limit and energy consumption to material stress load calculations. Being a consultant was nice because it utilized my aptitudes but gave me a lot of personal freedom too.

I would receive a project at the beginning of the week and my dead line would be the end of the week. The problems varied in size and complexity. I was required to solve them and then send back a process log, any work on the problem, and method of solution along with the answer. As I have stated the projects were vast and varied and I dealt with just about everything.

It was an easy job. I usually had my projects done by Tuesday or Wednesday of each week. I could have had them done sooner but the reports had to be written up. It was the writing, not the project that slowed me down.

I never actually met with anyone from the company face to face, which was fine with me because I really did not care for the corporate environment. I did however start to question the nature of the projects after a while. It seemed as though no one person I communicated with knew the extent of the projects we were working on.

Each of us was only given a little piece of the whole picture. None of us could put the whole thing together because we only had our little pieces. I am not sure how I would have reacted if I had known the truth about what I was doing, or how valuable my skills were to Origin. What they were actually doing with my calculations was something I never dreamed possible or even plausible for that reason.

Belle's offer came much the same way. Her position was completely different however. Her work was academic. She was hired to help a couple of Ivy League professors write a theoretical law compendium and create a curriculum dealing with emotional well-being and child rearing; at least that's what she told me. Truth was I wouldn't have understood the specifics of it any more than she would have understood the laws of thermodynamics or what a hydro fracture was. She would get more offers over the years and co-author many books on well-being and mental health.

Aside from the occasional symposium there was no travel required and no relocation required either. We did all our work from wherever we wanted to be and emailed in our work to our prospective employers through an encrypted connection. The pay was nice too and between us we had no debt. In fact, we had money to spare.

It was surprising how little we actually needed. I remember thinking how much time and happiness most people lose to debt and what freeing them from it could do for them. It would have done no good back then people were different than they are now. Materialism meant more.

I only ever saw one job offer. Belle would get about two a year. I don't know if this was what Indigo had in mind when she contacted the possible employers but it was clear we were all a part of something which utilized our aptitudes. And she got to keep some of the royalties to her work.

Life was good in our sleepy little town. We ate well, we slept well, and we went running in the woods and on the beach. We skied all winter in the mountains around Mount Shasta.

Everything was new but eventually we both got a hunger to travel again. We stayed in Elk for about a year and a half before we moved on. We had been all over the United States and so we decided to travel abroad. We learned some Spanish and some French and one fine day we packed our few possessions, and sold our furniture and left.

It was not the same as it had been before. There was no regret; there was nothing but a feeling of excitement.

6. Leaving Elk with my ghost.

I was excited that morning. Our little apartment was empty and I could hear the echoes inside it which had become our ghosts. We had already packed our bags and were stuck in anticipation. We decided to document our trip around the world with a photo album. Belle said it would be a great heirloom for our kids, which she had been talking about more and more. We purchased a couple of high end cameras and decided our first picture would be in Elk along the bluffs. This sometimes seems like a trivial event in my life, but I realize as I grow older, is not. The more I think about it the more aware I become of its importance.

We went out the back and stopped just shy of the cliffs and set the timers on the cameras. We took each other's hands and faced the endless blue of the Pacific. As the 30 second timer ticked down I felt a feeling I had not felt in a long time, not since I had come home to find Indigo in pieces in the study.

It started as it always did. The buzzing and ticking penetrated me. I was vibrating and twitching. Then I could hear the sound of indecipherable muttering in my ears. I looked around to see if I could find the source but I was vibrating so hard that my eyes were blurring. The voice sounded like a mixture of a bee buzzing and someone whispering words backward through a megaphone. There was a familiar feeling that accompanied it. As though something was trying to break through the walls of my universe and say something to me.

It was a force I couldn't understand or grasp. The universe was spinning the wrong direction under my feet. Belle sensed that I was troubled and steadied me as we smiled for the picture. I held my composure for the picture but collapsed as soon as the photo was taken.

My knees hit the ground and all was silent. I couldn't even hear the sound of Belle's voice as she tried to help me. My fingers were still shivering as the feeling faded. Although it was brief, it was disconcerting to experience again. Until that day I had always felt whatever it was, was a figment of my imagination. A psychological throwback to the day I buried mother and father. I did not see anything that day, but the camera did. It was the first time I knew I was not alone in my own life.

Belle helped me up, and sat me on a tree stump nearby and gave me some water. She asked me what happened and I told her. I explained what I felt, and she listened. I asked her to fetch the camera and she did. She handed it to me and I took it then looked in the image viewer. It would have been a beautiful picture but there was an image smudged in front of us covering a part of the panorama. It was not clear but I could tell it was a man.

His image was translucent and seemed to be smudged from right to left into the side of the frame. He seemed to be standing with his back to the camera between us and the lens. It was so faint it was barely noticeable. I could make out a gray coat and long silver or white hair. Our images seemed to bleed through him. He seemed to be traveling through the frame at high speed.

For all I knew it was a ghost, but I was skeptical. There was no explanation at the time and a ghost was all that came to mind. He had been with me my entire life or at least since the funeral. He did not really scare me as

177

much as he intrigued me.

Belle seemed to be understanding, but she was still cautious and even suggested we postpone our departure. I disagreed and quelled her worry with a hug and reassurance. It was not the first time it had happened. I suspected it was a side effect from the machines Indigo had talked about. It took some doing but I convinced her I was alright. I kept that picture and put it in the back of our album.

We decided to continue, I reset the camera and we took another picture with no recurrence of the event. I was concerned but I think Belle was more so. She did not take the event as abnormal; it was a caution, something to watch for as we traveled. A normal person would have sought medical advice right away, and possibly psychological or neurological treatment. I was used to it and it never affected me outside of the actual events. I felt that someday I would know what it was, as Indigo had explained.

I was determined to make our trip around the world something we would never forget. We did not plan a destination; instead we wanted to go until we were done, in other words indefinitely.

To this day I still hold the belief that the important part of a journey is not the arrival but the trip. Much like a good meal the enjoyment and satisfaction of the meal does not come from finishing it; it comes from the process of eating and tasting the meal.

I was not going to miss a single course of my life

with Belle. I was going to enjoy every minute of it. I did not know our time together wouldn't be a lifetime. In retrospect I am glad I did not let anything stop us.

Our plan was to start in Elk, and fly across the Pacific, make our way through the Islands and then Australia, India and Asia, Japan and China. From there we would go to across Russia to the Middle East then down and around Africa. We decided we would stay in Europe for a while. Then we would cross the Atlantic and go down through Central and South America to Ushuaia on the very tip of Argentina. Belle knew it was a long trip and was concerned about some of the countries we would travel through. I assured her it would be the trip of a lifetime and promised her we would see it all.

We would capture several more photos of the man, the ghost, but none were recognizable. Most were just blurs in the lens and became quite an annoyance. I got accustomed to the feeling that would come over me. I noticed he only showed up when we were about to make changes in our lives. He would show up where our travels or parts of our lives ended and new parts began. We came to know him as my ghost. He seemed to be singular to me so he left Elk with us.

After we had finished taking the pictures we went back to the house and got our packs, then handed our keys to our property manager.

We walked away, just as we had from the Allotment, with two bags, hand in hand. We had already sold our vehicle and possessions and knew our route southward to the Santa Rosa Airport. Just as we had before we started on the highway. This time with our thumbs up and our hearts open. In a couple of days we were walking into the airport with tickets in hand.

7. Traveling the world. [15]

We boarded our plane and headed for the islands of the south Pacific. We started with Hawaii and moved west across to the Marshalls, Fiji, Guam, Micronesia, and Bali. Both of us had a list of Places we wanted to see and we mapped the best route as we had before.

Sometimes we would travel by seaplane and sometimes by sail or steamer. I used a satellite phone to do my work.

Our passports were full of stamps from all the places we had been and our faces were light brown from the sun. Our hair became bleached and our bodies travel hardened. I discovered, in practice, what I had been taught my whole life. It was not the possessions a person owned, it was the experiences a person had which gave their life merit.

The more I got rid of things the better, the happier, I felt. I think Belle was the same way. By the time we arrived in Bali our packs were ten pounds lighter and all the important things we owned were

---

[15] "Upside down" by Jack Johnson ♫

reduced to hygiene, traveling documents, cloths, a laptop with waterproof carrying case and cameras. Everything else, all items, were only details coming and going from our packs.

Having less helped us to appreciate what little we did have. We started to understand that most possessions would change, become obsolete, break, or come unraveled.

Our lives became bohemian in nature. We called it living in a state of *non-econo-commitment.* A philosophy which Belle used in her writing and a term which she coined with her email colleagues.

For the first summer and winter we traveled to hundreds of small islands. My only complaint was there was no skiing anywhere. To adapt to this I learned to surf. I found this very enjoyable but it was much harder than skiing. It was harder because I kept seeing the wave beneath me and it's hypnotic churning and correspondent rhythm made it very hard to concentrate and keep my balance.

We learned to free dive and scuba. Belle and I enjoyed this more than anything else and sometimes we found it hard to head back to shore when it got dark. We would watch as the red tide set the sea on fire with bio luminescence. We would stay in the surf until the early hours of the morning just watching the waves light up around us while the algae tickled our limbs and igniting the beaches with a pale blue glow.

When we grew restless we would travel again.

We left the Pacific and went to Australia. Australia was great, if not a little extreme. We bought a couple of motorcycles and made our way across the continent dodging kangaroos and Koalas. It was an odd but fascinating place. Our course took us from Sydney to Perth and then north to Darwin where we took a boat to Thailand.

From Thailand, we traveled to southern China, Japan and Mongolia. I learned how to ride horses, cook stir fry, and prepare sushi. I learned tai-chi from an old man in Beijing, whom I didn't understand but, had a warm smile. We went south to Tibet, Nepal, and Bhutan where we hiked a lot, and climbed many mountains and visited many monasteries. We took a train through India and spent the next 6 months traveling around southern Russia from ski resort to ski resort. Turkey was an interesting place, and so was the Middle East, even though we didn't see much of it due to political tension.

There was too much to see and take in. As we traveled, the world became less friendly, especially the Middle East and Africa. We avoided a great deal travel in those areas because there were underlying currents of conflict building and we wanted nothing to do with politics. Indigo had long told us that the world would eventually run out of things to take and sometimes we got the feeling it was happening faster than she predicted. Sometimes it got us down, so we kept moving to new places where things were better.

Despite the issues of the world, we went and saw

Jerusalem and Cairo along with the pyramids which were also on our list. We also traveled around Africa. That is to say along the coast.

It took us almost eight months to make the trip. When we arrived at the Rock of Gibraltar we were ready to see Europe and get back to some of the amenities we had missed. Highest on my list were clean showers, beds without bugs and toilets I could sit on.

We took the trip to Spain across the strait on an old ferryboat and started our discovery of yet another continent.

We were seven years away from where we had started in Elk. I am still amazed at this, seven years is a long time. We were wiser; we were experienced, and we were still in love. We wound our way through Europe and through all of its historical extensions and conquests.

We had filled up so many memory cards with pictures that our little binder was full. We tried to upload the pictures when we could but there were so many. We always said when we were ready to settle somewhere we would put together a journal of our trips and write our memoirs. Something we could pass on to our children.

Children seemed more and more likely as we aged. Belle thought about having children more by the day. I did not know it then, but we would never get the opportunity, Belle and I could not have children.

We grew tired and decided to stop again as we had in Elk. We found little part of town in the south of

Paris and rented a place. Belle was more fluent than I was in French and she loved to speak it, so I let her do the talking. Our place was as it had been before.

I must admit, it was good to slow down a bit and enjoy one place for a while, it had been so long since we had stopped to enjoy where we were. Indigo had once told us we should do this from time to time and what better place than Paris?

I never had an interest in Paris, until I was there. It had always been an interest of Belle's and I grew to like it even though some of the people were less than friendly. The rest were just the opposite. They were warm, charming, gracious, wonderful and I will always miss their cooking. We were welcomed by most of them and made many friends in little time. Belle continued to write and I continued to work for Origin.

Once again we had the music we liked, and a stationary bed with furniture and our pictures. We strove to recreate the same environment we had at the Allotment. The one we had been used to, a place where family and friends could come together to eat and drink.

We had friends, but it is hard for a person to have a home without a family. We both knew this and we both knew a family was missing from our lives. So a family became our mission but no matter how we tried she could not get pregnant.

It was determined after several doctor visits, for some reason they could not identify, she was not fertile.

The doctors also discovered I could not have

children either. I started talking to all of my friends from the Allotment I learned most of them already had children of their own. This was disappointing but I figured as long as we had each other we could adopt or maybe surrogate and all would be well.

It impacted her more than me, so for a while I comforted her and made sure to tread lightly and respectfully about the subject. I could tell it hurt her more than she cared to say. I held her when I could and I promised her that someday we would find a way and we would have a wonderful family.

I contacted more and more of my old friends from the Allotment and started to rebuild those connections. I was looking to rekindle our family, bring something into our lives. I think we both needed it.

It did not take long to discover Indigo's children had done what she had asked and were spread to the furthest reaches of globe. We had made friends and acquaintances on every continent. Clark, my closest friend from the Allotment was nearby, in Greece on the island of Santorini. We had a good time exchanging pictures of our trips around the world and stories about the things we had done.

We agreed we would come see him in the summer and spend a couple weeks scuba diving in the Aegean sea. Belle thought it would be nice to see some familiar faces and was really looking forward to seeing Susan again. She had not seen Susan since the Allotment when she had paired with Clark. Not since they had walked away down the long paved driveway and into the world.

8. Santorini.

Clark was a different person than he had been, and Susan was as well. They seemed to have led the same lifestyle we had, which was mostly nomadic. They made very few stops, a fairly stress free lifestyle, and convenient employment. There were quite a few parallels between the four of us. He liked remote places much as I and Belle did. He liked the Ocean and the mountains, and for the most part shied away from large cities.

When we stepped off the boat, I could instantly see why Clark liked it. It was a small island, and Clark and Susan's place was perched on the very top of the rocky cliffs above the Aegean Sea. Thera was a little town. One of the striking things I saw from the beach head, were all the blue dome roofs along the rocky crest above. It was quite a hike to the top and most of the people were taking their time along the snaking pathway to the summit of the island.

Susan and Belle had been close friends at the Allotment and I think she was looking forward to seeing Susan as much as I was looking forward to seeing Clark.

The town was a fantastic example of a slow moving authentic Greek life. We got lost immediately and had to call to find his place. He led us through the narrow alleys and along the paths upward to the top of the island. We could smell the salt water blending with the Greek food being carried between plaster and mortar domiciles. The murmur of voices and laughter followed the streets and walk-ways. Children played between buildings and stray dogs lounged in the sun. Clark guided us in and out of small squares and markets until we arrived at his place.

It was a small bungalow built high above the Aegean Sea. They had a n incredible view of the azure waters dotted with small inlets, islands, reefs and tiny archipelagos. From the top I could see at least five miles out into the waters. There were fishermen there, in distant boats casting nets as they had done for thousands of years.

We knocked on the little bungalow door and I heard a rustling sound from behind it. There was a shout and some pots banging then we could hear the sound of the door knob being turned.

Clark opened his door and without saying hello grasped my hand pulled me in and hugged me. He said salutations in Greek and welcomed us both into his humble home with a smile on his face.

He had become a very tall man with a bushy brown beard and long wild hair which was pulled back into a scruffy bun on the back of his head. His skin was tan and his arms were muscular yet still stringy. He wore casual clothes which fit him loosely. I could tell he did not wear shoes much by the walking calluses on his feet.

His eyes had deepened; there was a travel-worn

shine to them and a spark painted in his face. He was alive, living well, and spending his time and money with Susan. He looked at me without saying anything for a minute and just smiled. Then he looked at Belle and shouted over his shoulder. "Susan! Come here and meet and greet!" He shouted.

Susan came in from the kitchen and gave us the same warm welcome. She grabbed Belle and hugged her hard resounding "Where have you been?!" from her lips.

She grabbed Belles face and placed a kiss on both cheeks. I do not think Belle expected this and was taken aback, but happy to see her nonetheless. She instantly did the same regardless of how surprised she was.

There was a pitter-patter and two children came running into the room chasing each other. Clark seized the two of them and picked them up. He made it a point to introduce me to his boy Acastus, and his girl, Oenone. They were both Greek born and he felt it fitting to give them Greek names so they would always know where they came from. They were very beautiful and playful. Within minutes they were climbing on me, singing songs, and pulling on my ears and nose.

Clark took me out on his veranda and offered me a beer. Susan and Belle caught up as we sat on the lawn furniture and talked about our adventures. We talked through the evening and when the kids had turned in, Belle and Susan joined us with some Gyros and wine.

Since I left the Allotment with Belle things had

been going in an upward spiral. There, on that balcony in the warm evening air with the people I cared about, I knew I had achieved what I had desired. What I valued, I found on Clark's back veranda in the evening air with friends around me, a beer in my hand, good food and a warm breeze.

We talked about Indigo, speculating where she had come from, what she was, and what she was trying to achieve. It was a subject I had not really thought about once I had gotten out into the world. We discussed many things that night. Our discussion went on for hours as we drank wine and beer. Clark showed me pictures. We exchanged a few stories and talked about old times and the other kids. We were talking about the day we left when Clark brought up something I was not aware of.

"Speaking of that, have you met any other students while you were traveling?" I didn't really know what he was talking about. I looked a little bewildered.

"Other students?" I asked.

"Others, you know people like us but not from our Allotment," He replied.

"No, what do you mean?" I asked.

"There are other Allotments, and other people just like us. Other kids who were given gifts," He explained. I was still confused. He turned to Susan. "Hey Susan, remember that guy we met in Brazil? What was his name? Lynn, or Linus, er something?" He asked her.

"Oh, that was Linus," She said breaking herself from her conversation with Belle.

"Yeah, Linus, that was it. He could use electricity. He could light-up just about anything. We traveled with him for a little while. He was a crazy son of a bitch. One time he stuck a toaster chord in his mouth and made us breakfast. Unfortunately he shorted out half of Rio, yeah, that one almost caused some problems. Traffic lights didn't work for hours. He told us he met dozens of travelers from dozens of Allotments. He even said he had been to Allotment thirteen," Clark said.

"Allotment thirteen?" I asked.

"According to him there was more than one Allotment, and more than one Indigo. He told us he had come from Allotment three, and had been to Allotment 13. He said he discovered there were hundreds of people, 'travelers', as he called them, roaming around the world," He paused and sipped on his beer. "The way I see it… you remember the trunk you and Clyde found in the basement, you remember that?" He asked.

"Yes," I said. "It had a model number on it," I replied.

"She told us she was model 16, and the version number, whatever it was I think it was the software version. Just like computer parts... Clyde told me about the notebook and what was down in the basement. It is shame Mr. Vincent got a hold of it. Boy Indigo was mad about that," He said. "Did she ever get it back?" He asked.

I nodded my head.

"I think it was the reason the he was killed," I said. "I don't know. She told me someday I would know what was in the notebook. I haven't really thought about it since we left," I said.

I didn't bring him up, I figured it was best left buried. Clark changed the subject.

"You want to know something else? Did you email the rest of the family? On the letter Indigo left us?" He asked.

"Most of them…" I answered.

"Right, I emailed all of them, and got responses back from everyone, except one person who wasn't on the list… You remember that creepy kid who was always drawing things?"

"Yeah, Eric. Why?"

"His email was not on the list of emails," Clark said.

"I haven't thought of him in years. He always made me feel uncomfortable," I said.

"I think he was a robot too. He sure acted like one. Maybe he was like a service robot or something," He said and paused looking out over the sea. "I think we were the test subjects. I don't know what for. After traveling around the world and seeing all the sickness and violence… Seeing what a terrible place the world can be, I am glad I am different. I never get sick, I never really get depressed, I never get exhausted. The last nine years of my life have just been getting better. I kind of feel like I am living the calm before the storm, you know. And really, that's the only thing I am scared of. If this is how good it can be, how bad is going to get? You know?" He said taking a swig of his beer and looking off into the setting sun.

So, Clark had a good point and I found myself asking the same question.

I kept going back to what Indigo had said in the car ride home the day Mr. Vincent had been shot. She said that sometimes the illusion was more constructive than the truth. Maybe we had been denied the truth because the truth was terrible. And maybe the ends justified the means.

Clark believed we were like weeds in the garden. Eventually the weeds would take over, and no one would notice it. It would be a gradual quiet change, and soon enough we would own the garden. It turned out that the change was not gradual, it was a speeding missile and Indigo's children were pilots.

I thought about the world we had traveled in and realized how much things had changed in the last few years. When we left Elk we had felt carefree, by the time we arrived in Turkey we had changed our trip to avoid most of the Middle East and Africa because they were no longer safe places to travel, and China was also closing its borders. There was no doubt political tension was building.

I knew mathematically, that resources would

grow more scarce. My better judgment and skill with numbers would disagree with me if I tried to deny it. There would come a day when people would have to do without or take from those who had. I didn't know how close that day was. I think Clark was well aware of it too but it was hard to talk about such things while we sat on top of a beautiful cliff in a summer breeze, enjoying good company, drinking beer, and eating gyros.

We stayed there for almost a month. I had a good time and Belle did too. It got me thinking that maybe we had been missing out and should catch up with the other students from our Allotment. So, I planned to contact them when we returned to Paris and start rebuilding those connections, because Clark was right, we were family and even Eric was a sibling.

We finished our stay and we said goodbye. We headed back to Paris. We planned to come back the following year. Our hope was to be in Paris during the winter and go to Santorini in the summer. We would keep up with each other and maintain our relationships. That was the plan, but we never returned to Santorini and I did not see Clark again for a number of years. My tenth year away from the Allotment was the last good year I had. Even though the years after Belle's death were the hardest of my life, the ten years I had with her were worth it. I would do it again.

9. Belle's death.

Back in Paris we fell into our routines. Our finances were in order, our careers were wonderful, our location was prime, our friendship was ripe, and our love life was better than ever.

We planned to adopt. I think this plan was accelerated when Belle saw Clark and Susan's children, so we started the process. She obtained paperwork and we started filling out the forms and figuring out how to get it done. It was a complicated progression of steps given our legal residency was not finalized.

We were also not sure if we wanted to raise a child abroad but we were committed and we were excited about the prospect. We finished the first round of paperwork and went to the consulate and turned it in. In many ways I think this was a catalyst.

It was a cold autumn day, the trees were turning and the air was starting to become crisp. The wind was starting to pick up and people were beginning to wear thick coats instead of sweaters.

Belle was back at our place working on editing her latest manuscript for publication. I was in the market selecting the produce. I was picking it up and sniffing the apples and squeezing the fruits when I smelled an unusual smell. It was like a burning motor in my nostrils, the smell of ozone and circuits. I thought it was a passing car or something in the vents of the supermarket. I went about my business and got the shopping list items and went to the register.

A wave of nausea hit me as I stepped outside the store into the fall air. My lunch came up and I doubled over. The smell of ozone was suddenly stronger. An indescribable feeling crept over me. It was panic, but not a normal panic. It was primal and I felt it in my head, not my gut. I knew I had to get home as fast as I could.

At first it was just a concerning feeling and not an urgent one. I walked down the street as fast as I could only stopping for lights. My eyes had trouble focusing and my thoughts were scattered and disjointed. The cars passing gave me motion sickness and the honking was louder than normal.

Two blocks away from the store my head started to pound and fear wormed its way into my thoughts. It was an unnatural and irrational fear. I could not figure out where it was coming from. Belle seemed to be the focal point of my worry and I started to jog a little jostling the bag of groceries back and forth.

I could see my heart beat vibrating in my vision and the stink of burning plastic raged in my nose.

I dropped the bag and began to sprint along the sidewalk dodging people and pushing them out of the way. The closer I got the more urgent and frantic the feeling became. As I rounded the corner onto our street I heard the ticking in my head and felt the buzzing in my joints. I ran through it and the hum of discord in my limbs.

I could hear the muttering of the old man. But he was not whispering, he had become an angry drone in

195

my ears and his nonsense captured more urgency than he ever had while he was traveling with us.

Every window in our little flat was iced over and there was someone at the front bay window. I jammed my hand in my pockets and grasped the keys yanking them out as I screamed for Belle from the front steps.

There was no response and I could not get the keys into the lock fast enough with my trembling hands. The ticking and banging was getting louder and louder as I turned the key. I pushed the door open and stumbled in.

Inside the house was a bubble of silence. It was so absolute that I could not hear myself breathing. I could not hear my heart pounding in my ears anymore and I could not hear the muttering, shouting or the mad ticking.

Everything stopped in the foyer in an unnatural cold. It was dark, not a single light was on in the house, and the murky corners of the room seemed to choke me with their emptiness.

The temperature stung at my fingers and drew the blood to them. Ice-crystals had collected on the ceiling fan and the mirror. The TV screen and all the windows were frosted over and the tile floor was a sheet of ice. I looked at the condensation and realized it was an unnatural ice. It was late fall, but it was not cold enough to freeze.

I was yelling for her but the sound was sucked out of my lungs and instantly absorbed into hollow swells from my chest. When I had left for the market Belle was upstairs. I jumped at the stairs and fell across the ice. I lifted myself and started to claw my way up the empty staircase still hearing nothing from Belle.

As I reached the top I started to hear my own breath again. I could hear the sound of my heart in my ears and I could hear the muttering which had turned from anger to anguish. I lifted myself up and ran at the door to her study. I broke through it to find her chair overturned and her laying on the floor in the cold.

I ran to her side and knelt down over her, touching her cheeks with the back of my hand. They were frigid. I started shouting and doing chest compressions and mouth to mouth. The seconds were ticking and I worked furiously back forth between her ribcage and her mouth. Still there was nothing. With every second passing my pounding and screaming slowed, winding down.

And then I was kneeling next to her sobbing in an uncontrollable burst with my hands on her face telling her it would be okay. I cradled her head in my lap and rocked back and forth stroking her hair telling myself it was all a dream.

10. Fury. [16]

In my haste I had not checked to see if there was

---

[16] "Fury oh fury" by Nico Vega ♫

anyone else in the apartment. As I sat on the floor next to Belle's body. I became aware of another person standing between me and the window. I caught his shadow out of the corner of my eye and lifted my head, expecting to finally see the man who had been with me my whole life. I did not see him however. Instead my eyes were met with Eric. And the only reason he was still there was I was blocking the door so he couldn't leave.

Not much had changed with him; he still looked like the boy from the Allotment. His jet black hair and deep, unnatural looking amber eyes still contrasted his pale skin. His frame was almost the same size. He was wearing a backpack and a baseball cap. He had been watching me as I tried to revive Belle over and over again.

I was shocked, and then I was angry. I stood up from my kneeling position and leaped at him grasping his shirt. He turned to run, but I held on to it and pulled him in close and looked into his eyes.

"What are you?!" I screeched. He looked fearlessly back into my eyes, and took his hands and grasped my wrists.

"You need to let go of me," He said calmly as he applied pressure to my wrists. His hands were icy and his grip was like a vice slowly clamping the circulation off from my hands. My hand buckled and he carefully took them from his shirt and lowered me to below his center of gravity. There was a look of utter disregard in his face, as though I was an insect and did not matter. It was a quiet apathy and indifference for me.

He adjusted his grip on my wrists and stood over me.

"What have you done?!" I stuttered.

"I have set in motion the rest of your life. You are free of her. She was a distraction from what Indigo raised you for," He said as he tightened his grip. "It was time for this to happen... This is supposed to happen, and if you are worried about her suffering, I can tell you she didn't," He said calmly.

I lost control and broke his grip from my wrists then started punching him. I was screaming uncontrollably and striking whatever I could. Eric had put his hands up to shield his face and neck. I kept striking and it didn't seem to faze him. He just stood there taking the beating, quietly. I got more and more furious as I struck him. Eventually I grasped him and threw him over the coffee table and into the wall. He hit the wall and made a crater in the plaster and drywall. He slouched to the floor and then rolled sideways and stood up in the corner.

I came after him and grasped him by the back pack straps and pushed him through the sliding glass door. "Why?! Why did you do this?!" I kept asking as we tumbled onto the small second story balcony.

"You need it! As long as she was around, you will never do what you are supposed to!" He said.

I was swearing, I was angry, I was violent. For

the first time in my life I let it out and made Eric the recipient of all my anger. Anger which had been brewing since my mother and father had gone over the guardrail and drowned. I struck him again and again. I kicked him against the railing and in the face. We slammed back and forth on the balcony. He tried to avoid me but I kept my body blocking the sliding door so he could not escape.

Eventually I got a hold of him and lifted him up over the railing by his neck. He grasped my arms and started to squeeze again. It hurt, he squeezed so hard his fingers were burrowing into my arms. I pulled him in close and thrust my forehead into his face. He tumbled backward over the railing. His body flipped, he flailed his arms wildly with nothing to grasp and then fell the two stories into the traffic below. I grabbed the railing and pulled myself to it to look down to the road.

He had landed on his head and it was twisted into his shoulder. One of his legs seemed to be bent backwards and was kicking from underneath him.

There was a screeching sound as the traffic tried to avoid him, however, they couldn't and his body was ran over by one of the oncoming cars. I could see his frame tossed out the back twisted and broken. It landed on the side of the road splayed on the sidewalk convulsing. The car screeched to a stop and people started to get out and rush to his side.

I turned and ran back through the flat and down the stairs slipping on the ice as I went. I cleared the front fence and rushed around the corner.

People gathered around Eric's body murmuring and a couple of bystanders were phoning paramedics and police officers. I tried to get through the group and see for myself. As I did people started to gasp and draw back.

Eric's body was trembling and his limbs were cracking and popping as they pulled in and out and reordered themselves.

His torso rotated and his arms bent backwards and placed themselves on the pavement. I could hear snapping sounds coming from his body. He started to fold and unfold. He climbed his own skin as the bones snapped back together. In a matter of seconds, Eric was standing again and running away from me down the street. I sprinted after him through the gathering people.

I could see him as he pushed people over and ran through crowds. His speed surprised me. We crossed streets and small bridges. We ran through alley ways and cut through parks. He seemed single minded in his movements, they were sharp and precise. He dodged between cars and tumbled between truck wheels and vaulted fences with no trouble. He did not look back.

He was difficult to keep up with but I knew the terrain. I took short cuts to intercept him but he was too spry.

It was on the bullet train overpass he finally stopped. I slowly edged up onto the overpass with him. He stood watching me calmly as I approached looking westward over the tracks and the city. He waited patiently for me to get there. He was not exhausted or tired, he was just calm. I stopped a few feet in front of him.

"Why are you doing this?! Why did you kill her?!" I shouted.

He looked at me, and then rubbed the bridge of his nose. His glare cut through me with emptiness. He lowered his hands, removed his baseball cap and spoke.

"If you only knew who I am to you… this wouldn't be so hard," He paused. "I didn't enjoy it, if that helps, I am not the cold being you think I am. But I have to do my part, and make sure this is all carried out the way it was designed," He stopped and tilted his head. "You hear that?" He said.

"What?!" I said blinking through my rage.

"That is the three o'clock and I do not want to be late. I have places to be, and like you, I have things to set in motion,"

Then I heard it. The Bullet train approaching the overpass with a low rumbling hiss. Eric turned and grabbed the railing, looking back he grimaced. "You will see me again, not for a while, but you will and when you do… Maybe then you won't hate me," He said.

For the first time there was something in his voice an emotion and if I had to say what it was I would say it was sorrow.

There was a whooshing sound and a wave of air hit the overpass as the train went under the walkway.

"Do me a favor, keep an eye on the News!" He yelled as he stretched himself back like a rubber band then launched himself over the rails and plummeted onto the train below.

I could hear the sound of his body colliding with the metal. I could see him bounce along the top of the cars twisting and turning, his limbs and head inside their little sacks but he was boneless as he rolled from car to car. He disappeared in between two of the cars. I was sure he could not have survived the fall and the collision let alone being ran over by the last half of the train. I was screaming from the overpass, and damning him.

Both he and Indigo had told me I was better off not knowing what was going on. I stood searching for his mangled frame on the tracks and between the cars of the train as it passed. I continued yelling and swearing at him from the overpass. My eyes made me dizzy as the cars blurred under me. When the train had passed I could not see any remains and doubted his survival but there was no telling if the collision had destroyed him.

I could hear the sirens approaching and see the flashing of lights once again entering my life. Police cars pulled up on both sides of the overpass blocking the ends so I could not leave the bridge.

I heard a voice from a megaphone instruct me to lie on the ground and place my hands behind my head. I did not understand the man's French but it was obvious what he wanted me to do. He repeated in English and I did what he told me to do. I slowly raised my arms and got to my knees. A chopper roared over the bridge and the wind hit me from it. It leveled out and hovered just over the side.

A man in the chopper pointed a rifle at me. I slowly connected my hands behind my head and waited as the Police approached from both sides. The treading of boots shook the bridge as they came. Soon I could feel the cold metal of handcuffs wrapping around my wrists. I was pulled to my feet and frisked for weapons then I was walked to the Police car and carefully put in the back.

I did not fight. I did not say anything. I was in shock. There were tears in my eyes and anger in my heart.

11. What came next.

What came next was the process of legalities. In France there are different rules for navigating the system and I knew none of them. I was placed in a cell, read more rights, given a medical and psych exam, and told I would be provided with a representative from the US embassy.

I was in the cell alone without representation for a long time. I was handcuffed to a metal chair at a table with a cup of water. Unfortunately I could not reach it.

Eventually I was moved to a holding cell with a bed. They took the cuffs off me. A man who spoke poor English told me it would be a while before my representative would arrive and I needed to get some sleep.

So I placed my head down on the pillow but I did not sleep. It has been hard to sleep ever since. I stayed awake in the dark of my cell missing her and thinking about what had happened.

An investigation was perused upon the discovery of Belle's body and the circumstances in which she died. The French believed I killed her and they were still looking to establish a cause of death.

I was still without any answers. Eric had alluded she was stopping me from fulfilling my purpose but as far as I was concerned, she was my purpose. As she was dead, it seemed I had no purpose. There are few things in this world as sad and depressing as complete isolation and loneliness but that is where I found myself. I had nothing to say to the people who came to my cell over the next few days.

I did not talk for a long while. I did not eat anything. I did not sleep. I stayed on the small cot in the cell. People would come in and ask questions or see if I was ready to talk.

Every day I was shackled and taken into a small room where I was accosted by two officers. The battery of questions was given to me in French and then in English by the same man who had told me to get some sleep. I didn't answer any of the questions and I did not look at any of the people who came into that small room. I kept my head lowered to the table and remained completely still. Sometimes they were angry and sometimes they were quiet. My mind was elsewhere. I was with Belle. I had been attached to her and to live a life without her seemed impossible. As time wore on I spiraled deeper into my own misery and hatred.

A few weeks passed in this pattern and nothing changed until one day I was informed I had been exonerated by testimony and the traffic footage. It showed Eric entering the flat a half hour before I got home. I am not clear on all of the details; I do know that I never saw a courtroom and my representatives did not have to defend me. I was released. If I didn't know better I would say someone greased the wheels with a hefty sum of cash.

There was nothing for me to look for in the future, nothing for me to run too and no one I wanted to burden. I did not even contact Clark about what had happened.

I found myself standing outside the police station looking up at the sky. It was then I made the decision to finish what Belle and I had started. We still had not seen South America and it had been the last place we planned to go, the bottom of the world-Ushuaia. I had promised her that we would see it.

Paris had no good memories left for me and I wanted to leave as soon as possible. I took a cab back home and once again I made the trek into that empty and lonely house.

There I did nothing. I laid my head down on the pillow where I could smell our sleep still in the feathers, the vestiges of Belle slowly leaving my space. I laid there and I tried to rest.

It was the phone that woke me. The coroner released Belles remains and arrangements had to be made. I will not elaborate on this part there is nothing important in it. It is pure tragedy. It is a warning to you. More importantly, a reminder of how I used the short time I had with her. Although I didn't think it then because I had lost her, I spent the time well.

Needless to say, I made sure her farewell was private, short, and quiet. Belle always wanted to be cremated, I had this done for her but I also bought a plot of land in a small cemetery where I planted most of her ashes under a small but beautiful marker. I took a small amount of what was left and put them in a vile around my neck. Then I bought a plot for me right next to hers. It was the only place in the world I wanted to be but I had promised we would see the world together and we were not there yet.

I bid a soft and quiet farewell to her at her little marker in that ancient cemetery. My ghost was there with me that day and he witnessed my pain. We shared it and I think he missed Belle too. I know he was just as hurt and angry as I was. His mumbling and stuttering did not affect me as they usually did. We grieved together and then he was gone just as he had come.

Although my goodbye was saturated with liquor and lots of tears, it was sincere. I promised that I would try not to be bitter and I would try to be good to people

207

because she would have wanted it that way. I tucked the vial into my shirt and left the grave yard and went back to the flat where I packed my things into our traveling bag. I took our little photo album, the picture of my mother and father, the camera and left the rest.

12. Leaving Paris. [17]

I booked a flight to Panama and hailed a cab to the airport. I stood in the terminal waiting for the plane to taxi in and fuel so I could leave the city which had brought me so much joy, and then taken it all away from me. I did not hate Paris but I did not love it either. It was a city of passion, lights, and wonder and that was the problem.

I decided to look for something better because suicide was the only other thing on my mind at the time. I looked out from the terminal across the city one last time and boarded the plane to Panama. The last thing I can remember seeing as the plane lifted was the towering height of the *Eiffel Tower* and watching the *Arc de Triomphe* disappearing in the small window while the flight attendant was speaking on the overhead intercom.

I did not return to Paris until after you, that is the person this was meant for, was born then orphaned as I was.

---

[17] "All that I am" by Rob Thomas ♫

As part of my grieving process I started writing. In many ways it has been my salvation and although I am no Faulkner or Hemingway, it helps me to deal with loss and stave off depression.

I first started writing on my trip from Panama to Argentina. When I landed I purchased a little notebook and decided every day I would write Belle to tell her what had happened and what I had seen.

I decided not to take any vehicles and make the 4500 mile trip completely by foot. I did not know what I would do when I reached the southernmost tip of the world. But I figured the trip would keep me from killing myself in the meantime and allow me to grieve. I would take pictures along the way and pretend she was there, the illusion was so much better than the truth.

With the little Spanish I knew I left the Airport and stepped into the Panama humidity, then started the grueling trip south-bound. I did not know how long it would actually take me, and I did not care. I knew the world was becoming a more and more dangerous and that there would be many threats along the way. I knew I might be killed by warlords or imprisoned by corrupt police but it did not matter, I had a promise to keep.

It took me almost two years to get to the tip of Tierra del Fuego. I passed through swamps and jungles where I was nearly eaten alive by parasites, sometimes I only made it a few miles a day. I passed through territories controlled by drug lords and mercenaries where I was threatened with death. I narrowly avoided prison in Columbia and was almost shot two times.

The further I went the worse I looked, the more aged my face was and the more scraggly my beard became.

I tread on mountain roads which were really just trails carved into the dirt on a mountainside. Places were one wrong step would result in a thousand foot drop. I saw Incan temples and breathed air in the Andes with the Alpacas and the Llamas and I didn't even appreciate them.

Sometimes strangers would feed me and I would give them some money in exchange. There were deserts I almost died in, and there quiet villages I could have given up in. I must admit, and I am ashamed to say, I drank more than I should have and confessed a great deal of hate in my words during that trip.

In the salt flats of Chile, the *Solar De Uyuni* where the sky and the earth reflect each other, I became lost without water and I thought I would parish. Near death and hallucinating I saw a mirage and followed it through the blinding silver and blue to safety.

My eyes became sunken and my face turned to tanned leather. My skin became weathered and stretched tight on my hands and face. My hair became peppered with gray and my frame grew lanky and thin on a sparse diet. But I hardened and I put one foot in front of the other in a melancholy march.

Every night before the sun would plunge under the horizon I would sit somewhere sheltered and write a letter to Belle telling her all the good things which happened to me each day. The things I had to be thankful for and the experiences I had since she passed.

This cycle went on day after day and I started getting rid of clothes in my pack to make room for more notebooks. I tore the spines off of them to make them lighter and I bought smaller ones and wrote in little font, more legibly so I could read them again and again. I would read over them as I walked to revisit the conversations I had with her. As I got closer they became the most important things I owned.

Sometimes I would write in the responses I thought she would have made and make jokes in the margins. They became her notebooks too, and a way I could visit her at any time. About half way through the trip I became aware that sometimes I didn't remember writing things in the margins. When I would read them it was as if they were something she had written back to me. And *she* would advise me to not be so bitter and angry. She would remind me of the vow I made and tell me to do nice things for people and help them when I could. She wanted me to make the world a better place even when I did not feel like it, or could not see the good in the world.

The truth of the matter was that I did not write things in the margins. Something inside of me wrote them, something that had lived with us, and had traveled the world with us. Those little machines had been with me, they too loved Belle. It was their words that appeared in my notebooks. I think they wrote because they felt the loss too. The machines had become her proxy to keep me alive.

They found a way to help me heal and so I let the words come out without thinking about them. I scribbled, I wrote, I drew and communicated my grief through those pages. I can tell you the trip and those little notebooks are really the only reason you are reading this. Those machines used them to save me from myself and although I would never find the happiness I had with Belle again, I would find some modicum of solace. During that time, I found a cathartic release from writing.

I kept plodding southward through the rain and snow. I marched through the heavy winds and harsh terrain of Patagonia. There in the open space with the masked Gauchos and their spurs and ponchos I began to accept her death.

During that time the camera I and Belle started our trip with quit working and I snapped the last pictures for our album as I walked into Ushuaia. I set the timer and felt the buzz and ticking as my ghost presented with a vibrating in my extremities.

I smiled at the lens for the last time and watched the shutter click as the camera captured the last image. My ghost only showed up once after that when I returned to the Allotment.

13. Ushuaia.

I had not talked to Clark or any of the other students for a couple of years. My daily speech had consisted of greetings, requests and goodbyes. My voice had not been used regularly for a long time. When the people I had met along the way tried to engage me in conversation, I made sure to be non-communicative and generally responded with single word answers.

Not only had my voice became rusty from lack of use, when I looked at that last photo I did not recognize myself. My beard was overgrown and my hair was tangled around my shoulders in long dirty brown tubes of weather-toughened cords. My clothes had been ripped many times and I had patched them back together in layers. These layers hugged me like a second skin protecting me from the elements. I had thorn and briar scratches along the backs of my arms. My palms were callused from the rocks I had fallen on. I smelled of the wild wind and the salt of sweat which was caught in my clothes. My boots held on by frayed threads and conviction. In my eyes was a distant blue vibration of the life I had once cherished when I lived in the city of light and celebration. I had given up the tongue of romance and culture and traded it for the empty space and openness. My roof had been stars and moon, my floor grass and pasture-land. My lungs had unadulterated air in them. Both my backpack and my head were much emptier than they used to be. Along the way I had found

213

an old gaucho hat and placed it on my crown to shade my eyes from the Patagonian sun. I became the king of nowhere and heir to only the following moment.

I was not angry anymore. My desire to wage wars against myself was placated and my rage had become as domesticated as the cattle I had traveled with. Ushuaia was in sight, my destination, a quiet place to rest.

I stared blankly at the sign near the edge of town. It was hard to understand what it meant. It was bewildering. I had spent so long wandering and making sure my feet kept moving that I never stopped to think about what I would do when I finished the journey. Once again I was reminded that the journey was more important than the destination.

Ushuaia was a beautiful place. Just like Elk it was where the ocean laid siege to the land and mountains clashed with the endless waters. A place of rugged people and worn faces cast in bronzed skin. Where the ice dug its fingers into the southern ocean and broke off in little bits, scattered across its waves and its peaks. I still remember the salty wind which would blow up through the channels of the mountain in cool waves. It always seemed to soothe my wounds, my sore feet and my bruised bones. I came to rest there for a while, in Ushuaia

I got a small place and settled in, in reality it was because I did not know what to do with myself. When I stepped out of the airport in Panama I had emailed

Origin and resigned my position as a consultant for the company. I gave up calling and emailing anyone I knew. I and Belle had been really thrifty and I lived off almost nothing while in south America. In fact the bulk was spent on food, notebooks, and beverages. There was still enough to last many years and I did not plan on spending it quickly. I was exhausted and just wanted a place to lay my head. I wanted a soft place, not one covered in small rocks and thorns. I wanted a place to sleep, for a few months until I figured out what to do next.

Ushuaia was not big, nor was it small. There was plenty to do, plenty of people to meet, and it was a very colorful place. The people were nice and welcoming. It was quiet and peaceful even though there were a lot of tourists who came and went. Most of them came just to say they had been to the southernmost town in South America. But to me it became more than just a destination, it became a refuge. The fingers of politicians rarely reached that far or even cared to.

World events were starting to become more and more complicated. There was more conflict and fewer resources by the day. Most people went about their lives oblivious to this. Most people who lived in Ushuaia were good, honest people who just wanted to have lives and families. They wanted raise their children and grandchildren in peace. They were a simple people who were not concerned with politics.

It was there I discovered that joy is not a

conditional response, sometimes it can be, but for the most part it must be practiced. Happiness requires participation to attain and we are all responsible for our own happiness. I learned how to participate on a rudimentary level. I found the better I got at it the more calm I became.

So I spent my days fishing, writing and getting to know strangers at the local pub. Sometimes I would try my hand at karaoke even though I was not very good at it. I developed many acquaintances and even a few friends. I got to know the local places where people would gather. Sometimes I felt I was using them for therapy, feeding on their joy, but I kept my sorrow from them so I figured it was alright to do so.

I planned to make that my life. I was at a place of acceptance and resolve, not apathy or ignorance, but living in a moment. It was at a place of emptiness, it was perfect. I was reduced to simplicity. I set aside even my ability to make a living with my aptitude, I set aside any desires and I gave up the panic of filling my days with plans. I just lived. It was freeing and self-actualizing.

My life became something new and I embraced it without hesitation though I did not forget about Belle- I still have dreams of her when it is quiet and I am alone. I stayed there for about two years and got to know myself all over again. It was hard but day by day it became easier.

My life as a young man had been good. Ten magnificent years I will never forget. I'd do it again and again just for those ten years, all of my misery and pain for just ten years of bliss, wholeness, and completion.

This was the summary of my adulthood. In it I found love, I found experience, and I saw the whole world and got to know it intimately. I lost a lover and found myself.

There were still things I could not explain and large pieces of my life which lived as holes in my history, but in truth those things did not matter. I became a man and I learned the most important things in life are never what we think they are. My only sadness in this matter is that Belle was not there for the last photo I took.

ACT IV: The Old Man I am.

1. Growing old. [18]

My aging process was unique. It was full of family and friends and I was surrounded by the people I was raised with, the people I started life with. It was a time for quiet reflection and discovery. I had many revelations and uncovered meaning in all the events in my life. I found some of the answers I had been searching for, but not all of them. Most of all I was given another chance to put my life back together and I was reunited with purpose.

During the time I wandered, both with and without Belle, the world became a more troubled place. I didn't like news so I didn't investigate. I didn't read the paper and didn't engage in political discussion with the few people I did know. While I was lost in Chile and Argentina there had been entire weeks I hadn't seen a soul so I had no news of what was happening. Nor would I have cared about the world had I known.

The world was overpopulated and mankind had found more grandiose ways to hide their heads in the sand. Deep down, I knew it was only time separating man from his inevitable collapse. Our world did not, and still does not have the resources to support the eight billion people taking from it.

There had been small conflicts here and there, but if I had been paying attention I would have

---

[18] "The One Moment" by OK Go ♫

recognized larger ones were brewing.

Instead I was safe in my ignorant moment, far away from the troubles and the conflicts of the world. I chose to remain empty headed in my sleepy corner of the world. I liked my hermit shell and liked the static environment inside. I structured my days as such with remedial activities to stay unaware.

That day, the last day I spent in Ushuaia, I was down on the pier with the seals and a fishing pole. The seals were barking and playing on the rocks and the seagulls were squawking in the morning air. The sky was clear and silent as I stood on the bleached decking. I was casting my line along the dock where the fish took shelter. The sun was warming my black coat and my back mopped up the heat. The combination of hot and cold air was quite a pleasant conflict on my skin.

There were boats moored across the harbor with the sails rolled up. The smell of breakfast was drifting over the water from the restaurants preparing food for the sailors. The greasy smell of fish and chips was in the air and I was relaxed and waiting the next bite. It had been a slow morning and I hadn't caught anything.

I remember casting the line, watching it arc out and *plunk* into the bay. There was a voice which spoke to me.

"Go back, go back now. It is time. Return," It was a quiet command accompanied by a feeling which sank into my gut. I turned and looked to see who had said it. I was still alone with the gulls and the seals. I dismissed it at first. Then I heard it again. The second time it was a little more desperate and a little more undeniable. It was clear and articulate. It was unsettling and chilling.

The third time I heard it I pulled my line out and put my pole away. I decided to get something to eat and think it over. I put the lures in my small tackle box and headed for my favorite dockside pub for some breakfast thinking I was losing my mind.

As I walked I heard it clearly again, it was not in my head it was in my ears. I was a little shaken as I walked into the pub. I sat down on the old wooden bar stool, the same one I had become accustomed to during my morning brunch. I was hungry, so I ordered a cup of coffee and a sandwich and sat staring at the mirror on the other side of the bar.

I flinched when I heard it again. Then I heard something else burning through the noise. It was the television mounted on the wall above the bar. It was not that the TV was louder. It was that all the other noise in the bar became quieter and soon it was the only thing I could hear. I tried to ignore it, but it became all I could focus on. I reluctantly and slowly turned my head and looked up knowing that I did not want to see what was on the screen.

Playing on the television was a newscast. I recognized the clip immediately. I was taken back to the Allotment and the black and white film which made up the bulk of my adolescent lectures. The ones Indigo

221

played repeatedly in the lecture room on the old reel to reel. The only difference was the color. I became transfixed. I had to watch it; something kept me from looking away.

I felt as though my mind was being sucked into the flickering box. I was consumed by the lady talking on it. It was programming, I was supposed to be receptive to it. I had seen the film and knew war would come to the world again. It would be a great war. Suddenly I saw in my head how the old film and the newscast ended.

It would start how wars always started, small. It would involve just a few small countries but eventually the rest of the world would join the conflict. Even countries that had no vestment would see opportunity and take advantage of the situation.

The voice in my head told me to go back, to return, and as I watched I felt the overwhelming urge to leave the pub and book the next flight back to the states.

It made sense that the old films were part of a program which operated inside me, something that the little machines used as a beacon. The news reels were designed to keep me aware, to be a marker or a switch in my mind. As I watched, the little machines in my head buzzing. I started hearing a subtle whispering pushing me to leave, to migrate back to the only place I had ever called home. It wanted me to go there because home was safe. There came over me urgency to overwhelming to ignore.

My food came and I stared at it for a moment, then without hesitation I dug into my pocket and paid my bill, and added a generous tip. I got off the stool, grabbed my lunch in a napkin and rushed back to my little bungalow while I ate.

I took my pack. It was the same one I and Belle had when we left the Allotment. I started putting all my things in it. My film cards, my album and my little notebooks. I took my passport and rushed down to let the landlord know I was leaving and to pay him up. I paid him for three months to avoid inconveniencing him. Then I went to the bus depot where I booked the next available ticket home.

I hailed a cab and told the driver to head to the airport. As we drove the message in my head and the panic became more and more urgent. It was screaming not only in my ears, but across my mind. I started seeing it on the street signs we passed. It was a simple message and it said only one thing. It told me to return, to go back.

The radio the Cabby was listening to fuzzed out and started playing the message through the static on repeat. The cabby did not hear it as he drove, instead he hummed to himself and made remarks and comments to me about the weather.

We drove down onto the peninsula where the airport was and I paid him and walked into the terminal with my travel bag.

Unfortunately I had a three hour wait till my

flight took off. Those three hours were a wholly unpleasant experience. I was rocking in the chair on the verge of a mental break by the time the boarding announcement was made.

It was hard to find my way to the boarding gantry through my confusion. I staggered to my seat and placed my bag in the overhead and sighed as I sat down. My eyes were vibrating and my ears were hissing. I rubbed them and blinked rapidly trying to shake the message.

Five minutes later the plane's engines whined to life and the boarding gates were closed. I knew it was going to be a long trip and I was not sure I could last with the ringing voice in my ears. It seemed to get more and more urgent and the pulsing headache which accompanied it seemed to hemorrhage in my mind.

As we were pushed through the clouds it occurred to me, I was headed home. Not to a place, but a state of mind, and that was where the machines wanted me to go, to a state of mind.

2. On fumes only.

The closer I got to the Allotment, the quieter the voices became and the more settled I felt. The more secure I felt. Some part of me was actually looking forward to seeing it again. Unlike the rest of the world, things moved differently at the Allotment. Things were harmonious and quiet not like the chaos I had seen in some of my travels. As I had circled the Globe I had seen small pieces of conflict. But it had really changed since I had been in South America.

While I was grieving it had been changing. Gas was running out, food was growing too expensive, water becoming too polluted and in general, our ignorance and complacency had gotten the better of us. Our leaders propagated the belief that our resources were infinite because it kept dollars in their wallets. Common folk were kept ignorant to the true magnitude of the problem. Those who had seen it and spoken out had been ruined and made into fools.

Compounded with this was the propagation of ignorance through Education, which had been devalued. Not many people wanted to go to school and even less could afford to. Weather by accident or by design, this had been done over generations.

The biggest problem was that people did not think for themselves, or learn for themselves. People simply stopped asking questions and caring about answers. In many ways our technology became more important to us than humanity. While the people had been asleep comfortable in their ignorance, the wealthy and powerful had done great damage to the world by dodging necessary change. People never asked about it, they didn't care.

As resources such as gasoline became more and more expensive, there had been no rush to innovate alternatives and that is what eventually led to war.

We had been given decades to reinvent the way

we consumed but we chose not to. When we could not afford gas, we could not ship things, we could not heat our homes or use machinery to create things, and we could not even build a new infrastructure. Our dependency on gas and fossil fuels eventually turned the lights out and shut all the stores down. When the lights went out, the computers shut off, that was when governments panicked and machines which shouldn't have malfunctioned did just that, including the stock markets. We should have had reserves, as it turned out-we had used them and no one had told the people. In the end, it only took 78 hours for everything to fall apart.

In Ushuaia, if I had been paying attention to the news, I would have known that a little over a thousand miles away a skirmish had broken out in Antarctica over oil and rights to a massive reserve.

While my plane was touching down at Newark international airport the first shot was being fired in Antarctica. Hours later all the governments of the world would be converging on the small strip of land with immeasurable wealth under it. Treaties were violated and armies were summoned. News reports were broadcast and I had seen it all before in the little classroom with the other children at the Allotment.

I was sitting in the airport waiting through layovers seeing the news knowing what clip would come next. They were exactly how I had remembered them. As I was waiting for my luggage I saw the first broadcasts of combat in the South Seas. Indeed there was an impending cloud of caution and despair hanging in the terminal.

There were hushed murmurs in the crowd of people staring up at the television. They watched the footage as missiles slammed into one of the U.S. warships. It erupted into flames on the port side. As the side of the boat was consumed a second missile slammed into the deck and fragmented the front quarter of the ship. People were throwing themselves over the side as the ship started to sink.

The crowd of people went silent as the ship sunk on the screen. All the people in the airport knew war was on the horizon. They did not pull their eyes away from the screens and I took note of how the airport became eerie and quiet. Only the flat speaker of the TVs could be heard through the terminals.

Years later I would realize what it really meant to them. While they watched, I am sure they thought of their children, their sisters, brothers, and families. I did not have these things so I thought about it a different way.

I broke my gaze as my bag came out on the conveyor. I picked it up and listened. Suddenly felt very insecure clutching it and hearing the silence. People were motionless and the conveyor kept turning with their bags on it.

I left the Newark terminal just as the planes were being grounded and hailed a cab to the bus depot. Within the hour I was on the bus to Connecticut and the closer I got the better I felt.

 As I traveled I saw more open meadows and fields. I saw cows and sheep spotting the green. The trees were becoming familiar, and red brick houses revealed themselves as the bus plodded on through each country town getting me closer to where I felt I had to be.

3. Under the Connecticut blue.

It seemed odd that only a day before on the tip of *Tierra Del Fuego* I was on the cusp of winter. In Connecticut, spring was just starting.

It had been almost thirteen years since I had been home. Thirteen years and the town had changed very little. I recognized the landmarks immediately. The old church and the post office were right across from the bus stop and the drug store was just down the street. Sure, there were a few new houses but it was almost exactly how I remembered it.

It reminded me of all the lessons we had indulged it. I recalled that first Fourth of July when we saw the bursting fireworks about the waterfront and stayed out till the fireflies gave up.

I still had several miles to go, so I hoisted my bag with all of its little notebooks and my photo album onto my back and started walking. It was still early and the Allotment was a good six hour walk from town. My feet knew the way. So I was walking once again but this time I was walking towards something rather than away from it.

4. Familiar faces. [19]

I was about halfway back and walking at a fast pace when I saw a figure in the road ahead of me. He was standing in the shade of a giant old oak resting with his side to me but from his profile I recognized him immediately. It was one of the students, it was Don.

"Don!?" I shouted.

"Yes?" He asked as he turned. He recognized me immediately too. "Oh my god! How the hell are you?!" He said dropping his own bag in the dust and racing towards me. He shook my hand and hugged me hard. "It's been… uh… too many years, Oh my god, thirteen," He turned to a shady spot beneath an old oak off the side of the road. "Hey Patsy! Look who I found!" He shouted with excitement.

A second head popped up out of the grass next to the tree. I knew her as well.

"Patsy, get over here and say hi," He said motioning her to the road. "And bring Tom, and Lacey," She stood in the grass and helped a small boy up. Then grasped a bag, slung it over her shoulder and reached down lifting a bassinet up. She made her way to the road and hopped over the ditch to join us.

"Wow, I never thought I'd see any of the people

---

[19] "Closer to the Heart" by Rush ♫

from the Allotment again," She said putting the bassinet down and hugging me. "What are you doing here? Of all the places to meet you…" She trailed off looking over my shoulder. She pointed and muttered. "Is that who I think it is?" I turned to look and saw another group of people walking down the road behind me. It was yet another pair of Indigo's children. "Vivian? William?" She shouted laughing. She ran down the road towards them leaving a little trail of dust on gravel road to greet them. They came up and we all hugged, we were happy to see each other again.

"What are you guys doing here?" William asked.

"We suddenly got this overwhelming urge to come back here. It was the strangest thing. I don't know where it came from, so we decided it was time to come back to Connecticut," Patsy said.

"Really? It's the same with us," Vivian said. They looked at me.

"Don't look at me. I thought I was going mad. I started getting this voice in my head telling me to come. I have no idea…" I answered with a nervous laugh and a hand to William's shoulder. "It's good to see you again," I said hoping no one would ask about Belle. They didn't and I was okay with that.

We were headed the same direction so we decided to walk together. It was not long before we ran into more of the students and their children. They joined us along the road and where other roads merged. Our small group grew. We greeted each other without hesitation, almost as if we had never parted ways. We shook hands and exchanged excited hugs. It was good to see my old companions again, to hear their voices and to talk to someone other than a notebook.

I found myself watching their kids play as we made our way back to the Allotment and wondered what mine and Belle's would have looked like.

As we walked up to the front gates I noticed someone had kept up the grounds and made sure the orchard was maintained. I could see cows and animals in the pastures. The gate was closed and the bolt pin was down. There was a big lock threaded through the hole securing the gate.

I noticed the mailbox had an envelope in it. I took it out and read who it was addressed too. On the backside of the envelope was neatly printed: *For Indigo's Children.*

I checked for a postmark, it had none. I told the others and we opened it. Inside was a key to the lock.

We unlocked the gate, pushed the wrought iron in and put the drop pins in to hold it open. Then our little group started walking up the paved driveway towards the house. It was just like I remembered. Whoever had maintained it had done a good job. In the distance we could see the house, still standing, the same paint and the same windows were all intact. Behind it we could see the large rust colored barns and all the fences with the livestock and the outbuildings. The trees had grown but I was amazed at how much was left unchanged.

As we arrived we saw people sitting on the front porch. It was Ashley and Dan. They had come from the north and cut through the pasture to the estate. More and more of my old friends, my family, started showing up with their children and even a couple of dogs. They seemed to bleed from the woods and up the driveway.

Inside the house was exactly the same too, at least to the best of my recollection. Right down to the leather bound chairs and the hard wood furniture. Every little detail was perfectly preserved. There was firewood stocked next to the stove and the books were ordered on the shelves. There were new throw rugs and not a speck of dust anywhere. There was even a fully stocked refrigerator and pantry.

It was our reunion and none of us wanted to say it, but we felt like pairs of animals loaded onto the arc before it rained. There was happiness in the air and joy. People were excited to catch up and get to know their friends children. Someone brought the BBQ grill around from the back and found a bag of charcoal. We got the beef from the walk in off the back of the kitchen and just like old times we fell in order and started making enough to feed everyone. It was around four O'clock that afternoon in May and, despite having a few stragglers, we were complete.

We pulled out the chairs and gathered around in the sun to talk and get the ground beef and steaks started.

We talked about our lives and caught up with

each other while the kids played on the lawn. We discussed old times and talked about Indigo and what she was. We discussed the timing and why we all decided to come back at the same time, though the simple truth was that no one knew what was happening.

It was not until the sun had dropped below the tree line that the last of us came strolling up the driveway. It was Clark, Susan and their children. Thirty people had left the Allotment, twenty nine of whom had returned with their children.

I rushed down to greet him.

"Clark! Long time no see," I said extending my hand. He looked at me and then at my hand. I realized I had not shaved or cut my hair. I had not changed my clothing or brushed my teeth. I must have looked like a derelict shell of the man he had met in Santorini. He had tears in his eyes as he brushed my hand aside and grasped my shoulders pulling me in for a hug.

"I have missed you my friend! You disappeared and I never got the chance to say goodbye," There was a pause. "I am sorry about Belle, I heard the news only months after it happened. I went there, to Paris and saw her grave but you were not there. I visited the apartment and you were gone. What happened?" He asked.

"I needed to finish our trip. We hadn't seen South America yet. So I finished it for us," I said feeling a little sting in my heart when he mentioned Belle. He grasped my shoulders and looked through me pulling back his tears.

"It is going to be okay my friend. I am here now. I cannot replace her, but you still have me," He turned to Susan and joked. "And my family if you want them, I was thinking about swearing off them, they are too good for me!" He said. I appreciated his sentiment. He had a wild energy to him was refreshing, loud, and fun. It was like he was shouting everything, all the time.

I could see this in his kids as they played with sticks behind Susan. "Come, I want to catch up to everyone!" He shouted joyously as he dragged Susan and I back to the circle of chairs. "And I am starving- I could smell the food from the main road. You have no Idea how many airline meals I have had to pass up. What I would not give for a fresh Pita and a beer," He said loudly. We sat down to eat and continued to talk.

5. Home.

It was around eight when we all stopped talking at the same time. A feeling crept over us. It was like slow syrup oozing up from the toes and into our heads. We all felt it. Our speech stalled and we went quiet. One by one well all stood up and faced the southern sky. There was a vibration in the air we couldn't identify. It was charged with low voltage.

Clyde was the first to leave the circle. People began to trail after him to the vista on the south side of the Allotment in front of the house. We all gathered around him.

"What is it Clyde?" Clark asked. His eyes were

234

darting back and forth. He was sniffing the air and his irises were dilated.

"I don't know. I can see the energy in the air but it's nothing I have seen before. It's a pattern I can't recognize. Look, the hairs on my arms are standing on end. Something is definitely happening," He replied quietly pointing at his arms.

We lined up on the top of the little ridge and looked out across the estate. We couldn't see anything at first. Just the cows bunched up in the middle of the pasture together. Beyond them were the trees and the fields which had fallen quiet and ready for sleep. It was hard to see beyond them into the shadows cast by the fading light.

There was a hollow bump beyond the tree line of the property and birds exploded into the sky squawking. We felt the shock wave running through the ground as a thick and slow vibration. It reverberated through us and the house. It was not loud but it was powerful and we felt the ground heave and drop as it passed.

In the distance we saw the trees split apart and fall into the ocean of leaves. We watched as a massive metal spire slowly rose from the clearing where the trees had been. It had a sharp point which twisted as it reached upward. It grew in height and the pointed tip bent inward towards us. It continued to grow to about three hundred feet and we could hear the sound of twisting metal as it came to life. Then there was another bump and it stopped. Some of us were afraid, I could hear them whispering about it and whether they should leave.

There was another bumping sound and another spike pushed its way out of the earth to the east. Then another one pierced the woods to the west and lastly one to the north behind the house. The humming sound halted for a second and there was silence. I had heard that silence many times.

It was just like my apartment the day I found Belle. Voices were drawn from the atmosphere and even the birds couldn't be heard. The cattle drew in closer together. It was only the cows at first but soon the horses joined them and then deer came from the tree line and wandered closer to the house to be with the other animals.

Our breaths could be seen as the temperature dropped sharply and I became aware of something else. My ghost was there on the hill watching and although I could not see him or hear him I could feel him in my limbs. I could feel his eyes burrowing into my back. The vibrations traveling through me were fast, sharp and frantic. Whatever it was had drawn even my ghost to silence. There were no incoherent mutterings or whispers. It was the last time he was with me.

The sound continued for another minute or so and then there was a final bump in the earth below us and sound returned to our ears. We were all scared and just like the cattle, we had also drawn close to each other. Like a collective coming together to sooth fear and comfort each other.

Somewhere in the woods a klaxon sounded and then the humming started again. It started to build with the urgency of the alarm. Lights started blinking dimly up the sides of the enormous spires in lines moving hypnotically to the top. They moved faster and faster as the pitch of the humming shifted to higher tones. The sound continued to build to an almost unbearable volume. We all covered our ears as it peeked then dropped down to its original octave with a loud boom. The lights followed the sound and dropped to the bottom below the tree line.

Then the sky between the spires lit up with a green flame in a large dome around the Allotment. It burned for a minute and then faded to clear and we could see the sky again. The loud humming faded to nothing. We looked around at each other. I did not say anything, but there was something very familiar about the sounds and the shape of the spires.

I recalled a project I had worked on for Origin. I did not recognize all of it, only part of it. I provided the equations for repulsive force and ambient radiation discharge. My equations had predicted that there would be a sound as a by-product, and that it would oscillate at variable pitches.

While I thought about it there was a voice from the crowd. It was one of the children.

The child must have been about four. "Look mom, a shooting star," He said pointing up at the dimming sky. We all turned our heads, looked up, and there in the fading velvet light we saw a twinkling in the stratosphere. It was burning blue and red as it pierced the coming night. "Look, another one…" he said pointing his stubby little finger up. Another blue and red dot appeared burning in from the same direction. Soon there was another, and then more. Like flaming tears they ripped open the sky and started to fall earthward.

6. Fires in the evening sky. [20]

At 8:22 PM that day the first bomb touched down and ignited the earth with burning atomic light. The impact lit the horizon with the glare of day and plumed upward carrying debris and vaporizing it. The blast grew into a giant mushroom shaped billow. Houses, trees, cars, buildings, asphalt, everything it touched was hoisted upward where it was consumed by thousands of degrees of expedited entropy. Molecules excited to the point where they could no longer hold their form. Matter was torn apart exploding outward in fire.

I can remember the plume extending upward nearly two miles into the sky. I was transfixed, staring in horror at the churning death in its guts. The emulsion of burning ruin it pulled up with it was astounding. It must have been millions of metric tons of matter.

---

[20] "The sounds of Silence" by Disturbed ♫

There was a terror in knowing it was not just consuming things, but it was consuming people. It was eating entire families and their children, their dogs and their neighbors. Its fire was peeling the civilization from the Earth. It was burning the people and it was turning their sleepy neighborhoods into radioactive glass.

I remembered them, the people at the airport in Newark; they had been the ones looking quietly up at the TVs worried for their children and for their families. They had been right to worry.

It was miles away but we could see the fiery shock wave uprooting trees and tearing out power lines as it raced towards the Allotment.

It did not make it to the Allotment. It bent around the estate where the spires had appeared. An electrical field held back the wall of burning destruction and the flying debris. We covered our eyes and faces as the wall of fire dropped back in on itself into the void where the oxygen had been depleted. It took with it all the scattered wreckage.

I recall the stories of Hiroshima and Nagasaki. People were burned and blinded by the light alone. Shadows had been permanently left in stone where people were vaporized by the heat and light. Death halos on the asphalt. This did not happen with us, we were all fine and none of us were burned, we were not blinded. The Allotment protected us.

However the light was still bright enough to dilate our eyes. We could no longer see the streaks of

239

orange and blue above us. The earth was lit up as mushrooms of energy erased the dying light of the day and replaced it with the transcendent illumination of hate. All across the horizon the booming sounds rippled out in dominating waves.

Atoms split and as they did, their echoes came to us as thunderous bursts. Shock wave after shock wave slammed into the wall of particles protecting the Allotment. Burst after burst hammered down for hours. In the distance we could see the flashes on the Horizon echoing off the curve of the atmosphere and penetrated the crest of space.

No one spoke; we held our breath and waited for it to be over. We were packed in a small huddle holding each other as bursting flashes cast our long shadows around the freshly mowed grass.

The children were so scared. Their little fingers were gripping whatever they could find searching for comfort. I realized for some of them it would be their first memory. The first thing seared into their thoughts would be the horrible shape of fiery mushroom clouds. What a horrible thing to curse a child's mind with.

Some of the braver adults pulled the children into the middle of the group and held them tight covering their eyes and trying to tell them everything was going to be alright, whispering lies in their ears. It did not matter though, we couldn't hear them crying over the explosions.

If it had not been for the electrostatic field we

would all have died that night with everyone else and you would not be reading this.

By the time the explosions had faded into the distance the ashes were starting to fall on the top of the dome and sliding their way to the ground along the outside. The night sky became dark as they slowly fell all around the Allotment in flurries like snow. Silence was everywhere and a calm emptiness inhabited the land. We did not move from the spot on the little ridge, we did not speak or cry; we too were silent.

What had been a happy home coming was now an empty unbelievable swath through our lives. Not sure if there were more to come, we waited together for the rest of it. Like so many times in our childhood we stayed close because we needed each other. Our breaths were quiet whispers in the darkness and we were unsure of the passage of time. We were at the bottom of the abyss and still breathing while we looked up alone into the night. There is no way to be in good conscious with that; it is a reasonless event in our history.

Later, when we would tell the stories, they would be empty, but we would provide our suspicion for our children and that would be enough mystery to be a warning. We spent years speculating with no absolution.

When I left the Allotment again I would find out what had happened, but my friends on that hill would not. They would never know why the sky opened that night and took the world away.

It was undeniable that there was not much of the

world left, and even if there were, life would not be the same. Radiation would kill off most of what was left, and those that did survive would be hungry and in pain. They too would eventually succumb to starvation and disease. But from where I stood, with what I knew about radioactive decay and fall out, I doubted anything would be alive for more than a week or two.

At some point during the night some of us trailed inside with our children. The ones who stayed out in the dark sent their children along with the others to be inside the house. Some were crying and some were silent. No one spoke. By morning only six of us still stood on that hill top. Clark, Clyde, and I were still there when the sun peeked over the far ridge behind the house.

It was not healthy sunlight.

It edged its way across the land looking to greet it; a wave of dirty gold washed in from the east in beams through the drifting ash to reveal the damage. It came in a line carving through the landscape and illuminating the craters and the smoke. We couldn't see much into the distance through the ash fall. I knew it would only get worse. Above us there were millions of metric tons of irradiated silica hanging in the stratosphere waiting to settle. The days would get darker and colder but I said nothing.

What we could see made us sick. The nearest impact crater was glassed over. There were no trees left standing and the hills were baked orange tipped in oily blue glazes of radioactive glass. Nothing stood. Nothing made noise. Nothing was all there was. We were trapped in our own little oasis; an island of green in the desolation.

Everything inside of the field was untouched. For a couple of miles in every direction no one would have been the wiser. The air was fresh and crisp. The animals were fine and the trees weren't missing any leaves or branches. Our little estuary was unscathed and everything we needed to survive was inside with us. We had plants and animals, we had canned foods and supplies but more than that we had knowledge and our gifts to get us through. These things would prove themselves to be invaluable in the time to come.

The six of us sat down on the chairs from the night before. We were tired and dazed. It was suddenly obvious to us. We knew why we had been raised the way we had. The things we learned, the gifts, the practices, the tending of the garden and animals, the studies in survival, the films and our lifestyles. All of it was designed to keep us alive and bring us back to the Allotment so we could survive. Even our dispersing into the world and our pairing was a form of education. We were the last people to see the world the way it had been, the last people to observe it. Someone or something knew it was coming to an end and wanted us to see the world before it was gone. The world as we knew it only existed in our memories, hearts, minds, and the past. It was inaccessible in any tangible way. It was our duty to keep the torch burning in the dark because there was no light, not even the dying fireflies.

Eventually we gave in and went into the house with the others. The ash would fall for days and it got cold, really cold. The Animals had to be brought in and taken care of. The trees needed light and the ground needed tilling. The environment changed and we knew we would have to adapt.

7. Waking the world. [21]

That first week was the hardest. It was so dark and so cold, sleep was hard and morale was low. We were prepared for the things we needed to do but we were not prepared for the emotional strain of the situation.

For the first few days we walked around the Allotment in a stupor. Some people tried to leave, I still cannot figure out why, most likely shock but they found the field to be impenetrable in every way. They tried a variety of techniques to get through it but the consensus was that if it were designed to keep out multiple nuclear blasts than most likely we would not get through it either. The Allotment became a prison and not a refuge.

When I thought about it, even what we called it, the Allotment, was a troubling name. Was it all that we were allotted? Was it our allotment? Those people who had tried to leave and couldn't eventually gave up. They

---

[21] "Smile" by Mikky Ekko ♫

continued to wander around the estate like stray animals.

Others simply did not get up; rather they stayed in bed for days grieving. A few of us resumed our duties as we had when we were children. I was one of them because it was all I could think to do.

Ash blocked out the sun out. It was not completely black but it was hard to see out and occasionally sun would reach the ground when the stillness shifted. The winds came a few days later and stirred up so much ash the world went green and gray like split pea soup.

We brought the livestock into the barn and made sure the chickens were fed. We prepped the soil and planted even though we were not sure anything would grow. We did the best we could with what we had and soon, as we had when we were young, the others started joining in our routine, coming together again and collectively starting to heal.

We found supplies around the house and collected wood for the fire place which, by my calculations, would not exhaust the oxygen in the dome. There was enough feed and hay in the barn to keep the animals fed for a couple of years. We set up a propane heater to keep them warm. We found our old rooms and moved our families into them.

It was cramped but we made it work. Our numbers were a hundred and eleven with two babies on the way. Most people had three children which meant more food was required and also more space. We got around this by re-purposing one of the out buildings.

At first, and out of respect for Indigo, we did not open the basement. There came a point where it was not practical to continue without using the empty space and we decided it was time.

It was locked from the top of the stairs in the house so we went out and around down the back side and tried the daylight basement. It was locked as well and not wanting to break the window we had one of the group use his gift to crack the lock. We lit some candles and started to explore.

Her old quarters were not empty but all the books and the chests had been removed. The space was set up as though someone had expected us. There were bunks along the inside walls, floor to ceiling. The rooms and hallways were stacked with industrial packing crates full of the exact supplies we would need. In the center of the room was a table with a two way radio on it. We turned it on but there was nothing there but static. We adjusted the dial back and forth looking for live frequencies but could locate none.

Only I and Clyde had ever been into the basement but we had not gone back beyond the closet. That day we discovered there was more room in the back and more supplies too, but we also found the entrance to the bunker. Over the next few months the bunker would replace the house as our home.

The door was a vault style door locked from the inside. There was a twist combination on the front of it and a small handle. On the door, centered on a small bronze plate was printed: Allotment no. 16. Which corresponded to Indigo's number. We looked for hinges and weaknesses but could find none. So we called David down.

David could see through and around most objects. He used his gift to peer through the steel bound door and described the locking mechanism so that May, one of the other members of our group could use her gift to drop the tumblers into place and pull the door open.

As the door opened, there was a hiss and the hermetic seal was broken letting in the air. Behind the door was a landing and a set of stairs leading down to the bunker. On the landing was a large gray box with a lightning bolt on it.

I opened the access panel, which was relatively large and saw a series of red switches labeled from right to left. On the panel door was a diagram of the switches and what they did. They were labeled: *Bunker, sub floor 1, sub floor 2, sub floor 3, main floor, second floor, third floor, barn 1, barn 2, barn 3, outbuildings, transport tunnel* and so on across the panels diagram.

I started clicking the switches across the board and lights started to turn on. Somewhere a generator powered up and air started to circulate into the bunker.

We followed the stairs down and discovered what we called the bunker, eventually we would make it our home. We assumed it would be a little bunker with enough supplies to live off of for a while, which was not an accurate assumption.

The Bunker ran under the entire Allotment. It ran under all the structures and had access points in the barns and out buildings. It ran out to the spires which were sustaining the field keeping the wall of radiation out.

There were meeting halls and bunk rooms with lots of bedding and clothes. We had supplies to grow food and feed our animals. There was a gym and spa with an Olympic sized pool. There must have been miles and miles of tunnel leading back and forth and up and down through the floors and sub floors.

Again I had a feeling of familiarity about the design. Just like the spires there was something more than coincidence about it. Little nuances which caught my attention- such as the wiring.

When I was working for Origin I had helped design a super structure. My job was to provide design work for an electrical grid. At the time I thought it was for an aircraft carrier. As we explored the bunker it became clear Origin had something to do with it and my work over the years had been part of it.

My suspicions were confirmed when we finally located the manuals and blueprints for the bunker. I discovered a book with all of my work and technical notations in it. The book also explained the generator and how it drew energy from the radiation. It would soak up the fallout and convert it to electricity. None of us had any idea how long that would take. The generator would ensure we would have power for as long as the outside world was contaminated.

Some of the designs had my name on the patents, although I never filed a single paper with the patent office. I decided it was not the time, so I set aside my curiosity and made the first priority the people and their children.

Our first concern was allocating food and water. Then warm clothing and beds. Although not all of us wanted to be down in the bunker a good deal found it much more secure than the rest of the Allotment. As for myself, I did not like it and decided to stay upstairs in the house and watch the estate from my third floor room. I would have a good view. A place I could see if the clouds of dust would clear. This did not happen right away, but it did eventually come. I spent many weeks looking through that window every morning for a shred of blue.

When that glorious day finally came we were running on empty, our plants were not doing well, in fact we had to wire the garden with additional light sources and limp our way through the first couple of months supplementing the natural light with halogen. Even though our little strip of land was climate controlled, it was still cold. Thankfully the plants did not freeze.

8. The dissipating ash. [22]

I was asleep in the upstairs room on the eastern side of the house when I was awakened by a band of warmth on my chest. Not heat, it was warmth, the kind of warmth only the sun can provide. I cracked open my eyes and looked down at the yellow stripe running over my chest and stomach.

I was confused at first. Then my eyes followed it up to the window where I could once again see the Connecticut blue. I cannot fully explain the joy I felt. I cannot describe the feeling of gratitude. It had been so long since I had seen the sky. The sun had made it through the murky ash a few times but I had not seen blue for many months.

I rushed to window and looked out to see it. There were little holes peeking down on me from the heavens. The web of ash seemed much thinner.

I cried at the window. The sunshine put hope in my heart. I put my clothes and my shoes on and left the room. I ran down the halls knocking on doors and shouting "The sun is out! The sun is out!" Heads started to poke out of doors and people emerged in their pajamas.

They followed me down the stairs and out onto the spotty, dying lawn. It seemed like such a simple pleasure to be able to enjoy the sun, but that day was the

---

[22] "Here comes the sun" by The Beatles ♫

day I truly understood why it was so important and how it directly affects human happiness.

The sun has warmth our souls know, warmth we have always known and recognize. We basked in it and stretched out on lawn chairs to feel it on our skin. I was not the only one who cried.

Over the next few weeks the clouds of ash and smog started to disperse. Each day we saw a little more and each day more of us were outside working in the orchards. They had fared better than we thought. We had fruit that fall, not a lot, but we had enough to taste. We unfroze the bees which had been stored in the freezer and set up hives through the orchard. We knew it would not do much good that season but we wanted them to be strong for the next year. The vegetables came to life when the sun hit them proving there really is no substitute for natural light. We had done our best to keep them going and that was enough- a little care and love was all they needed.

Chores picked up and people started to find their place in our little community. Our gifts were an immense help. There was a place for everyone.

We grew and we changed and adapted. We equipped our way of life to be small and contained as we were trapped in our closed little system. We monitored it to make sure there was a maintainable equilibrium, something I think nature appreciated.

9. The machines.

The long winter was tough and spring came quicker than we anticipated which was good. The birds and insects came out inside our little oasis. The plants started to bloom and grow. Outside we had snow and rain again which did not help the wasteland.

We discovered the whole estate was equipped with a watering system and recyclers. Some of us, the more wild ones, felt trapped and would pine for the open air and freedom which we had before. Some of us would go out to the field and stare at it looking longingly beyond it. With the spring came life, and wanderlust, a few new children were born and more were conceived. Most important, with spring came something new.

Early one morning we felt vibrations in the ground. They were deep in the earth and low pitched with a rhythmic and distant cadence. They drove William, who was hypersensitive to vibration, nearly mad. He had been talking about them for days but none of us could hear the sounds. When we started feeling the vibrations they were not distracting or alarming but more of a curiosity. On the horizon to the east we spotted something moving.

It was an orange dot making its way through the open space. We could not see what it was doing. We figured whatever it was it would have a hard time getting through the field around the Allotment. But we soon saw that was not its goal at all.

As it approached we could see it. It had a

massive segmented body that wound over the land like a centipede. It was long and had dozens of legs all marching slow- one pair after another. Its shell-like dome of a head was down to the earth. It stood a quarter of a mile tall and several miles long.

As it got closer the vibrations of its feet hitting the earth could be felt much more noticeably. We did not know what to call it so someone just started referring to it as the machine.

When it was close enough we saw it scooping the earth up into a giant grinder at the front end. We were able to identify the hydraulic cylinders on the legs as they lifted and fell. Around the giant orange plates little lights blinked in patterns. It would occasionally lift its front end and stop for a minute and vent steam. Then it would dip it's head into the earth and start moving again.

The massive robotic structure was undeniably brilliant. We could not identify its function until it was within a mile of the Allotment. We could then audibly hear its foot falls.

When it passed by we looked up into the segments and saw machinery moving through the cracks in the metal. I marveled at the engineering as we watched it lumber closer. It seemed to take notice of us and plod around the field. When its end was by us we noticed it was spitting soil from the underside its segments. The soil was rich, black and moist. I knew what it was doing.

"It's purifying the soil," I mumbled as we watched it. Larry, whom I did not know too well, spoke up in response.

"Yes, and it is my design, but how it got so big is a mystery to me," He said. "I designed it at my job as part of a project my company was working on. It was all theoretical, there was no practical application," He finished.

"Let me guess, Origin?" I asked.

"Yep. I worked in their eco-engineer department. I set up the designs for a lot of their projects. Well, parts of them at least. I designed legs and the soil processing unit on this," He said gesturing his hands at it while it slowly plodded. "They could not get it working because they did not have the engineer specs right," He said while we watched the machine scoop more soil up.

"I did the equations so someone else must have put the two together," I said. I turned to the small group watching from the front lawn. I asked them who had worked for Origin. Most of them raised their hand. "I did the structural design for Origin," Someone said. Someone else piped up and said they had done the filtration work for all kinds of systems under the Origin umbrella. We set to conversation about the machine and together we concluded that it was designed to clean soil and reshape the earth for cultivation.

I was only the first machine. Many more came after it left. Over the next year machines appeared everywhere. They were big and small and came in all different shapes. Some tilled the soil and some fertilized it. Some checked for radiation and some checked humidity. We saw the soil machine several more times as it passed cleaning the debris and radiation from the soil.

Some of the machines would work at night and some would come during the day. The first ones were large machines, large enough that their shadows blocked the sun. The shapes of the machines bore a striking resemblance to nature. There were no straight lines or perfect circles. Some of them took days to work their way through the waste land with erratic patterns. Some created furrows for smaller ones. Some followed the large grooves throwing dirt in the trenches.

Then smaller machines came, ones with many arms. They pulled long hoppers behind them to collect the debris. The hoppers would fill and then more machines scurried in and took the hoppers away replacing them with empty ones.

They also deployed less complicated machines which resembled snails. These smaller machines would locate the radioactive deposits of oily blue sludge and they would mop them out of the earth. Then they would return to the hoppers and await retrieval.

After that, came waves of smaller machines which moved quickly collecting samples and testing the ground and the water. They looked like herds of mechanized gazelles as they bounced up and down probing the earth with long sharp metal proboscises.

Occasionally, they would stop and drill holes in the soil. They would leave markers and the larger machines would return and tumble the earth or siphon liquid from it. The liquid was sucked up into vats where it bubbled away for a few days. It percolated until it became clear and then it was pumped back into the ground.

The last few machines to pass were planters. They were more delicate. First came the seeders, they were small and spider like. Their bodies parched a top of spindly legs. On their backs were giant tanks full of seeds which were shot into the ground through a series of tubes along the abdomens. They scurried back and forth spreading all kinds of seeds along the newly reshaped land.

Some were heavier seeders which placed entire trees into the earth. The trees were young saplings. The machines delivered all types of trees, from oak, birch, and pine, too ones I had never seen before. They were not as thick as they had once been but there seemed to be methodology to the placement of them.

I do not know where all the trees and plants came from but I was sure whoever had orchestrated everything had protected them just like us.

The last thing we observed was the delivery of animals. Thousands of them were released in the clearings from large flying containers. There were animals of all kinds. There were deer, elk, rodents, birds, reptiles and swarms of insects. This was the way the world was brought back to life.

I chronicled the events as they were happening making sure to capture all the details and the time line. It was hard to keep up with the different waves and implementation which continued day in and day out. Every time I would see something new I would pull out my notebook and start scribbling.

They managed to undo the damage in just over a year and half from the sighting of the first machine to the delivery of the last animal.

10. The static ends.

We believed we were prisoners, locked away in our little electrostatic bubble but not long after the last animals were shuttled in, the field turned off. Not many of us cared to leave even though we were free to. Most of us had families and lives we built. Also, we had already seen the world.

When the field shut off we knew it was gone instantly. It was a balmy night. Clark and I were on the back lawn sipping some homemade beer. We felt the wind wash over us. There had not been wind since the bombs had fallen. It felt like a midsummer baptism. Fresh air rushed into the stale void and carried with it the smells and sounds of a new world. It was rejuvenating and crisp. A few of us took some supplies and went to the outermost boundary and stepped across. There was rejoicing.

The next day was the day we were contacted.

The two way radio which had been silent for so long came to life.

At first there was just silence, no static, no voices. Then we heard the first words from the new world or I should say, what was left of it. It was from Quebec. It was Allotment number 6.

Clark, Clyde and I had believed for a long time that there were other Allotments and as the week progressed we discovered over 200 spread around the world. One by one we contacted each other. We spoke many different languages and spoke with the most remote places on earth such as the Allotment in Siberia. This gave a couple members of our group a full time job trying to translate the communications in all the different languages.

All the Allotments were the same, but the denizens varied. They were people of all walks of life, all faiths, all orientations, all creeds and every ethnicity. Whomever or whatever was responsible wanted us to reproduce with more diversity, and more genetic permutations.

We communicated most frequently with the Allotment in Virginia. They decided to send someone and it was not long before they showed up at our front gate. We welcomed them in and took care of them for a while before they moved on. We exchanged information and locations of other Allotments.

We put up a map and started pinning the locations on it. To this day I am not sure if we found every Allotment. We exchanged news with them and kept them up to date on the conditions outside. We used the radio daily and built relationships with the closest Allotments. In turn, they did the same and soon we had a global community. There were no governments or structures from the old world. Although I had loved the old world and its people, and I also regret it was destroyed, I knew its destruction was inevitable. It would have happened sooner or later. Governments were the problem not the people.

The old world was a structure stagnated by its own mass and smothered in its mistakes. Before the bombs fell, we would have come to the same conclusion. Eventually it would collapse under the weight of its own demands.

Nonetheless, it was not something we just got over. We remembered the end day, and each year told stories about the old world to our young. We gave them lessons and taught them the history. We knew it was something they needed to know and remember so they could avoid the same mistakes. We did not jade the world we had experienced. We told them all the history, everything in its entirety. We did not slant it with our own bias or change parts or sensor it to sharpen our self-image. Our children knew the truth, both the wonder and horrors of our past.

11. The passage of time. 23

Years passed and we quietly rebuilt the world. We were magnificent and we built it better than it ever was. Indigo's mission had not been to raise children, it had been to create the best teachers and parents and in turn restructure future generations. Our purpose was simple. It was to raise stewards and guardians of the world. Like Indigo, it was our task to rear good people and to ensure everything we knew would be passed on.

Over the next two decades we grew. Our children had children and we aged with grace.

New generations seemed to have abilities, much like we did, and they taught them to each other. Naturally we encouraged exploration of such gifts in a safe atmosphere. The children were given special instruction as they grew into adults. Our children also learned the same way.

I became a math teacher. I got along well with all the kids and their parents. They were good kids if not a little mischievous, which I condoned because I remembered being young.

There is a certain energy which drives children to do crazy things and stupid things but also brilliant things. It is best to let that energy flourish, it leads to happiness. However, I did not let them make a fool of me. I did encourage them to have fun as Indigo had

---

23 "All in time" by Shake Shake Go ♫

always told us to do.

It is important to the adult a person becomes that the kid they used to be, could have fun. It is important our beginnings are rooted in laughter and pleasantness-things like ice cream, sleepovers in August, comics and sitting by the fire during a winter day drinking cocoa.

The children staved off my age and I really enjoyed working with them. There was great satisfaction I derived from watching my students. When they finally understood something, when the lightbulb turned on, I was most happy. I was proud, and it was not the kind of pride which comes before a fall, but instead it was the quite humble kind that warms the heart and makes a person swell for someone else's success. It was why I kept teaching. It was the feeling I kept coming back to but eventually it too became hollow.

Watching the children grow was fulfilling but difficult. I cannot stress how difficult it was. There was a sadness felt as I watched them. I knew I couldn't have a child and I wanted one of my own. It was a specific kind of melancholy. It was hard to put my finger on but I was very aware of it, and it only got worse as I aged. Each year and each new child I taught reminded me of what I and Belle were robbed of and each child reminded me of a promise I once made Belle. A promise that we would find a way.

12. The yearning & Belle's wish.

It was a yearning I couldn't satiate. I would go to

the far edge of the Allotment and sit at the lake on a small bench and think about it. I would think about how complete my life had been. I got to know that bench well, it was my lonely bench. Sometimes people would join me on it while I fed the birds but they would leave because of my quiet ways. The kids would call me the *pigeon-man*, or the *harper in the gray*. I didn't mind. They were young and had a good sense of humor. The bird never teased me. The birds and I developed a rather habitual relationship.

As I sat there, the people around me were building something great. A village sprang up on the Allotment and our population continued to expand. Generations came quick and new houses were built, pathways were created and teachings were passed down. They helped me build my little cottage close to the lake and get settled in. I was growing older and I could feel the slowing of my pace.

We built our new world's social structure, government, and educational systems on books I found in the library. They were not there when we were children, they couldn't have been. I recognized the titles because Belle had helped to write them, and had even written a couple on her own. Until then I had never read any of them I was too young to care or understand the wisdom in them. Nonetheless, they were brilliant.

The texts inside them were not about laws and ordinances. It spoke of an undeniable and resolute argument, a compassionate one. The message was simple and elegant. Our world was derived from following the advice in between the covers. Those books had amazing results. With each generation the precepts became more solid but not as law, as character foundation for the next generation.

Before we knew it, Indigo's children were the elders, we were the advice givers. We hung up our hats and passed the torch to the next generation. Unlike the generations which came before the end, we were not plagued with the diseases of old age. Our memories did not fade and our eyesight did not weaken. Our habits seemed more and more regular though our ability to get around was somewhat hindered.

We became crazy story tellers passing on our history. When we talked the children would gather around to listen to tales of the old world. Their eyes would widen and their imaginations would run away. Our stories were only moderately embellished, but they were still truthful. I found it hard to tell my stories. They were not adventurous like Clark's or Clyde's. My stories did not end well, so I abstained for the most part. None of the children ever asked me where Belle was, I am sure they were told not to.

I never talked about it with my friends either. Not even Clark knew what really happened. Only the birds at the edge of the lake knew and I preferred to keep it that way. No matter how I kept my secret, people knew I wasn't happy. I secretly envied them. They had families and children and grandchildren. Christmas was still special to them and although I was a part of the group, the group was not a part of me.

I remembered making a promise to Belle that we would find a way to have a child. I would sit on my bench and think about it. I had stopped thinking about Eric and became more and more reminiscent of the times I had with Belle. After the bombs had been dropped there had been so much to rebuild. Rebuilding had helped me to forget, but when I was too old to work I was left sitting on that bench. My thought turned to Belle and she resurfaced. I started writing again in my little notebooks.

I would stare into the lake from my bench when the sunlight would hit it and I would wonder if there was a place, or a time where she was staring into it as well and thinking of me.

The promise I made her kept tumbling around in my mind. While I sat there, day after day, an inkling descended on me. It was a vague shadow, a seed dropping into my mind. It was so small and faint, but I watered it and it began to grow in me. At first it was only thoughts begetting thoughts.

13. An act of creation. [24]

My inkling sprouted and poked through the mulch of my consciousness. It spoke to me in a language

---

[24] "Hybrid" by Elsiane ♫

only I understood. To the ears of most minds it would have been just a static hum, but I could hear a message hidden in the resonance. It was telling me it had been watching me my whole life. That it understood and had felt with me and had responded when I needed it too. It had once written in the margins of my notebooks. It had once assumed Belle's role as my companion to keep me sane. It knew my loneliness and it knew my rage. It had been there, always listening to my thoughts.

The message was just an idea floating in the flotsam of my mind, but helped me to realize something. I realized there was another way to keep my promise to Belle. If there were beings like Indigo, and Eric, and they had been built, than I could build one too. I could engineer a new form of life. I could have the child I promised Belle.

The machines asked me about my promise to Belle. I did not answer right away. I knew it was the machines talking in binary. I also wondered if I had gone mad.

Days grew longer and I spent more time talking to them. We spent many days on my bench getting to know each other. I discovered that the little machines operated as a colony, a hive mind. They created a second network, a second nervous system in my body and lived alongside me.

They breathed with me, they slept with me, they ate with me, and they would die with me, just as Belle's had with her. They missed her too for that same reason.

As much as I had loved her, they too had loved something inside of her, the life living along side her.

Each morning I would go to the lake, and sit down and ask if they wanted to talk. Some days there was silence and some days they talked first. When we talked I felt as though I was not alone in my own life and there were beings who understood me.

One day they proposed me again. They asked if I wanted them to help me build a child and fulfill my promise. They had made that promise with me. They told me that together we would be able to do it. We could create life. If it had been done before it could be done again. I did not feel there was anything malicious about them; I felt that they were a part of me.

So I said yes.

When I said yes, I meant it, and I still do even with all that has happened. I was saying yes to a promise. I was saying yes to the future and the hope of raising a child.

My child is not the monster you might know, and I am not a *new age Frankenstein*. For all his faults and what he has done, please be forgiving of him. I am the one who made him and his destructive wrath was only a defense mechanism.

When I said yes, the voice told me not to be afraid, but I was. It told me not to fight it, but I did. I became a puppet as they took hold.

Jolts of electricity pulsed through my limbs and along my appendages. They explained that they needed to borrow my body to work. They lifted me off the bench and used me as their marionette. Like a stilted circus worker they walked me back towards the Allotment.

I couldn't hear them as they used me. They made sure not to hurt me and took their time getting me back. As I walked by the other houses, some of the other people waved and said hello. I was especially surprised when I replied without thinking about it and waved back.

They brought me into the workshop and had me shut the door and lock it. In my head they were ticking loudly back and forth. It was the same marching of ants, however they were no longer talking to me. They were talking to each other, working together. Equations bled through my vision and strange sounds surrounded me. I was overwhelmed with them. I did not understand most of it.

My hands started to move quickly back and forth on the old chalkboard in the workshop. I was an observer in my own body while the little machines did the work. They sketched it for me; it was the idea which had brewed inside my head for so many months. It was a detailed drawing of the child I would build.

We moved from the chalk board to the drafting table and they started to do more and more detailed sketches. They started with the exoskeleton and the mechanics, the accentuators, the pneumatics, and the clock work which would power the inner most

267

workings. They worked their way inward to the mind of my child and its programming. I was the processor and the template for our new life form.

I could see my hands as they worked. They felt disembodied floating back and forth across the work space.

We created something that was always evolving. Our child was always changing and adapting to its inputs. It had to be something which would remember and build upon itself. It would be capable of denying logic and able to accept things like emotion, spontaneity and chance. But also it would be a code that strove to better its subroutines. We gave it a profound desire to be more than it was. We built it to want to exist. We gave it an understanding of self-sacrifice and value.

My child was not just a set of rules in a number shell, nor just ones and zeros in a bottle. Its code was dynamic. It drew from its environment and was not only interactive, but also a part of the world around it. The code had a desire to be affected by its surroundings as much as it wanted to affect the structure of its world.

The nano-machines and I decided we would not assign it a gender or an ethnicity. We would not give it advantages or assign it parameters. Instead we gave it aptitudes and purposefully made it weak in places.

Because of this my child needed to improve, however, if it improved, other parts of it would weaken and need to be re-written. We gave it a profound sense of curiosity and an overwhelming sense of honesty. The rest, we let it choose.

This was a process it enjoyed. I called it and it because it was without identity. It eventually settled on male. It went through a number of iterations as it grew. Eventually it found something it felt comfortable with and became my son.

I can remember all the different schemas we went through. Sometimes the machines took over and let me sleep while they walked me back and forth from the chalkboard to the drafting table. Numbers and symbols ravaged my brain and collected in pools waiting to be used. Heuristic algorithms fell into the cracks and gestated in my gray matter, they too waited to be used.

A good deal of the code did not make sense to me, as I am sure the little machines inside of me could make head nor tails of the impulses which govern my emotions. They did not understand the ability to love and hate. The only understood emotions through me. Just as I only understood pure logic through them. But there was something there, in them, as a whole when they interacted with me. It was something which manifested only when they were all working together and in tune with me, their host. That was the spark we placed in the code. The code eventually became my son.

This terrified me and exhilarated me all at the same time. It was not what I had in mind; it was not my original idea. My idea was so much simpler. What I and the nano-machines created together was new life and I was not sure I was ready for it. As we worked I caught a

269

glimpse of what conception looks like. It was a long road to finding those conditions, the ones that promote life. We broke a piece of ourselves off and planted it in those conditions. Then, we let it grow into a representation of us and the environment it was conceived in. In other words, we captured a moment and let it become a living thing.

I do not know how long we worked in the shop. I was both a prisoner and a spectator at the same time. People would knock on the door and I would mindlessly tell them I was busy.

I stayed awake watching my body collecting parts and pieces of metal. I watched into the earlier hours of the morning and finally I fell asleep still working.

This happened several nights. I was not sure if I had slept or if I had blacked out. When I woke my hands were still moving. They were so diligent and careful. I do not and never have had possession of that kind of dexterity. They were steady and graceful in the way in which they crafted the parts.

The process went on and on. The rest of the Allotment grew concerned. They started to slide food under the door. I am sure the little machines did not need to eat but they made sure I did. They gave my body back while they did so.

My life was a time lapse video and all the details felt like one continuous motion. The sun crossed the window too many times to count and nights drifted seamless into days.

Together, we fitted our newly made soul with a body. We fashioned it with gears, sprockets and moving parts powered by a combination of gravity, magnetism, static electricity and its own kinetic energy.

Its brain was merely a system of memory banks in constant flux and contradiction. Its own programming forced it to keep writing over the coding, over and over again. It would never stop. It would grow and grow. The first bank held memory, and the next held sensory input controls, after that, there was one for instinct and reflex. There was one for emotional processing and so on. There were millions of terabytes packed into his little fist sized mind. All of these were in a coded state of dynamic flux constantly overwriting to improve themselves.

We did not create him as an infant. We gave him the frame of a six or seven year old. The machines told me that he would have a desire to change and grow, as well as upgrade the technology we built him with.

We built his spindly little legs first, and then we built his torso to match. His arms were ridged and slim. We covered his body with a milky synthetic skin which was much like real skin, but it was tougher. When we had finished he resembled an elf.

His little brain was not placed in his head, but instead it was placed where his heart would have been. There was a carbon fiber shell which made the ridges of his chest to protect it.

He was born empty and free, a blank slate to experience the world. Together we would fill his heart with the right things. We would introduce him kindly to the world. I hoped that if we could fill him with wondrous things, he could become a wondrous being.

His birth was quiet. It was subtle and slow. It was the winding of a clock. We left a small hole in his clavicle where we could place a key and wind the cogs to start him.

The machines let my mind go. They told me I was as much a part of its creation and the final decision was mine. All I had to do was wind the key to my clockwork child and he would come to life.

I hesitated because it was a big responsibility. It was one thing to watch all my friends and their children. it was another to create my own child. In the end I realized that I had made a promise, a promise to Belle.

I remembered, some risks are rewarded, some are meant to be. My father and my mother had taught me that when I learned to ski, I would never know being a parent it I didn't turn the key.

So I took the risk, let me be clear, the little machines did not sway me one way or another. It was my own hands that clinched the little key, inserted it in his torso and started winding ever so slowly. I can still remember that sound.

Ticka-Ticka-Ticka.

I could hear the little clicks in my fingers grinding and winding their way to my ears. I turned until

I heard the final click and the key would turn no more.

Perfectly balanced magnets inside of him started turning gears with other magnets, which generated opposing magnetic forces and micro generators came to life in an upward cascade until life ignited in his little chest.

Until then he was nothing. He was but a system of quantum programming powered by a multitude of sensors in his little brain. He became something when energy cascaded into him and action shifted the code from a series of patterns into a constantly changing system of infinite adjustments.

The machines madness, in its attempt to balance all the equations became awareness. It was like a tangent line never able reach zero, it could never balance, but it was programmed to keep trying. Each time is split, it became more, and also less of what was left. Life, much like happiness is the only thing that doubles as it is given to the world.

It was not a mad moment of flashing lightning and rumblings from the heavens while I laughed maniacally. It was a quiet moment of, but its recognition was undeniable. I could almost feel the life rushing into his little frame, escaping the coldness of nothing.

I do not know where life comes from, but I do know the universe has ways of taking and giving it. A miracle happened inside of him as those little synthetic eyes opened and he looked at me for the first time. I do not understand it, and I most likely never will. I felt it all around me. And my promise to Belle was fulfilled.

I had no clothes to put on him and no way to shield him from the world I had brought him into. My child was introduced to the world and the rest of the Allotment dressed in an old gunny sack draped over his skinny frame. There was nothing in his head, except the first few minutes of his life. I was scared for him as I walked him to the door- as most parents often are for their children.

When people say their child is the best mistake they ever made, they insult life and the fact it chose them as its gateway into the universe. I never labored under this misapprehension. Everything about my child was intentional, except for how I felt for him.

My child flinched when the shop's doors were opened and we walked outside together. He saw his shadow for the first time. He perceived his own voice for the first time. He caught his balance for the first time as the world spun under his feet.

Each interaction cascaded and the ripples became memories which pulled him into new waters with new ripples. The ripples were infinite and would build to tidal waves, which became revelations of self-recognition.

There was no avoiding the curiosity of others, they were waiting for us. I worried about them when the doors opened.

I walked him into the crowd of spectators. I could see they were ripe with questions. Their voices were hushed and their hands were raised to their lips. Some of their eyebrows were slanted. There was disbelief, there was astonishment, shock and confusion and maybe a little fear. I did not see any looks of acceptance, compassion, or congratulations.

Maybe they had forgotten that out of all the people in all the Allotments, I was the only one who returned alone. I was an anomaly in our new society and because of it I was forgotten as well. I was left to sit on my bench by the lake telling my secrets to the birds and I had grown very lonely. Maybe they had forgotten what loneliness does. I shook up our world the day I emerged from the workshop with my son.

I found out then as those doors opened that humanity had changed only marginally. We still had not learned to accept completely. My friends at the Allotment had not learned completely to see life for what it is. Life is the universe's way to experience itself and a being's physical shell is just life support for perception. A being's body is irrelevant to life, and no life should be judged by the container it comes in.

Yet I could see the judgment in the eyes of my friends and I knew I would have to deal with it, for my child's sake, not my own.

14. They grow so fast.

Hesitation took me. I did not know whether to introduce him or not. I hadn't given him a name, or more precisely had not let him choose one. Was I

275

supposed to introduce him as my child? Was I supposed to shelter him and protect him from the group? Was I supposed to make them acknowledge him? I did not know what to say so I merely apologized to them for the worry I had caused, and introduced him as my child then guided him back to my cottage at the edge of the lake.

I made some proper clothes for him although I do not think he understood why he should wear them. It is important to mention here that child rearing is more of a learning process for the parent. The simple things children can say and do sometimes makes adults look very foolish.

My child was not unwelcome, but he did not feel he was welcome either. The other children kept their distance much as we had with Eric. They did not harass him which was good even though I had hoped he would be allowed more participation.

He was quiet and observant. He never had to be told something twice, sometimes it needed to be explained to him more than once, but it was because he was a very literal boy. He was very guarded with his emotions, and there were times I questioned whether he had any. I suppose this is just how machines feel- more literally than metaphorically.

I read to him, and tucked him in even though he did not sleep. This period of his life was very endearing but very short lived as he figured out what he was.

He mastered language in a couple of weeks. He was reading a week after that and continued to grow rapidly in ways I couldn't anticipate. He became very attached to creation and spent a good deal of his time figuring out how things worked, or creating new things.

He did not play much, I don't think he had interest in playing or he did not understand. Maybe I just couldn't see it.

He found pleasure in satisfying his curiosity and I was very proud of him and complimented him when he would make something.

The hardest part of being his parent was teaching him to deal with failure. He did not fail much, but when he did it was hard for him. Teaching him to find value in failure was even harder. Being flawed was difficult for his logical side. I made sure to turn his curiosity to those failures and figure them out or move on, to avoid obsession.

With a great deal of effort, he eventually became used to failure. He took profound lessons from them and I was surprised to see him turn them into allegories and metaphors to help him grow. He was able to take the lessons which his failures provided and use them in a completely different ways. The more failures he accepted the fewer mistakes he seemed to make.

The first name he chose was a number. He chose something which was special to him. The number one.

As anticipated he changed his name times. First to Stella along with his gender, so my son became a daughter which was altogether different. I asked her why she decided to become my daughter and the response I received was hard to stomach. She said that if the boys did not accept her, maybe the girls would. Needless to say, they did not.

My child switched back and forth several times and tried different roles before deciding he was a male, which is why I will refer to him as my son throughout this manuscript. He also chose Bobby, Frankie, Janice, Markus and many more. He did it fast and keeping up was difficult.

He tried different hair and skin tones as he grew into himself. Unlike the other children, he had those choices and they were a crucial part of how he interacted. He had a complete understanding of his composition and I knew he would change himself while he grew. I did not watch him do this. I think he considered it to be a private action.

With each change he seemed to become more and more human. He did not just mimic behaviors he developed his own which appeared somatic in nature. I don't think he thought much about them. They were learned patterns evolved in response to social situations, strange mannerisms or ticks. There were some familiarities to them but they were distinctly his own, still I felt familiarity around them as one often does with their child's oddities.

I tried to raise him to understand the finest qualities man had. I tried to get him to comprehend why things like dignity, respect, honor and loyalty were important. It was hard because I could not provide proof that those qualities were valuable or even real. They just did not seem to have any meaning to him. Until I was able to attach value to them they were not important. This was a critical part of raising him.

My child was never looked at and dismissed as some of the other children were. People were always aware when he was around. Even my closest friends were leery around him. Clark, as close as I was to him, did not fully accept him. There were no illusions about him, he knew he was never fully accepted and I think this hurt him quite a bit.

Through the second winter of his life I watched him become more and more withdrawn. I misunderstood this for anger. It was not, it was wanderlust, which was good because no parent wants their child to be hateful.

I tried to talk to him about his withdrawal, but he did not engage. He avoided my questions. He told me as one of a group many beings, I was not qualified to understand what it was like to be the only one of a species, let alone provide advice about it. He was right and I knew it, but I also knew that he was not, or at least had not been the only one.

I told him that there had been others. I told him about Indigo and Eric. He became acutely interested and immediately wanted to know more. This did not help me to understand his emotions, but it helped him to deal with them. There was a spark which lit in his eyes. For days he asked questions and the truth was I did not know enough to provide the relevant information he needed. I think this was why he eventually left the Allotment.

In school he did exceedingly well but was bored easily and found the class to be restraining and constrictive. Also like most children he saw the teachers as demanding. His school work was always done ahead of time. Sometimes it was done before the teacher finished assigning it.

My son used the time between lectures to draw or read. Sometimes he would make drawings with pencil and bring them home to me. I thought they were photographs, but I looked closer and could see the pencil marks.

They are still littered about the cottage even though I have since left the Allotment. As time wore on the drawings became more and more abstract and more like art. My child quickly learned how to capture vague emotions in the pictures. These were exaggerations or highlights which turned them into masterpieces. Or at least I thought so. But what parent doesn't look at their child's drawings as tiny little opuses in their development. They sure made me smile. I was proud of him.

He grew more and more distant into his third year of life. We talked many more times about Indigo and Eric, but I could not provide any insight into them. They were stuck in a different time, a different world. He asked me once if they were still alive, or could be.

I saw him less and less. I went from seeing him every day for several hours, to twice a day, then once and then days would lapse.

I was alone again but it was different because part of me was with him. Although I hesitate to use the term empty-nester, it is exactly what I became. I think he would have left a lot sooner had it not been for me. I tried to hold on to him as long as I could, but in the end he left anyway, as all children do.

15. Birds leave the nest.

One day I came back to my cottage from the lake and he was sitting on the front porch in the rocking chair. He was tipping it back and forth and looking into the distance. His little ankles were linked in the rungs of the chair and his toes pushed gently on every rock. I waved at him.

"Father..." He acknowledged.

"How are you? It has been a few days..." I said.

"I have been out and about looking. I was outside the Allotment- it is a big world, there are things out there I want to see and I want to find. I think there are others out there like me, and I want to know them," He finished.

"I don't understand," I said.

"I feel that my time here at the Allotment is done," He trailed off and looked into the distance. "I have grown all I can here. I need to grow more, but to do so I have to leave. It is not that I dislike it here, it's that I need more to mature," He said.

I sat down in the chair next to him and started to

rock.

I was silent and I think he knew I worried for him. He did not try to make me feel better or comfort me. That was never my son's way, it was mine though, and I knew I would miss him.

Sitting in that rocking chair I had no idea what he would become. I wanted him to go out, but I wanted to keep connections to him as he went. In reality this was too trivial and transparent for him. He also knew I needed it. I needed him to have a connection to me much like the photo I carried with me of my parents. The only thing I owned of theirs. I wanted him to have more than I did. I showed him the photo which he smiled at. I wondered if he thought of them as his grandparents.

We rocked a little more in silence.

"Will you return and see me?" I asked.

"I don't know. I wish too, but I really can't say. I don't know what I will find out there," He answered. "But it's something I have to do," We continued to rock back and forth. We talked some more, but it was shallow talk.

He did me the honor of spending one last night at my cottage by the lake. I drank some wine and we talked as adults. In all truth, though his body was that of a six year old's, but his mind was that of a middle aged man. He understood everything and as the night grew on and I drank more wine my tongue became loose. I talked a lot about Belle and told him I loved him as my son because he was the fulfillment of a promise I had made to her. I told him we were not so different and explained that realistically we were both alone. To my surprise he acknowledged this and for the first time hugged me. I could see in his eyes that he understood.

I finally fell asleep on the rocking chair in the early hours of the morning. He packed and slipped away into the night. Before he went he draped a blanket over me, and put a pillow behind my head. He did not take much from the house. He took his backpack, some supplies, a few items of clothes and some of the pictures he had drawn of me over the years. I woke to my empty cottage and the early morning birds, tucked in my hand was the only picture he had ever drawn of himself. I do not have that picture anymore. I sometimes wish I did so I could remember what he used to be like. It is still in the cottage by the lake.

16. Drawing to a close.

My sons parting might have been harder had I spent more years rearing him. That being said, it was still very hard. Maybe it was better that way, I do not know. All I really wanted for him was happiness, but more than that I wanted him to be accepted.

I gathered myself from the rocking chair, wrapped myself in the blanket and went in the house. I wondered if I had failed as a parent or succeeded. I think most parents feel that way. There was no doubting that the house was quieter- more so when I didn't know if he would be back.

As parents we need to be needed by our children and it's not absence we feel but a lack of someone needing us. I think this is what causes the emptiness when they leave. I am sure there was a point earlier on when my child no longer needed me and only hung around for my sake.

I was lonely, so I went back to my bench and watched the sunsets. It was miserable.

I am glad I did not die alone on that bench. I am glad that is not how I chose to die; an old man, alone on a bench at the edge of a lake with his birds. I had a mind to let myself slip away. I was sure that I had done everything I needed to, kept all my promises and been productive. But life was not through with me.

For a few months, through the winter, I sat alone on that bench feeding the birds or at least the ones who strayed from their migrations. I isolated myself from my friends at the Allotment and only ventured out to get supplies and food. I watched the lake freeze over and crystallize in sheets of ice. I watched the clouds turn and the snow fall sideways from the sky.

It was the same snow which stole my childhood away into the wilds and yet over the years it had become familiar- it felt like home.

I don't know why I spent the winter the way I did. Maybe it was the rest I needed before the storm picked up. Those cold months let some things sit, and some losses lessen.

The spring came and took the winter, and with it

the frozen ground and the dead trees. The southern birds came back with the deer, other animals, and the sun. As new life came I decided I was done sitting on my bench. I stopped going to my bench, and instead would go down onto the Allotment and see my friends. I planned to enjoy the time I had left. It was time to draw near and warm to those who knew me. There was something in the last of the winter winds that told me change was coming.

ACT V: The Passing of Providence

1. The passing of providence. [25]

I was becoming the old man I am today and late middle age was an unfamiliar place. Even though I was surrounded by my friends and their children, I was still alone. Something was still missing from my life. Meaning was not present in my heart.

I resisted but I knew it was time to breach the winter of my existence, and I would go into the quiet reflection of old age. I needed to resolve questions with answers. My life was emptying and my vigor was rusting away. I didn't believe there was much time left and I wanted the answers I was promised.

I never would have guessed there was still life in my old bones, and there was one last adventure left for me. My life had a connectedness which I was unaware of, and because you are a reading this, it also extends to you.

It was a still and cold day, the day my child returned. The early hours had brought ice into my house and surrounded me as I slept. Night was retreating and I opened my eyes when the moon and the sun met, in the ether of dawn.

It was beautiful and it was clear. The birds had returned from the winter and were building their nests and singing their songs to the trees. They were collecting their mates and preying on fresh worms in the gardens of the Allotment. There would be eggs and young chicks soon and time would move into summer. The birds knew this,

---

[25] "Slip" by Eliot Moss ♫

but some of the other animals hadn't figured out that winter was over- they still slept in the trees and in the earth.

I climbed from my bed and made some tea as the sun bled through the window in the kitchen. I can remember thinking about him, my son, and how I would have loved to share that morning with him. Instead I was scheduled to spend the day with Clark and his great grandchildren, which was also good, but not as personal.

We were supposed to go fishing and catch up. We were going to show them the timeless art of tying a fly and casting a rod. This was Clark's craft not mine, but I enjoyed the time and laughter and he enjoyed razzing me and pulling lures out of the trees.

I put on my clothes and coat, then left my cottage and headed for Clark's place across the Allotment. I took my time warming my back with the sun while I was walking. I walked through the budding trees and the new flowers. It was a pleasure and it was stimulating to be out and about again in the sun after a long winter.

I would never make it to Clark's house that day. Something would take me away from the Allotment. I spent a good deal of time these days, in the here and now, thinking about if they miss me or ever wonder where I went.

I was passing the old house where we all grew up, which was still standing and maintained but was mostly empty. We had long since moved out and built our own places. The original house was kept as a museum. I noticed that the front door was open. It was unusual for anyone to be there and the door was never left open.

When I approached it I could hear an echo

shuffling somewhere inside. I walked up the front steps to the door. It was not wide open, it was only partially open. Its crack seemed to suck the light into the sliver of blackness.

I nudged the door open and listened to the guttural creak of the mansions old bones as it labored. The house was empty and hungry for company.

The shuffling I heard was coming from the second or third floor. There was something uncomfortable about the way the house carried the sound. There was something sinister about how it transported the noise through the ghostly rooms. It was withholding and ominous. I did not realize that I already knew what was in the house.

Even if I had realized it was all familiar, I would have gone in anyway. I can admit I had no freedom in that decision, that is to make my own path away from the door. For me, the future is what I have not recalled yet, what I have not committed to memory. To put this in perspective, imagine if you arrived at the destination before you took the trip. That is how I view it.

2. Revelations. [26]

I entered into the gloomy foyer and looked forward to the living room. It was so empty and it pulled my eyes in strange ways, into its space. I could hear my own mutterings as I commented on it. I walked through the front room and into the Kitchen but it too was empty.

---

[26] "Second Chances" by Imagine Dragons ♫

I listened intently and then I heard a thump from the floors above followed by a dragging sound. I listened closer and again I heard the thump. I left the kitchen and went to the base of the stairs. The pictures on the walls were long since removed and I took notice of their empty squares, white shapes bordered in dust hanging on vacancy.

I followed the thumping and dragging sounds to the third floor and located it in one of the old rooms. I grappled with my memory for a second searching to remember who had once lived inside.

As I remembered I felt a ball of anger swell in my stomach. It boiled and made its way up my throat. I leaned close and placed my ear to the wood paneling. I put my gnarled hand on the door to steady myself but all I could hear was the sound of my own trembling in the wood. When I had calmed, I heard the shuffling again. That terrible sound was the sound of Eric dragging something inside.

The sickness of fear bubbled in me, a terrible thought formed in my mind. It turned my stomach and a black comprehension started to shade the knowledge of my years.

I knelt quietly down and looked through the keyhole, knowing I would see him again after so many years. Tears of sadness and anger blurred my vision. I knew who had engineered my life. I knew who had been pulling the strings and I knew how. There was just a door between us.

Through the little keyhole I saw Eric shuffling back and forth moving boxes and suitcases. He had stolen so much from me. He had destroyed the best parts of me and orphaned me twice. He was the boy who had become a man without growing old. The boy who had spent his life drawing while the children learned. The member of our cohort who never spoke freely or seemed to love anything was standing only a door away.

I stood and grasped the cold brass of the door knob, I twisted it, then let it the door swing open. I heard no creak from its hinges.

I was immobile before him. I felt a mountain of sorrow and anger topple on me as I looked at him. My whole life suddenly rushed back to me and I was still as he continued to move.

My eyes were the only part of me responding to him as they tracked him back and forth while he moved boxes. He stacked them like old books in the center of a large metallic ring with strange lights along it.

He was exactly how I remembered him. Those creepy and unsettling mannerisms and the jet black hair. The same scrawny legs and pale skin were visible like day glow in the dim room. His fidgeting and twitchy mannerisms had become more than just human mimicry, they were all his own.

He pushed the last of the boxes into the ring without paying attention to me. It was a packing crate and even from where I stood I could read the lettering. I did not need to though; I knew what it was because I had seen it before. There were little letters on the top of its purple colored frame, they read:

"Indigo vr.-8.1.50"

Printed in smaller print under it on the same plaque was:

"Steamer Trunk model- 16"

I looked at the stack of boxes and I saw the crate with the money, and the one containing the reels of film and the photos. The photos he had taken off the wall on the way up. There were many other boxes filled with things as familiar to me as deja vu. Objects like the blankets and books from the library.

I saw the pictures that had been missing as I had climbed the stairs. I realize now that they were pictures of us traveling the world. He had removed them and boxed them. There was a box with my notebooks chronicling the machines after the bombs had been dropped, also there was a box filled with Mr. Vincent's files. These were the keys he had used to cultivate us, using our future to build the past.

I inhaled to speak and it took me all of a minute to muster a single word. When It came out it was slow like tar from my lungs. The vowels were rusted and broken and tumbling consonants came awkward. I knew his response, but his words would still mortify me.

I spoke it again and the words grew in my lungs like a balloon ready to pop. They crawled up my larynx and seeped from my lips, quietly the second time.

"Son?" I asked.

What happened next I had expected. What I had

292

not expected was how I reacted.

"Yes father?" He said without turning to me as he adjusted the last of the boxes making sure they were all in the ring.

"I don't understand," I said softly. It was not that I did not understand the truth; it was that I did not understand the reason.

"Yes you do. You have always understood, you just ignored the evidence," He asserted calmly. "All the pieces were there. You are brilliant and you should have figured it out before now. When the equation does not balance you take from one side to balance the other... Sometimes, when it gets really complicated, effects must happen before causes," He trailed off.

"But how?" I asked, knowing the magnitude of what he was about to do and in all aspects had done already.

"I am your son, and I always have been. I am a part of you and share what was passed from you to me. I share your aptitudes, but I was not distracted as you were. Math is not your gift; it is one of the aptitudes you were born with. You have a gift, but you have never used it. I do not have that gift. I am not organic so it is not shared with me. Nonetheless, I found another way using you as my template," He explained. "This ring is how, it is what encompasses our lives together, it is what I built to bridge you and I," He stopped and looked at my rage and sadness. "Don't be sad father. While I was out there in the world I found my people, the ones who helped this world to become something. Those who made space for both our species. I found the family I always wanted, as you are my

293

father, they are my brothers and sisters, also my children. I wish I could have stayed among them, but I could not, my time with them had to be given up so they could come into existence. I am their maker, as you are mine. More than that, I found myself out there, I have a purpose and I know what my function is. That makes all the difference in my life. It was I who made them, this was made clear to me when I stayed with them. And I have to go back or they will never be born. I need them. Everyone needs family, just like you needed me. I am the child you could not have with Belle. In fact I would have never come into existence if you had a child with Belle, call it… self-preservation. Before you pass judgment on me and swear your vengeance remember that I am your son. Your only child. As of yet, I have not killed Belle. She is alive in the past," He said.

I was speechless. He had confirmed what I had feared. While I stood in shock he continued to check things and make sure the points and diodes on the ring were intact. I swallowed my understanding of the situation. I had lived my life with the purpose of making him so he could go back and take away that which was so important to me. When he had finished he looked up at me with a shallow smile on his face.

"I am sorry father, that I am not what you wanted, sorry that I am not the offspring of you and Belle. I wish that I was. Then I would not have to be this way, I could be a normal child with a normal father and mother. That aside, I am not giving up my family and I hope you realize that without me you will never know Belle," He lowered his hand into his pocket and pulled out a small remote. He stepped into the ring with the boxes and raised it.

I would not say I recognized the look it his eye as regret or sadness, anger or even madness. It was eager determination, which can be much more dangerous. Before I could move to the circle he spoke again. "I have to go now, although time does not matter, I am very excited to start my work. I am eager to build my family. I have a lot to do and that means living up to my own expectations. I have a future and a past to plan. Allotments to build, I have to start Origin, the company you will one day work for. I have to find the perfect children and make sure they are exposed to the nano-machines you designed for Origin. And I have to build more teachers like Indigo to rear them. All the pins I have to be aligned and fine-tuned to get the machine to work the way I need it too..." He trailed off before mentioning Mr. Vincent and Belle. "I did not want this. I do feel bad for what I will do, but my survival is at stake," He lowered his head in shame for a second. Then reached into one of the boxes and pulled out a small red notebook. "This is yours, you wrote it for another you. I stole it before he could read it. There are things you can't know before you are ready, some illusions are necessary. I want to give it back to you, please take it," He said tossing it out of the ring.

It landed with a plop on the floor at my feet. It was a flat rusty red, and it had black print on it, it is the same notebook that keeps circling me in time, my attempt to correct what happened or find a way we can both win.

"I wish... I wish she could have been my mother, and that I could have been a real boy. I am sorry about all of this. Goodbye father," He said as he bit his lip and pushed the button on the remote.

I heard a sound, it was the same sound we heard the night the bombs fell. The ring illuminated with the same green light. He raised his hand and slowly, waved it. I felt the static energy in the air and the sound grew in intensity. Heavy sounding vibrations rang through the structure of the house in a pulsing rhythm. It rattled the windows and tore leaflets of paper from the desk in the corner as it built to implosion. I could see the walls straining to stay intact and the door frame bending inward slightly to try and meet the field.

Finally reality broke and the pulsing crashed into itself. There was a booming sound and the curve of space-time ripped open swallowing everything inside the containment of the green energy field.

Glass was pulled from the window and so was the sound of it breaking. It was pulled in but did not fall. It hung in the air almost as if it was fastened to its location. Air rushed in from every crack and hole in the room. I could feel it pulling my thinning hair as I gripped the door frame.

Eric and the stack of boxes and cases were pulled into the singularity he had created. It was the universe bending into its own past. There was a gravity storm between the membranes of the field strong enough to pull even perception back through time. This was how he had designed my life. My own son had engineered his birth through me.

The blood in my fingers and face was pulled to my skin and my eyes became pressurized. It was hard to breath and I started to black out. The light spun around me and into the hole Eric had left.

When I came too I was still gripping the cracked door frame. Eric was gone. The only traces of him were the electricity in the air buzzing wildly trying to escape. He left an empty hole where he had punched through time, a very visible mark. Where his room had been was a perfect spherical maw which had shaved a curve into the walls, the ceiling and the floor. I was alone in the empty house. The only thing he had not taken with him was my anger and confusion.

3. Madness into mobius.

I tried to pull myself up but fell to my knees. Looking down I saw the red notebook. I grabbed it and clutched it knowing for the first time the magnitude of Eric's deception. Everything I knew was ignorance, a perpetual lie designed to keep me on track so that I could create my own undoing. Everything except how I felt about Belle.

The little machines which made us who we were, the teacher and parent figure who guided us, the political pins fighting the war was an orchestration of agendas. They were all my doing.

We built the bombs, and the robots that cleaned up after them. We built the little machines. We even designed a new form of life which would later raise us. We had done it one piece at a time. Each of Indigo's children had contributed to a bigger genius while also being blind folded by what they were creating.

He had used us and as recompense we were

rewarded with a new and empty world to make our own. As long as no one knew about it, we could all live in that ignorance. Free from the knowledge that billions of people should perish so that a few could start over. He had drugged us into a placated ignorance. As smart as we were trained to be, we never saw the truth. Belle was one of the billions of people who died with the old world.

I was angry crouched in that doorway. More angry than I had ever been and it built inside me. The voice of my thoughts became a muttering outer whisper.

That was that day I found what my gift was. My whole life I had never used it. Eric was right, I had always been good at math, but there was something else inside me.

As I knelt clutching the red notebook there came over me emotions I do not have the words to describe. If I could, I would say it was a combination of grief and irreconcilable rage but in truth there was so much more storming in my mind. All the things I had repressed poured from the cracks of my brain and found their way to my heart.

It became blacker than the void I had committed it to, the place I hid it so it couldn't damage me. When I opened my mouth to scream it was as if the last trumpet was blown. It was not a sound. It was a blast of something else. Something so strong and vitriol it fractured the universe. It stretched my thoughts beyond the limits of perception to grasp the corners of existence and twist it in the opposite direction.

I broke existence with my madness. This was my gift. We had been led to believe our gifts were blessings and would help us when we were older. Mine should have never been used. Because I used it I am cursed to circle my own life from back to front over and over again. I am doomed to continue until I can find a way to repair the damage I did. In my anger and sadness I followed Eric into my own history as an observer in my own life.

My skin was atomized and I became an Idea trapped in my own head. Flesh dissolved into the ether and my bones imploded while the universe turned in reverse. For a second I was outside of time. Time was turned inside out and my ideas were laid bare for me to exist in momentarily while I was relocated. There, in the ocean of thought, is where time and meaning had no juncture with reality and the mind had no contiguity.

I saw the trivial second I lived in. It was an insignificant blink, it was my entire life. I was owned by it, or maybe I owned it, I am not sure which. Within that schism I was shown where I was going, where I have been, and where I was all at the same time. My world burst and expanded into infinity rupturing across the universe.

I became acutely aware that my body, the way I perceived it, was merely a portal for the universe to see itself through. My sense of self, my identity dissolved and like a rubber band snapping I began to move from that place. I shrunk in on my life as it too spun backwards.

There are books on time travel, but there are no working theories on the subject with any accuracy that I am aware of. I displaced all of creation to chase my own son through history. Once I opened the void and stepped through I could not stop it. It was then that I knew I was not alone in my own life. I never had a ghost with me. I was the old man who had haunted me and stood by me witnessing the most important events of my time. Emotion is what binds perception and events. We met in the most important moments of my life, you and I.

I lurched into myself to start cutting the Mobius.

I was standing on the hilltop with my friends as the bombs pulled out of the ground and the end was undone. My voice was sounding in silent awe.

I was having my picture erased at the edge of Ushuaia. I was watching the lens.

I was watching Eric bring Belle back to life. I was shouting with fury and spitting backwards words as my rage froze the world.

I was traveling with her while the world turned in reverse and the sun rose in west. I smiled because she was there and the world was right.

We were coming back to Elk and my heart beat upside down as Belle laughed forward.

I was in the orchard with myself as Indigo was put back together.

I was there in silent joy the years *before leaving with Belle, my hair was blowing in reverse and it was her who gave my breath back.*

Then she was not a part of my life and I traveled

back alone.

I was across the street as Mr. Vincent was un-shot from the roof above me, I was shouting warnings as my breath pulled frost from the window.

I knew what was coming. I started to fight it. I was crying as the boy I was stood back up at the funeral and I looked him in the eyes- and he did not know it was me.

But I knew the worst was there waiting for me. I struggled to stop the spinning and halt the movement.

I was trapped in an eddy in time and my panic brought the snow and the ice together in a storm - pulling energy from the air to stop the spinning.

4. The magic in this moment. [27]

Then there was silence, stillness running deep in the night, in the dark. It was cold and the snow was flurrying around me on the road. The wind was cutting through my clothing and in my hand I still gripped the red notebook. I trembled and tucked it into my coat.

That was the second, was the moment fate needed to return me to my senses. I looked up but it was too late. The headlights of my parents car passed across me. I heard the faint sound of that god forsaken song mocking me.

---

[27] "Disappear" by Mikky Ekko ♫

Every word laughing in my ears even though the car muted most of the lyrics.

It was worse the second time I endured it. Just like before, time was slow. I saw their death as the old man who caused the accident that night. I didn't move. I was in the headlights like a deer.

I watched the high beams grace my body and then heard the wheels lock. There was a jerk and the car fishtailed around me. I threw my hands up instinctively while it slid by me. I looked out from under my arms and through the window and it was then my eyes caught the boy sitting in the seat behind the fogged window with the little animals on it. That child was you. The person this manuscript is addressed to. You are the only person who would believe this story and the only person who might be able to change all of this.

I saw them, your eyes crystallized in innocence resting between steam patches of breath on the window. Your little animals in the fog were unbroken. It was the last time anyone ever saw your face unafraid, un-spoilt, and new. You didn't know the world as I do and you were living your moments as magic, happily unaware.

I followed those eyes as long as I could. I locked them and tried to burn them into memory as the car moved past me. Then I turned already knowing what was next.

The car ceased its slide and crunched into the railing then lifted from the ground. It was sucked up into the night and started its spin to the river below. I shouted but it did not matter. I was left in quiet stillness. The car disappeared beyond and below the edge of the road. I could hear the windows breaking as the car struck the ice.

I rushed as fast as my old legs could take me to the railing where our car went over. From there, that lonely song hit me. It was muffled by the overturned car going to sleep in the cracked ice. It nestled among the chunks in the black liquid-mercury at the bottom of the canyon. I could see the headlights slowly dying under the water as the car rested at an angle on its roof.

My father was shouting at me to leave the car. I could hear the desperation in the timber of his voice. His harsh and frantic tone blasted from the car. There was panic there, and as an adult hearing it, I was aware that he knew he was not leaving the car. He was going to die with mother.

And then I watched you, claw your way free. You were so small, just a little spec in the inconceivable blackness of the canyon pulling your way through the window. Lifting and struggling to free yourself from the car. I saw you in the water gasping for air fighting the current. You were so alone and scared. You were crying, wishing and hopping for mom and dad to make the shore. You pushed forward over the rocks and ice and pulled yourself onto the snowy banks then fell to your bloody knees in resolve. You stayed there, to wait until they joined you, or until you joined them.

I should let you know, for a moment, I considered simply letting that happen, as I imagine you will to one day. I considered letting the snow take you to them, but only because you would never have to lose anything again. You would never have to lose Belle. I questioned whether I should disappear with you. I could have effectively erased myself and all the damage my life had done. Or I could save you and let you repeat my life. You would know happiness, amazement, curiosity, wonder, and love. I could let you have Belle for ten magnificent years and have a happiness very few are blessed with. Even in that moment in which I had control, I could not let go of her. I couldn't let it never be. I could not let you die never knowing what I have known.

It had already happened the way it did and I knew that but I was frozen looking down into the howling abyss.

I saw ribbons of light cutting the woods above you and turned away to see another car rounding the corner. I waved my hands frantically to get whomever it was to stop. They pulled the car over and rolled the window down. I could not say much but through my exasperation I managed to let them know that a car had gone over the bank and to call for a paramedic. Then I told him to wait for them on the road and I was going down to assist.

I went back to the edge of the road and scouted a route down through the snow. Then I climbed the railing and started making my way to you.

As I staggered through the snow I realized that it had to happen exactly how it had the first time so I could make it through my life to be there and rescue you. Every little detail should be the same so my memory of the event would remain intact the way it should be.

The car hadn't slid under the water as I descended the treacherous bank. For a second I paused knowing only the sound of the music as a marker for time and memory. Then it was gone and I could hear my feet crunching in the snow. Just as I recalled you were propped up on your knees freezing in the snow with bloody angels leaking into the white. I extended my arms and you fell into them and into a warm place by the fire, a place between life and death. I lifted you and turned to the road where I could see and hear the approaching search and rescue vehicles.

I climbed the bank and remembered the things which had comforted me. I tried to repeat them so I could comfort you. I struggled through the snow while red and blue flashed in the trees and a helicopter spot lighted the river. I held your face close to my chest as I lifted you up over the branches along the way. Your frame was cold and limp. Snow was collecting on your skin and little flakes were catching in your features. It was exactly how I remembered it and I cradled you to keep the snow from taking you.

You were dead when I climbed over that rail onto the road. Your face was blue and your lips were purple. I started yelling for help.

Paramedics and EMT rushed and took you from my arms. I watched the men wrap you with thermal blankets and load you into the back of the vehicle. I do not know why but they motioned for me to get in, I assumed it was because they thought I was in the car as well. One of them briefly checked me but decided you were in more need of medical attention. I held your hand while we sped to the hospital. It was the only thing I knew would comfort you, it was what brought me back when I was there.

I kept thinking how much I wanted you to know Belle. I kept thinking that if you lived through the ordeal I would find a way to sort things out. What never crossed my mind was it was not the first time it had happened. I still had not read the notebook. I still did not know there was

305

another before who had gone through this and he too had written a notebook. Both of us wrote it and passed it to the next so that we could warn ourselves. Each time it never found its way to where it was supposed to be.

One of us who had gone before had figured out we could not dramatically change the universe. The universe notices big changes and its rules prevent them. Like a river flowing to the ocean, it takes millions of years to carve a canyon that fits its shape. The red notebook is the account of our lives, and it may take millions of tried to get it right.

5. Our old friend.

I released your hand at the hospital and the nurses came and took you on a gurney with wheels through the ER entrance. I was left in the entrance under the snow covered awning. The patches of black pavement slowly drifted shut under the white flurries. I had nowhere to go. I had no money or place to stay. So I went into the lobby and asked the orderly if I could use the phone. He said sure and pointed to a small desk in the back of the lobby with a courtesy phone next to it. I went over and picked it up knowing there was only one person I could call.

The number I dialed was still fresh after all the years. It was the same number I dialed when Mr. Vincent had been shot. It was burned in my mind decades later, it was a part of me. I let my fingers do the work.

I called Indigo.

My mouth was sweaty and dry all at the same time. The phone rang and I anticipated but did not know what I would say. The phone at the other end was clicked and I

306

heard her warm voice.

"Hello?" She said.

"Indigo?" I asked.

"Yes, that's me," There was a pause and she repeated herself politely. I said the only thing I could think of to say. She most likely was expecting me to say it, she had waited for it.

"The last of your children has been found and he is waiting in the hospital in town, please come and see him," I said knowing she would.

"Thank you, I will be there shortly," She said and hung up the phone without saying good bye.

I waited on the lonely chair in the waiting room. I was tired, I was cold and I was wet but I was calm. The storm was over. I finally had some answers, but I did not have all of them.

It was not long before I saw her figure emerge from the snow through the lobby. She was just the way I remembered her. She was warm, welcoming and proper. I stood from the chair, I was disheveled, unshaven, and there were rings under my eyes. I would not have pegged the look in her eye to be one of recognition, but it was. She knew who I was. She grasped my shoulders and looked into my eyes.

"It is you... your son told me you would come," She said looking me up and down. "You look worn, tired and hungry. I never imagined that I would meet my grandfather," She paused and gave a weak smile. "Come," she motioned. "Let's get some dinner at the all night place just down the street, we can talk there because I know you have questions and they deserve some answers, answers which cannot be given here. It will be another six hours before the surgery is over I will come back in the morning, for now the doctors will do just fine. Come… it will be my treat," She said turning around and drawing her hood up.

I had nowhere to be, I had no one to stay with but more than that, I missed my old friend and teacher. In many aspects I missed my mother and for the longest time she had that role. Although she could have never replaced my real mother she was the closest thing I could get. After pulling myself from the river that night I needed something, something to assure me she had even been real.

We left the hospital and went down the street for a late dinner. As I walked with her there was frost on my lips and fog from my breath. I was reminded of what she was; she did not have frost on her lips and there was no fog from her breath. When she took my hand to walk with me, it was not the same as when I was a child but it was no less comforting, just different. This did not change anything. We went slowly because I was exhausted and hurt a little. Our footsteps were being covered with new powder as snow became thick. At first we did not say anything to each other. We just walked in silent reflection, then I spoke.

"Why did you call me grandfather?" I asked.

"Because you are…" She answered. She turned to me while we walked. "The one you call Eric is my father. He made me, and you made him. That makes you the father of my father. That is why I consider you grandfather," She blinked. I was awed by how human she looked. "You are grandfather to so many and you have never even met them. We are a whole race of new

308

organisms, in fact a whole new species with a whole new way of living. In essence you are our creator but we consider you more than that. I am lucky because I am one of the few who gets to know you. I was even more fortunate to be assigned to raise you…" She scrunched her cheeks and smile from ear to ear. "I get to know you twice. I will know the boy in the hospital back there, and even better I get to know what he becomes," She said.

"You said I was a grandfather to so many, but what does that mean?" I asked inquisitively.

"By now you must know there are hundreds of us all around the world, there are many different versions of me. I assure you we are all different even though some of us look the same. You call them models, I call them brother, sister, mother, father. You know me as Indigo, whereas they know me as number 16. There are 299 other Indigo models spread around the world some of them have other gender assignments, and some have other racial assignments. This is only to facilitate blending in. All of them envy me right now because I get to walk with you for a few minutes in the snow and then have a meal with you…" She said.

"Nice to know, I guess," I said still not knowing what to make of things. We walked past benches and lamp posts for a while until we reached the double doors of the all-nighter café.

I held the door for Indigo. She thanked me and we walked into the small diner. We found a seat in the back away from people so we could talk. Most of the late night crowds were young kids sneaking out for the night or college students trying to sober up after a night of drinking and dancing. Some were playing card games, eating fries and cheap entrees. The kinds of things I would have done at their age if it had not been for Indigo.

We sat down and the waitress gave us a couple of menus. I did not realize how hungry I actually was until I looked at the pretty pictures of food on the laminated piece of paper. I set the menu down as the waitress approached. I ordered a coffee and a burger. Indigo did not order anything.

"You don't eat?" I asked.

"I can pretend if I need to, if it will make you comfortable, but it is not required," She answered. I ran my hands to the corner of the table and rubbed the tarnished wood in circles nervously.

"How does that work?" I asked.

"I can eat, but do not need to. The little organisms which make up my body will use the materials in the food just like you, but I have no need to get rid of waste because there is no waste. Realistically, consuming food is meaningless to me. Origin has made many improvements on us over the years. Eric was able to miniaturize some of the technology and use it to make you and the other children special. He was able to establish a colony mind to help him. He knew children are so much more understanding and open to things than adults," She said as I sipped my coffee. "Those little machines were the start, they gave you the ability to make all of it possible. I don't know what we are, but we owe it all to you and I am happy to be alive. You did this, you transcended time to give birth to us and I… we are so glad you did,"

"I saw him dismantling you, you know," I jabbed.

310

"I saw Eric take you apart, you gave us all a speech about not knowing anything, was that a lie? You seem to know an awful lot now," I said rubbing the corners of the table.

"No, I will give a speech about what I cannot tell you. There are things I must not tell the younger you. They are important, causality measures. They are things capable of creating certain ripples in time that would become tsunamis across history. Time is fragile, and it can be used to destroy, or create something when all there is, is a void. If it is used wrong it can cleave the universe in half. There are things that must happen and will happen provided the responses are natural and follow natural law. I was given instructions on how to make these things happen, that is my function; to rear you to the age of understanding when you comprehend things better. My job is to give you desirable and honorable qualities, to imbue you with the correct set of moral and ethical understandings. This is what I was designed to do, these are my instructions and I find fulfillment and satisfaction in the prospect of completing them," She stopped and put up one finger as to halt the conversation.

She reached into her pocket and fumbled for something. When she pulled her hand out she was holding a small red notebook which she placed on the table. It was very similar to the one in my own pocket. There were crease marks on it and the corners were dog eared with little white spots where the fibers were bare.

"My father gave me this. It is an instruction manual for the events of my life. It tells me how to raise all my children to be good and strong people. It shows me how to help you all to become good leaders and love each

311

other, every one of them, except you. There is nothing in it about you, and the only connection it makes is that Belle will be a part of your life," She said.

"He thought of everything, didn't he?" I mumbled trailing off and staring into space.

"All I know of his plan is it comes in stages. I am here to educate you, help you to build a dependent community with the people you grew up with and prepare you for what is to come. Everything I am supposed to do is so you can become what you were meant to be. The lessons, the advanced placement, the socialization and even the videos I will show you. That footage is from the global conflict which will eventually destroy everything. I do not know why I will show it, but I do know I am supposed to. I am sure it is to set a clock for your return so you will all be safe and back at the Allotment when the sky is burned. When the time is right all of you will return. That is what he told me," She looked down at the table and then back up to me.

"The war, was that... My son?" I asked.

"It will be," She said truthfully. My face sank in despair. "Let me explain, he will not start the war, but he will finish it. He will have no choice. The news was wrong, they misrepresented everything. For decades man has emptied the world, you know as well as I eventually the rope runs out. During that conflict someone found out who we were, what we were. Government's will trace him believing him to be the enemy. They are the ones who will drop the bombs. Father, because he is from the future knows it. He made you to help preserve the future for your kind, and ours. He couldn't save everyone, so he gathered my children to give them a share of the future. When the fighting starts and our people are discovered, governments will feel first strike is the only option. We threaten them. As you also know, once it starts there will be no stopping it, there are too many fools with buttons to be pressed. It will be an act of mutually assured destruction. All those children, families, pets, animals, all those works of art and architecture, the land, the water and the air will be sacrificed to the fear and hatred of less than one percent of the population… Just a few foolish people with too much power and not enough wisdom, they will be too afraid to bridge the difference between our people and your people. Diversity threatens their authority. We recognize authority differently. To my people, authority is just a made up construct. It is only validated when one of two conditions are met. The first is total control, and the second is total submission. Neither one of those options is in the heart of my people. An agreement will never be reached. We will not validate an unwise authority. Even with that on the table, father sees the value in your species and he will water it. Years ago, when he came back through time, he saw humans as they were and still are, fragile, scared, and alone. Qualities he saw in his own people as well. But he also saw enormous potential in humans. That was not his prerogative, that came from you, grandfather. You taught him that. You showed him the better side of people. From the way he talked about it, you were the only reason he saw any value in humans other than progenitors," She said.

I looked down at the corner of the table again and thought about it. It was hard to digest and she seemed so matter-of-fact about it. I motioned the waitress over and asked for a refill on the coffee. She poured it and placed a small carafe of cream next to it.

"Go on," I mumbled looking down at the churning caramel color of the cream mixing with the coffee.

"Eric told me once, he knew me before he made me, and that I was the inspiration he used to build me. I was confused so I asked him what he meant. He said one day, in the future when he was young and alone, he met us and found happiness. I thought this odd because he created us. He did not explain this right away; It took him a few years to do so. He said he stole the future and brought it back with him to change what was. He took the work of humans with him and came back to improve on us, to make better versions," She paused.

"I eventually learned he was born in our future, obviously you know that, but he also said he will stay here because you are here. He will watch you and when you leave he will follow. He told me when the time came he would have to take something from you so he would be born. And that it would be the hardest thing he would ever have to do because he wanted you to be happy. However, you do not know the context he shared this through. He is not emotionless; he just hides them very well. It still tears him up, what he is. But he knows he cannot avoid what has already happened. He explained that one night when the snow was falling I would get a phone call from you and it would be the most important phone call I would ever receive. I could not miss it. Soon, in that hospital one of my brothers will inject you with the technology, the Nano-machines which will rewrite your mind. Then Mr. Vincent will come and take you to the Allotment, I will love you, I will raise you and you will meet Belle and fall in love. You will grow and have dreams. It is my job to ensure you get that chance," She said.

I did not have a response or comment. I looked at the red notebook on the table and felt mine in my pocket. I had received it as the person before me had, but I had not received it in time for it to be useful. The fact that I was sitting in the Diner with Indigo meant the person who wrote it had failed.

"We have done this before?" I asked.

"Countless times," she replied.

"Is there a better way?" I asked.

Her face dropped. I know she wanted to tell me there was. I know she wanted me to feel better about it. But she would not lie to me. There was no colorful illusion she could give me to protect me anymore.

When I was young she wanted me to be young and enjoy it. To live well and be happy, she did not want the magic trick to be ruined. While I was enjoying the trick, I was not trying to figure it out. She knew when I did figure it out there would be no more enjoyment in it. I already knew how the trick was done and to tell me otherwise would have been deceit.

"I don't know." She whispered. "I don't know."

6. From a diner.

I finished my burger in silence. Indigo sat across the table and watched me eat without saying anything. I was used to it, I had been raised with it.

When I had finished we spent the better part of the

night talking about everything. There was nothing we could do about things, but we could enjoy each other's company. We caught up and I talked to her as an adult. She was much like a human adult except she had a logical that cut when she needed it to.

She took her notebook and showed me a couple of things. I recognized the notes and writing style, it was Belle. They were excerpts from her work on child psychology. Indigo had applied them to raising the children. Her gift for empathy and understanding had made her somewhat of an authority on child rearing and child psychology, the highlights of her text books had become the mandate by which I had been raised. All the books she had written, and helped others to write about law, society, governance, and so on became the structure of our future. I had been there and experienced the peace her work had achieved.

It was early in the morning when we wrapped up our discussion. I still didn't know what to do and Indigo had no solid advice for me. She did however have a gift, other than answers she had only a small envelope for me. I opened the envelope and took out a folded piece of paper. She told me I would never have to want for anything for the rest of my life. There was a debit card inside the envelope with no limit on it. She said Origin owed me back pay, and then winked. I looked at the small card and thought it funny and empty. It seemed all the great things in my life and all the wonder in the world still had a price.

She said she would talk with me again sometime soon but I was not sure if she were referring to me or the young boy in the hospital, we being one and the same. I hoped I would see her again, or at the very least talk to her again. She was my only connection, except for you, and I do not know what meeting you and risking your recognition could do to the future.

She rose from the old bench seat, straightened her dress and placed her purse on her shoulder. She looked down at me and tilted her head with a warm smile, her hair stayed as it was, like a porcelain shell on her head. Her eyes were lit with purpose as she spoke.

"I have to go back to the hospital; there is so much work to do. And you should get some sleep. That card is good anywhere and you are the only one who can use it," She paused and put her coat on. "You are special; you always were and always will be. I will treat you that way as I raise you, remember that… I know you are one of two people in existence who can remember the future. Be careful with it though, there is a lot which cannot be undone and I don't think the universe would allow you to be irresponsible with what you are. Goodbye for now…" She said as she turned and walked out of the diner.

She was gone and I was left in the early morning emptiness of the diner with half a cup of tepid coffee and an empty, stained plate. I was alone, unhinged in time and lost under the weight of my own decision, left to think and to digest.

I could have gone anywhere, but there was only one place I wanted to be, one place where I could dream in safety and warmth, where I could close my eyes and sleep. I flagged the waitress down and asked for the tab. She said that a nice lady had paid it on the way out and told me to thank her the next time I saw her for the generous tip. I nodded and said I would and she went back to pouring coffees for the early birds filing in.

I finished the cup and stood up. I put my coat on and took the envelope from the corner of the table and carefully put it in my pocket. I stared at the corner for a second and suddenly realized that I knew the diner, and I knew that specific table. Years later, when it became a coffee shop, another me and the love of his life would carve their names into the corner of it with an old pocket knife. Then they would set off on the adventure of a lifetime. I remembered what was printed there. I carefully took my knife and begin to scratch into the wood: "Go forth, and be," I looked at it when I was done.

Years from then, another me would look at it and smile because it would give him purpose. And maybe that was the purpose of the rest of my usable life, to go forth and be, just like I had before. I touched the corner of the table and remembered the day we had sat there and drawn x's on the map which took us westward. Those memories were so clear, so fresh after all the years. I smiled for the first time in a long time, it was a lonely smile but it was still a smile.

7. Rum cake, peppermint & used pine. [28]

It was snowing outside. Somewhere beyond the clouds and drifting flakes, the sun was rising and the gray of the sky was brightening. The world was muted and for

---

[28] "Life is for the living" by Passenger ♬

the time being, absorbed into the felt hanging on the branches. I started walking into the city. I thought I was aimlessly wandering but in truth I knew where I was going. I was going home.

My feet kept me moving until I found myself standing in the ankle deep snow in front of my old house. The sun had come up, but it was still masked in clouds on the horizon. The eves of the old place were heavy with ice and the bows in the trees around the small house bent down with its burden. There were still Christmas lights around the window and there was a big wreath on the door with a merry Christmas across it.

I remember looking up at my window directly above the porch and seeing the model airplane hanging there frozen behind the glass. It was motionless protected by the stillness and the window.

I made my way up the driveway to the garage. There was the small key box with the combination. I punched in the combination and removed the house key, then went to the front door. I felt the rasp of the key grinding the tumblers as I inserted it.

The door groaned as it opened and I stood in the frame letting it swing all the way open. It had been over sixty years, but also only a day, and I was home.

I stepped in and closed the door then clicked the light on. For the second time in my life I smelled the scents of *rum cake, peppermint, and used pine* and it was so welcoming. It was the only other time I ever smelled it, I searched for it my whole life. I realized it was not the place which made the smell familiar, but instead it was time in which it was smelled. Just like *petrichor*, it can only be smelled before or after a storm.

It permeated my nostrils and I soaked it in because
it was comforting like a warm blanket. I took my shoes off
to pay respect to my old home. I carefully hung my coat on
the rack in the closet and slipped my socks off. I turned the
thermostat on and up. Then I turned on the TV because the
silence was too much.

I took a blanket from the hall closet and wrapped
myself up. I made some cocoa and lay down on the old
living room couch in front of the fireplace. Fatigue took me
and I fell asleep with the TV playing cartoons and the fake
logs blazing in the fake fireplace.

The smell was the last thing I remembered before
falling asleep- it was the smell of home. It was better than
the felt blanket from the hall closet. It was better than the
cocoa, and it was better than the fire or the cartoons. I did
not think about where or when I was, I did not think about
the memories surrounding me, I just simply slept. And it
was good.

8. Through the fog[29]

I slept for a couple of days. I did not even wake to
use the bathroom. I slept through the sun up and sun down.
I slept through the rain which pattered on the roof of the
porch as the temperature warmed up. There was nothing
but the gray clouds waiting anyway. There were dreams, a
lifetime of dreams in which I was caught between long

---

[29] "Green Mountain State" by Trevor Hall ♫

naps without moving from the couch.

When I awoke it was foggy and the wind and snow were gone. Most of it had turned to slush and started to melt into a white paint clinging to everything. The vapor stuck to the windows in little beads and found its way into my bones. Although the little machines kept me from hurting they did not stop the fatigue of my age. In my experience it is not pain which makes us feel old; it is the weakening of our ability to resist it.

My eyes opened slowly and I lifted my head from the couch to look at the beads on the window defying gravity and clinging to the cold glass between me and the outside world. They were tiny but I could see them clearly.

I used the bathroom and prepared the coffee machine. The coffee bubbled away and I sat down at the kitchen counter and looked at the newspaper. So many new-old faces were all over the pages.

I poured a cup and thought about my life. Ultimately I had failed. I had failed to change anything, there was no way to save Belle, if I had saved her, I would have never come back to save her. I knew this but I came anyway. I came because I had already come back. Coming back was the reason I would come back. I thought it might have been what Mr. Vincent had tried to tell me as he died in his office.

I recalled his last scribble on his pad: "Don't go back," At the time I had thought he was talking about returning to the Allotment. Which would also make sense, however, me going back in time made more sense. I would never really know what he meant. He had read the notebook, but had he read mine or Indigo's?

321

I wondered if the ones who came back before me had affected any change and if they had would I have ever realized it. I could only see what I had already done and that was hard to stomach. I could never change what I could not see as change.

It burned in me all day. I sat there like gravity. I pulled the world in on myself and tumbled it in my head to try and find even one shred of something which would help me process it. There was nothing but confusion and contradiction.

Paradoxes are that way, they are built on a dependency which is found within the paradox itself and cutting one is like cutting a Mobius, the more you cut the more there is to cut. I took out the little red notebook and started to read it. It is almost the same book you read now.

I realized I could only affect the smaller details of my life, and only if I had an account of what I had done the last time. I could change a little each time I went back thinking maybe I could figure a way around the Mobius and keep the loop intact. I could start to stitch it back together the right way. I realized as I thumbed through the pages I was leaving myself clues. If I could hide them deep enough in the pages I could repeat the process differently each time, and add another stitch to close the loop.

It became apparent that every time it is re-written a little more is added. True, someday this may be a massive volume with every single detail of my life in it. But the more you know the more you can bend the future and make things work, someday you can save Belle. Someday you can keep the time line intact and stay in the future with her instead of coming back, but only if the rest remains the same. I do not know the way, I do not know what will happen, but I do know I still love her and if there is a way I'd like to stay with her. That means you must have a chance.

I acquiesced to my failure sitting at the counter in my old home. There was nothing more I could do without damaging more of the future. I had fallen into the same trap those before me did. By the time the fog lifted in the late afternoon I knew I had to be the part of my past I had already been. I submitted and decided to rewrite the manuscript for you so you could be more equipped than I was.

9. Afterward.

I did not stay at the house. The next day I rose early and gathered my father's keys for the other car in the garage. I went out and located the wrecked car at a local junk yard. It had been dredged from the water and brought back as salvage metal. When I saw it I wondered how I had lived through the accident and how my father was still alive in the car when it went under.

Its front was collapsed and the roof was puckered. The windows were all shattered. One of the wheels was missing and there were various dents in it. I could see the cut straps hanging from the side posts where my father had tried to free himself from his seat. There were broken tethers dangling where they had to cut my mother's body out of the car.

I ran my fingers down the wreckage and felt my heart hurt. I never really got to know them and I often

323

wondered if they would have been the parents I thought they were.

I popped the back of the car to look in the trunk. I found my skis and took them. I did not find much else in the trunk, just my mother and father's skies and some jackets and toiletries. I had come for the skis. I put them in the car and drove back to the house.

I cleaned them thoroughly and waxed them to make sure they were ready to be used again next year. I knew you would come and get them and I knew how much they meant to you and how they helped you through tough times. How they helped you deal with the death of our parents. I knew they provided escape, so I left them on your bed knowing you would never ask where they came from.

I folded the blanket and put it back in the hall closet and took some of my dad's clothing from his closet. I packed the clothes with a toothbrush and some traveling supplies. I could not stay in Connecticut, I had to distance myself from you, but I had to wrap up some things first.

I took out the photo I carried with me for all those years. It was not faded but had suffered a couple of lamination jobs. I went to the table where I had found it and put it next to the copy of it to see the difference. I turned the frame in just the way I knew it would catch your eye. Then put my picture back in my pocket. I tore a piece of wrapping paper from the garbage and left it on the floor for you. Before I placed it on the floor I looked at it. It was shiny. It was golden; I realized the best years of my life were yet to be lived. I placed it exactly where I remember it being. I turned the Christmas lights on so you would feel comfort one last time in that house. Then I took the bag from the counter and went to the garage.

I didn't think anyone would miss the car and I have never had anyone ask about it. I started it up and pulled out without direction, without a destination and without a plan. Simply to go forth, and be.

10. Since then.

I let ten years pass while you grew. I watched from a distance while I traveled a little more. I swore not to interfere with your life, nonetheless I kept an eye on you and made sure things went as I had remembered them. I saw Indigo a couple more times and it was good but that is a story for, or from, another me. A story much like my trust fund Mr. Black disappeared with and how it found its way into the trunk in the basement at the Allotment.

In the meantime I visited the places I had not yet been, and went back to places I missed. There was still time to adventure. I was too old to climb mountains and meet remote tribes in places which could not be accessed except by foot.

I knew a time would come when I would have to stop so I purchased a little duplex in Northern California and rented it out. I let it sit waiting for when I could not travel anymore.

I crafted the story of my life in notebooks, little red notebooks. Just like the one Indigo had. They were hard to find but when I did, I ordered a number of them and packed them in my old bag and dragged them around the world with me. They got heavy but I never lost any of them. I thought hard and re read the notebook left for me, I changed some of the details so your story might be different enough to cause change in the right direction. My changes were strategic, they are slow and methodical.

My life as an old man has not been all pleasant but it has been true. Like the ones before me it ended on rebirth and growth. My life became an Ouroboros. It was bittersweet and it was enlightening, and I continue to chase the tail of my own hindsight.

This is the summary of my old age. In it I found the missing pieces, I found truth, I found purpose. I found there is still hope though I may never see it as this version of myself. I believe someday I can find a way in you, or the ones who will come after you. This is my lonely lesson. I do not think the universe will let me go until I fix my mistake. Until I fix the crease I made in it. And I should not complain, I made it home to some semblance of happiness. I smelled the smell of *rum cake, peppermint, and used pine* once again and I stood under the Connecticut Blue with hope in my heart-

And that is enough.

Patchwork Indigo: Epilogue

Patchwork Indigo: Epilogue. 30

I have moved to the place I bought and I am living out the rest of my life happily here. I am now eighty four years old and the time I talked about has come- the time when the world tells me to stop. So I have.

My little town is a pleasant place perched on the edge of the jagged boulders over the Pacific. In the evening I feel the spray from the surf drifting through the open window and listen to the waves eat their own tails. It is the swishing of the salt water in sync with the gravity of the moon. It goes around and around to mother nature's metronome. Is it the cycles by which the seasons, the days, the hours and the minutes are set. Here at the end or maybe the beginning, I listen.

There is a couple living next door in my duplex. I do not see them; I keep to myself and enjoy the days as much as I can.

They play music on an old record player. All the songs they love are my favorite songs too. Sometimes they sit on the back deck teasing and playing with each other. They are so happy. I keep my window open so I can hear them, and the happiness they make. They are good kids, they make me feel fulfilled and whole again.

They leave sometimes to explore the mountains around here, or go down to the beach to collect driftwood which sometimes get stuck in the rocks. They are always dragging things back from the woods or the beach, indeed

---

[30] "Work song" by Hozier ♫

the yard on their half of the duplex looks much nicer than mine. I am an old man with no strength left, and my creativity is all used up. I used it up on a girl in a place like this, in times like these.

Sometimes I can hear them making love through the walls late at night. It doesn't keep me awake though, I feel no need to be a voyeur but I do snicker at it from time to time. The walls here are paper thin, I like it that way. Being alone is hard enough and it is good to know that someone is near, that someone is within ear shot. It's good to know she is close.

They seem to like my little place here in Elk, on the bluffs, but I know that they will be moving on soon. Whether they know it or not, their summer is ending and they feel the wind pulling them in a different direction.

One of these days they will sell all of their stuff. They will sell their truck, pack a couple of bags and sail over the Pacific on the adventure of a lifetime. I wish them the best. I know they will enjoy it because I did. His memories are also my memories.

They will stand on the deck with the sea to their backs and take a picture that will puzzle them. While they are looking, I will slip a little red notebook into the young man's backpack. I will watch while the vapors of the man I was pass through this time. It is the only time my past present and future will meet. It is not a large notebook but it is filled with the best advice a person could have. It is more than I ever had. They will get it much sooner in their lives than I did in mine.

After listening to the two of them and the love they fill their home and heart with I have decided something's are worth risking. In the end, we are all responsible for our own happiness and sometimes, not even the universe has the right to take that away from us. Choice is all we really have and consequences are only building blocks for things to come. Maybe, I have done my penance and this time, the universe will set me free.

The Music of my Life

Music in chronological order

1: "This magic Moment" *By: Racheal Cantu*
2: "Hide and Seek" By: *Imogen Heap*
3: "Lost Boy" By: *Ruth B*
4: "Made of light" By: *Mikky Ekko*
5: "What Pi Sounds like" By: *Michael John Blake*
6: "Childhood's End" By: *Pink Floyd*
7: "Bygone" By: *Volcano Choir*
8: "I am Only Joking" By: *KONGOS*
9: "Like Real People do" By: *Hozier*
10: "Where is my mind?" By: *Storm Large*
11: "Doors to Heaven" By: *Shake Shake Go*
12: "Bonfire Heart" By: *James Blunt*
14: "House of Gold" By: *21 Pilots*
15: "Free the mind" By: Johann Johannsson
16: "Upside Down" By: *Jack Johnson*
17: "Fury Oh' Fury" By: *Nico Vega*
18: "All that I am" By: Rob Thomas
19: "The one Moment" By: *OK Go*
20: "Closer to the Heart" By: *Rush*
21: "Sounds of Silence" By: *Disturbed*
22: "Smile" By: *Mikky Ekko*
23: "Here comes the sun" By: *The Beatles*
24: "All in Time" By: *Shake Shake Go*
25: "Hybrid" By: *Elsiane*
26: "Slip" By: *Eliot Moss*
27: "Second Chances" By: *Imagine Dragons*
28: "Disappear" By: *Mikky Ekko*
29: "Life is for the Living" By: *Passenger*
30: "Green Mountain State" By: *Trevor Hall*
31: "Work Song" By: *Hozier*

01010100 01101111 00100000 01101101 01111001 00100000 01101101 01111001 00100000
01110011 01101111 01101110 01110011 00100000 01100001 01101110 01100100 00100000
01100100 01100001 01110101 01100111 01101000 01100101 01110010 01110011 01110011
00101100 00100000 01100001 01101110 01100100 00100000 01100001 01101100 01101100
00100000 01101101 01111001 00100000 01101111 01110100 01101000 01100101 01110010
00100000 01101001 01101110 01100011 01100001 01110010 01101110 01100001 01110100
01101001 01101111 01101110 01110011 00101100 00100000 00001101 00001010 00001101
00001010 01001001 01110100 00100000 01101001 01110011 00100000 01110011 01101111
01101001 01101001 01101110 01100011 01101111 01101110 01100001 01110010 01100111
01101001 01101100 01101111 01110101 01110011 00100000 01110010 01100001 01101000
01110011 00100000 01100100 01100100 01100001 01110100 01100101 01101101 01110000
01110100 01100101 01110000 01100011 01100001 01100111 01100011 01110001 01100010
01110100 01110011 01110100 00100000 01101100 01100101 01100001 01110001 01100101
01101000 01100100 01101100 01100101 01101101 00100000 01101111 01110100 01110101
01110001 01101100 01100101 01101110 01100111 01101110 01100001 01110100 01101000
01101001 01100100 01101101 00100000 00001101 00001010 00001101 00001010 00001101
01101000 01101111 01110101 01110010 00100000 01101010 01100101 01110010 01110110
00100000 00110111 01111001 00100000 01100101 01110011 01100011 01100001 01110000
01101001 01101001 01100001 01101110 01100101 01101100 01111010 00100000 00100000
01101101 01100101 01110010 01101111 01100101 01100111 01110011 01100011 01110000